THE OFFICER GIRL IN BLUE

THE OFFICER GIRL IN BLUE

Fenella J. Miller

An Aria Book

First published in the UK in 2021 by Head of Zeus Ltd
This paperback edition first published in the UK in 2022 by Head of Zeus Ltd,
part of Bloomsbury Publishing Plc

9 7 5 3 1 2 4 6 8

A CIP catalogue record for this book is available
from the British Library.

ISBN (E): 9781838933494
ISBN (PB): 9781800246294

Typeset by Siliconchips Services Ltd UK

Printed and bound in Great Britain by
CPI Group (UK) Ltd, Croydon CR0 4YY

MIX
Paper from
responsible sources
FSC® C171272

Head of Zeus
5–8 Hardwick Street
London EC1R 4RG

www.headofzeus.com

For Jean Fullerton, great writer and great friend

I

Bulstrode Park, Buckinghamshire, June 1941

The train from London had been delayed and by the time Charlotte arrived at Gerrards Cross the transport that she'd been expecting to find had already departed. She propped her kitbag against the station wall and went in search of the stationmaster. She found him skulking in his office, his feet on the table, drinking tea and reading the *News Chronicle*.

'I require a taxi to take me to Bulstrode Park,' she said in what she hoped was an authoritative manner. It seemed to do the trick. The fact that she was quite obviously a WAAF made it simpler for him to identify her.

The boots slammed onto the boards and the corpulent, middle-aged man heaved himself to his feet. He seemed unfazed by her abrupt tone.

'Righto, miss, I was told there would be another one of you lot arriving on the London train. Bert's outside waiting to take you to Bulstrode Park.' He smiled cheerily, nodded and then resumed his place and picked up his newspaper once more.

'Thank you,' was all she could think of in response.

Sure enough, a dilapidated taxi was waiting on the forecourt but there was no sign of the driver. She heaved her belongings onto the back seat and then went in search of him. She was surprised and delighted that a vehicle had been provided for her personal use – she thought that petrol was only available to the military nowadays.

Eventually she located Bert smoking a Woodbine and gazing across the fields. 'Excuse me, I'm already late and would be most grateful if you could drive me to Bulstrode immediately.'

He took a last drag on his cigarette, carefully pinched the burning end off, and pushed what remained into his top pocket. 'The other ladies went an hour or more ago. The lorry hung about for an hour and then scarpered.'

The car coughed, rattled and roared into life. Bert drove like a maniac; she was flung from side to side as there was no strap to hold on to. He turned into the imposing driveway, sending gravel in all directions, and was waved through by the armed soldier lounging at the gate.

Charlotte disembarked with relief and only just had time to step back before the car drove away. Didn't Bert know that the faster you went the quicker your petrol would be used?

She looked around with interest at the place she was going to begin her training to be an officer. The house was magnificent, and every bit as pleasing as she'd expected from her research. A string of dukes had owned the property and added and subtracted from it, but the house she was viewing now had last been altered in 1865 by one Duke of Somerset.

The mansion was of red-brick construction, was more than three storeys high, had several spires, an interesting roofline and a plethora of single-storey additions that no doubt housed the kitchens, laundry room and so on. There were probably dozens of outbuildings at the rear but she couldn't see these from where she stood at the front.

She mustn't dawdle here but register her arrival inside and then find her accommodation. Several Women's Auxiliary Air Force and Royal Air Force personnel wandered past but none of them acknowledged her. The interior of the massive building was equally impressive and, despite it being June, she shivered. Like her own family home this place would never be warm even in the middle of summer.

She completed the necessary paperwork and was told that her billet was on the top floor, and that she would be sharing with three other girls. The admin clerk had been friendly and not at all put out at her tardy arrival.

Charlotte picked up her kitbag was about to head for the stairs when an attractive WAAF, a little shorter than herself, with red hair and green eyes rushed up, her hand extended.

'I'm Marion Russell. I just arrived myself.'

'Charlotte Fenimore,' she said and shook hands with Sergeant Russell.

'Jolly good. I'm glad I'm not the last to arrive. Shall we go in search of our beds and get everything tickety-boo before we go and look for the others?'

'I'm somewhere on the top floor. Where are you?'

Marion held up the piece of paper in her hand and Charlotte was delighted to discover they would be sharing.

Despite being in perfect health and physically fit they were both red-faced and panting by the time they eventually located their quarters.

There were four beds all neatly stacked as they should be but nothing to indicate which ones were occupied and which were available for them. However, there were tin hats, gas capes and greatcoats hanging on the pegs by the two on this side of the room. The linoleum was highly polished and the metal lockers allocated to each person were dust-free.

Marion hurried over to the two under the window and checked. 'These are empty, Charlotte, so they must be ours. Do you have any preference?'

'None at all. I don't suppose it makes any difference in the summer but these beds would be hideous in the winter as the windows don't fit properly.'

'I don't suppose it'll be much fun sleeping here if it rains either. Never mind – it's only for a few weeks.'

Half an hour later their kit was neatly stowed away and they were ready to go in search of the remainder of the group who had been sent here to be turned into officers.

'There are no bathrooms or WCs on this floor – I need to find one before we go out,' Charlotte said.

'I wish you hadn't mentioned spending a penny. Now I'm desperate too.'

They found the ablutions on the first floor. 'I hope I don't need to go in the night,' Marion said with a smile.

'It's a pity they don't supply a chamber pot,' she replied. When they reached the entrance hall the first thing they heard was the sound of voices coming from the passageway on the right. 'Good heavens, it's six o'clock. Let's go in search of sustenance.'

Her new friend agreed that food was the priority and followed Charlotte in the direction of the racket.

They had their tin mug and irons – cutlery – with them so all they needed was something to eat and tea to fill their mugs.

The mess hall was half-full. The RAF personnel sat on one side and the WAAF on the other. At least they weren't completely segregated as was often the case. She noticed that there were two serving hatches – one for the men, one for the women. Fraternisation was obviously frowned upon.

Several girls nodded and smiled but they were all too busy eating to stop and talk. There was bubble and squeak, sausages and gravy. It looked palatable and certainly smelt appetising. The two of them threaded their way around the tables and sat at one of the few empty ones on their side of the room.

Like everyone else Charlotte concentrated on eating and not talking until her plate was clear. 'I'm going to have some spotted dick and custard. Shall I get you some?'

'Yes, please, and I'll replenish our mugs.'

The mess was now heaving and nobody lingered at the table to chat as there were others waiting to sit down. After rinsing their irons and mugs, she and Marion went in search of the recreation room.

'How many of us are there doing this conversion course, do you know?'

'There are about thirty, so I've been told. Did you know we only spend two weeks here and then, if we pass muster, we get sent elsewhere to complete our training?'

'I didn't know that. Thank you for telling me.' Charlotte indicated a pair of double doors just ahead from which feminine voices could be clearly heard. 'I'm hoping we'll be able to identify the other girls and they can give us the gen. Do you have any idea where we go next?'

'Not the foggiest – no doubt the powers that be will inform us in due course.'

There was a distinct lack of RAF in this part of the house – yet another indication the two sides of this service were kept apart. She hoped there would be a dance at the weekend as there had been at her previous posting. Not that she was particularly interested in flirting but she did like to dance when given the opportunity.

One of her best friends, Nancy, was happily married to David and already had two adopted children and a new baby in their family. Her other good friend, Jane, was hoping to get pregnant whilst she and her husband Oscar had an unexpected six weeks' leave. He'd broken his arm in a minor accident with his fighter and Jane hadn't taken any leave for months.

This meant she was the only one of the trio who hadn't found someone to fall in love with. There'd been ample opportunity to mix with RAF officers of various sorts but none had appealed to her. Most of them were either too young and brash for her taste, or too old. And besides, falling in love with an RAF pilot was likely to end in heartbreak as the fatalities in this branch of the services were horrendous.

In that moment, as she strolled down a draughty corridor with her new acquaintance Marion, she came to a decision. When she was promoted, she would apply for a posting in London and make an effort to meet chaps who worked at the foreign office, were in government or some such thing.

Maybe there was a medic just waiting for her as David had been for Nancy.

'I say, old girl, you look a bit vacant. Have you got a headache?'

Marion's comment dragged her back to the present. 'Sorry, lost in thought.' They stepped through the doors and were immediately greeted by waves and shouts from a group of girls sprawled in various chairs at the far side of what must have once been a grand drawing room. It now had only plain, utilitarian furniture and none of it looked particularly comfortable or inviting.

'Hello, I assume that we've finally found the rest of our cohort. I'm Charlotte Fenimore and this is Marion Russell. Have we missed much?'

'Nothing at all. It doesn't start until eight o'clock tomorrow morning,' a small, plump girl said with a smile as she shifted over, making room on the floor for them both.

'Good show, don't want to blot our copy books so soon. Have we got an itinerary of some sort? I wasn't given anything but the location of my billet.'

'Drill in the garden in slacks and PE tops first, then a two-mile run around the grounds followed by what will be a much-needed wash and breakfast,' another girl told them.

Half of the group were doing something hush-hush so they couldn't discuss their work. No doubt there were girls working in RDF like her and others plotting the routes of the incoming and outgoing aircraft as Jane was doing. Some were employed in admin, catering, and other boring duties. However, their group also included a radio and a wireless operator, an aircraft hand and a sparking plug tester.

Watching the cathode tube, following the little blips

shown on the screen and then relaying the information to others in her team was a valuable task but the flickering light had started to give her the most appalling migraine headaches. The medic on the camp had said she couldn't continue and her skill and training would now go to waste. Using the brilliant radio directional finding system that had helped the RAF win the Battle of Britain last summer had made her feel she was doing her bit for the war effort.

It was lights out at ten o'clock so in ones and twos they started to drift off from nine o'clock. Marion worked in admin – had been in charge of a hotel full of new recruits – and Charlotte rather thought this was something she might apply to do when she had her commission. Maybe administrative duties when you were an officer wouldn't be quite as boring as she thought.

The next week was crammed full of mostly physical tasks, teambuilding exercises where they had to take it in turns to lead a group of four other girls. Points were awarded to the winning teams and so far her band were heading the board.

There was no mingling with other trainees of either sex. By the end of the fortnight the original thirty girls had been reduced to twenty. Those unfortunate enough to fail at one or other of the tasks were tapped on the shoulder, not given the opportunity to say goodbye to their peers, and just returned to whatever position they'd previously held.

'Have you decided where you want to be sent at the end of all this?' Marion asked her on the last day of the two preliminary weeks.

'I want to be in London. When I volunteered two years

ago I remember being impressed by the efficient officers at Victory House who marshalled us from place to place. I'm going to ask to go there.'

'Although the continuous bombing has stopped, it's still a dangerous place to be.'

'Not nearly as bad as where I was posted previously. We were bombed most days and I think any base is fraught with danger.' She smiled. 'And not all of it from the Luftwaffe. I'd rather like to be somewhere I wasn't constantly pursued by eager RAF pilots.'

'Golly! Most girls would give their eye teeth to be on a fighter base surrounded by the gods of the air.' Marion pulled a face. 'Not me, though. I expect I'll be sent back to manage another horde of trainees. That's the problem – if you prove to be good at something the powers that be are reluctant to move you anywhere else.'

'I would much prefer to have continued with my special duties but I can't do so for medical reasons. I have the option of retraining in another branch but I've decided I want to do something more administrative in future.'

'At least we know where we're going next even if we don't know exactly what hoops we'll have to jump through this time,' Marion said as she rammed the last of her kit into the already bulging bag.

'I've never been to Loughborough. I hope we get a few hours off occasionally so we can explore the area a little.'

Marion laughed. 'We're not going on our hols, old girl. If the past two weeks are anything to go by, we'll not have a minute to ourselves. Let's hope neither of us get the dreaded tap on the shoulder.'

The other two girls who'd shared the cramped attic room

had been unfortunate enough to be culled so they'd had the room to themselves for the past week. She hefted her kitbag onto her shoulder and joined the stream of WAAF heading for the entrance hall.

There'd been no necessity to make friends with anyone else as Marion and she were already best pals. Charlotte had always found connecting to people difficult, which was why her close friendships with Jane and Nancy were so important to her. Maybe over the past two years she'd mellowed a little and that was why she was now able to open up and enjoy Marion's company.

She dumped her kitbag against the wall and dropped her tin hat on the top. The row of bags looked a bit like drunken sailors, albeit rather short ones. They were breakfasting first today as the transport lorry was expected at seven thirty.

The hundred-and-fifty-mile journey in normal times would have taken less than three hours, but there was a war on and delay was inevitable. It was late afternoon when they disembarked, all desperate for the ablutions and something to eat. They'd been told they wouldn't be collected from the station until five, which gave them almost an hour to wait.

'I'll join the queue in the ladies' room, Charlotte, as my need is more desperate than yours. Can you get something for us to eat from the café?'

'I'll do that. Shall we meet over there, under the clock? Can you manage to stagger across and dump my kitbag with yours before you dash off?'

The jolly woman serving behind the counter in the café was happy to fill their tin mugs with tea. 'Saves me the washing-up, luv, so glad to do it. There's only spam sandwiches but I've got a couple of nice Eccles cakes you can have to go with them. Only came in today, so lovely and fresh.'

'Thank you, we've not eaten since breakfast. Even spam sandwiches sound absolutely spiffing.' She gave the woman a handful of coins and with the brimming mugs in one hand and the sandwiches and cakes balanced precariously in the other, she headed for the clock under which she'd left their belongings.

Marion arrived moments after she did and beamed when she saw the largesse. 'Golly, a feast indeed. Here, let me have the tea and things whilst you dash off to the loo.'

Charlotte took the opportunity to wash her face as well as her hands whilst she was there. She stared back at her reflection. She doubted her estranged family would recognise her now. She was slimmer, fitter and her expression was that of a confident and happy young woman.

Both her parents had died some time ago and she'd never been close to her older brothers who were now, no doubt, brigadiers or colonels in the army. She'd not communicated with either of them since she'd volunteered at the start of the war almost two years ago. They didn't even know that she was a WAAF and about to become an officer.

Her family consisted of Jane and her lovely husband Oscar plus Nancy and her husband David and their children. For some reason none of the men she'd met stirred the faintest interest in her. Maybe she was destined to be an old maid.

As she sat with her friend, using her bag as a chair, munching happily on their picnic, she realised that despite everything at that moment she was perfectly content with her life.

'We've talked about everything else, Marion, but I've not asked you anything personal. Do you have a young man somewhere in the forces waiting for you?'

'No, not interested in romance. I don't need a man to prop me up, to make me feel special. I'm hoping to rise up the ranks and have a lifelong career in the WAAF. What about you?'

'I'm not sure. I do know that I don't want to get involved with an RAF officer. That's why I've decided to ask to work in London, hopefully at Victory House.'

Marion drained the last of her tea and brushed the crumbs from her immaculate uniform. 'Have you ever had a serious relationship?'

'I've not had any relationship at all. I was away at school until I was eighteen and then spent a year at home riding and enjoying my freedom. There was a dearth of young men in my circle as they'd all volunteered by then.'

'Same here. Being pawed over by any man just doesn't appeal to me. I'm glad that you feel the same way.'

There was no time to answer, as Charlotte saw the other members of their party rushing off across the concourse. The transport had obviously arrived earlier than expected.

2

The train steamed into Loughborough station and this time the waiting lorry was only for their kitbags. The girls milled about uncertainly for a moment, wondering if they were supposed to form up in files and march to Loughborough College or make their own way.

Charlotte thought this might be part of the course and after a quick word with Marion the two of them stepped forward.

'Right, ladies, form rank. We'll show the good citizens of Loughborough town what a file of WAAF can do.'

Marion stood ramrod straight beside her, every inch a sergeant on parade. 'Hurry up, we don't want to disappoint those assessing us. I'm certain this is part of the selection procedure.'

This was more than enough to galvanise them into action and within a couple of minutes two lines of eight smart WAAF stood behind her. Charlotte was in fact the highest ranked amongst them so they had no choice but to obey. Marion was one of three sergeants but the other two made no demur when her friend took her position at the rear of the column.

'Eyes front. Quick march.' Charlotte led them, confident

that they made a splendid sight as they set out in unison. Fortunately, she knew exactly where the college was having asked the lorry driver before he drove away.

With arms swinging, perfectly in step, they entered the grounds fifteen minutes later. The guard at the gate sprang to attention and saluted smartly. She returned the gesture without losing pace. At no time had she turned her head but had seen in her peripheral vision that their progress had been noted and admired. In fact, there'd been a few spontaneous rounds of applause and several catcalls from watching servicemen.

On one never-to-be-forgotten occasion when she'd been drilling a group of WAAF, she'd been distracted by an officer asking her a question and forgotten to give the order to about-turn. When she looked up, to her horror, her ladies were almost out of sight. They'd heard her shouted command and she hadn't lost them over the hill. This would never happen again on her watch.

The building they were approaching was similar to the one they'd left that morning – early Victorian, red-brick and with numerous miniature towers and Gothic protuberances. The grounds they were marching through were immaculate. From what she could see from the corner of her eye this looked a perfectly reasonable place to spend the next few months.

She halted the women neatly. The driver of the lorry had unloaded their kitbags and they were piled haphazardly outside the front door. She gave the order to fall out and collect their belongings.

Marion joined her. 'I say, old bean, that went absolutely splendidly. We certainly turned a few heads on the way here.'

Without needing to discuss it they both waited until the mêlée around the luggage had dispersed before heading to pick up their own bags, which were now the only two there.

'I hope we're billeted together again,' Marion said as she hefted her bag over her shoulder.

'Let's go in and find out, shall we?'

An officer with one narrow gold stripe, indicating she was an assistant section officer, approached them.

'WO Fenimore and Sergeant Russell, your arrival was noted and appreciated. You will be billeted together on the first floor. Get yourself stowed away and then head straight for the mess. The itinerary for tomorrow is pinned on the noticeboard over there.'

They both saluted – long way up, short way down – as they'd been taught when they'd first joined up two years ago. The walls here were panelled as at Bulstrode Park, but the house was a good deal smaller and so far she'd seen no RAF wandering about.

'First floor and only the two of us,' Marion said with a happy smile.

'This must have been arranged before our arrival. I think from this we can assume we lead the pack as far as kudos goes,' Charlotte replied.

'You're the only warrant officer so you have seniority. The other two sergeants are more recently promoted than myself so it could just be done on our ranks not on our performance over the past two weeks.'

'It doesn't matter which it is. I'm just glad I'm sharing with you.'

This time the room was substantially larger, had an iron bedstead against each wall on either side of the window and – luxury of luxuries – an actual wardrobe and chest of drawers into which to put their belongings. There was also a washstand with a decent mirror standing on it and a couple of wooden chairs.

'Pity we don't get an actual mattress and real sheets as well. I wonder if senior officers get a proper bed or if they still have to have biscuits like us?' asked Marion, gesturing to the three small, hard mattress squares on each bed.

'Let's hope we find out at the end of this course. I'm going to make up my bed after I've emptied my kitbag. I doubt that we'll get any unannounced inspections.'

This time they were on the same floor as a bathroom and WC, which was an improvement on the last posting. With stocking seams straight, shoes freshly rubbed to a high shine, the two of them headed downstairs to find the mess.

About half the group were already there, and there were still empty spaces at the table. Supper today was shepherd's pie, carrots and, of course, cabbage. The vegetables were horribly overcooked but the pie looked all right. They had the hall to themselves as it was still an hour before the usual time for the evening meal. God knows what the vegetables would be like by the time everyone else arrived to eat.

They were greeted with enthusiasm and soon discovered their immaculate arrival had definitely put them ahead of the other two groups also being trained to be officers.

'That's good news, Gladys, thank you for telling us. I didn't stop to read what's happening tomorrow – can anybody tell us?' Charlotte took a mouthful of the pie and nodded in appreciation.

'Drill and PE at seven then breakfast at eight – just like before. We're going to have lectures on organisation, administration, pay, legal assistance, discipline, travelling, hotel management, accounts, signals, costing, administration and equipment.' Gladys paused for breath and grinned after reciting the entire syllabus. 'I spoke to someone in another group who is three weeks ahead of us and it seems we also get something called historical development of the nineteenth and twentieth centuries, art, literature and music. Don't know what these have to do with being an officer but sounds like fun.'

Gladys, despite having a name not associated with the upper classes, spoke with crystal-clear diction and had a definite plum in her mouth. Heaven knows why her parents had given their daughter this name and not called her something more appropriate, like Sarah or Elizabeth.

'It's going to be like being back at school. Do we get exams as well at the end of each section?' Charlotte rather liked the sound of the syllabus and was looking forward to her stay here.

'I expect so. I'm a duffer at written tests so rather hope we don't. I much prefer to be quizzed in person,' Gladys said as she returned to spooning up the last scrapings of her apple crumble and custard.

As the weeks rushed by she and Marion became the natural leaders of the group and, under their guidance, everyone flourished and no one was sent home. Charlotte's head was full of useless information on things she was certain she would never use but, amongst this dross, were also facts and figures that would help her become a first-class officer. For her, the promotion would be just one step higher, as an assistant section officer was only one rank ahead of a warrant officer. For Marion it would be three steps and for the corporals – who made up the bulk of the trainees – it would be four jumps.

When they mustered out as junior officers they would all be on a par, but she was confident that both her friend and herself would climb more rapidly than some of the others. She aimed to be at least a squadron leader before she left the service at the end of the war – whenever that might be.

The day before they finished, all her group safely through the written and verbal tests, she was summoned to the office of the commanding officer – one Group Officer Webb – and she was curious as to why she'd been singled out for a private interview.

'Sit down, my dear, there's something I wish to discuss with you.'

Charlotte wasn't sure if she was more surprised at being addressed so informally or by the fact that any officer would consider discussing something and not just giving the order. She took the seat in front of the desk and waited politely.

'I see that you've asked to be moved to admin because you can no longer return to the special duties you were trained for.'

'That's correct, ma'am.'

'I also see that you declined to retrain for special duties in another area? Could you explain why you made this decision?'

'Although we're not supposed to talk about what we do, I know what other things are involved. I don't want to be a plotter or filterer and work underground. I know I could be a wireless or radio operator but that these would require a further few months' training.' She paused to gather her thoughts.

'I'm good at organising, at commanding. I want to put these skills to use by, hopefully, working somewhere like Victory House.' She looked squarely at the officer on the other side of the desk hoping to convince her of her sincerity.

'I was very impressed by the efficiency of the officers working in London and would relish the opportunity to prove myself in any capacity.'

'I see, you've put it very clearly. I have a posting for you that will suit you. Victory House wants an officer who can drive and has an excellent education. You appear to fit the bill perfectly.'

Charlotte's heart sank. This sounded like an admin job but this was her choice. She'd been offered retraining in something more interesting and had refused. Should she have agreed to become a plotter as it would have been something more interesting and worthwhile?

'Thank you, ma'am, for thinking of me.' She thought her voice commendably firm considering the turmoil inside her.

'They asked for my best candidate and that, my dear, is you. I'm not exactly sure what your duties will be but it won't just be shuffling papers. You specified you wanted to be in London so I thought of you immediately.'

'Thank you for recommending me. It sounds exactly the sort of thing I want to do.' She hoped she sounded sufficiently enthusiastic as it was entirely her own fault she'd been given an admin posting. Being in London was what she wanted so she was determined to be pleased.

'Another thing, you won't be officially billeted. You will be given a *per diem* but have to find your own accommodation within walking distance. Will that be a problem?'

'No, I can stay at an excellent hotel I've used several times before. It's in Whitehall and very close to Victory House. Will that be acceptable?'

'Perfectly, my dear. Good luck – but I don't think you're going to need it. You have been the outstanding candidate this summer. I'm certain you'll soon be promoted again.'

Charlotte got to her feet, saluted and marched briskly from the room when really what she wanted to do was turn cartwheels.

Marion was waiting for her and wanted to know what the summons had been for. 'You look cock-a-hoop, old bean. Did you get the posting you wanted?'

'I certainly did. What about you, do you know where you're going next?'

'I'm to report at Victory House and will be posted from there. We get a week's leave before we take up our new positions. As we're both going to be in London anyway, would you care to spend the week gallivanting about the city with me?' Marion was really turning out to be a terrific friend.

'I'm going to be working at Victory House so we'll report after our leave together. I'd love to spend some time with you. We can go to the cinema and maybe a nightclub or two. It's a pity all the paintings have been stored for the duration of the war, otherwise we could have visited the National Gallery or the Tate as well.'

'Have you ever been to Palm Court at the Ritz for afternoon tea? They still do it you know, and anyone in uniform gets in half price.'

'I haven't set foot in the Ritz – my family used the Savoy when they came to town. I want to visit a friend, Nancy, who lives in Chelmsford. I'm sure she wouldn't mind if you came with me. We volunteered together but she's now a wife and mother.'

'If you're quite sure she won't mind a stranger being foisted on her then I'd love to come with you. Then that's our week planned out. There's going to be a formal dinner tonight. Then we have our passing-out parade and this time we don't have to march back to the station but will be driven. I've really enjoyed these past three months, haven't you?'

'I have. Obviously I've learned a lot and am now ready to be an officer. Half of what we learned will never be used but it got the old brain cells working. It seems a long time since I was studying for my higher certificate.'

'Shall we start packing now so it's not so much of a rush tomorrow morning?' Marion asked.

'Good idea. Why don't we walk into town after lunch? I don't know why we couldn't have finished this morning as there's absolutely nothing going on today apart from the dinner.'

It hadn't rained since the beginning of August and it was now September. The grass was burnt brown from the sun. Everywhere looked dry and sad. It had poured most of July and doing drill outside had been rather unpleasant. Last winter had been freezing and she sincerely hoped it wouldn't be the same this year.

There had been another group of WAAF doing the course

who'd started a day after them. She supposed it made sense to delay the departure of her own set by a day so there only needed to be one formal dinner and one passing-out parade, instead of two.

'I'm not changing my shirt, Marion, just putting on a clean collar. I'm nipping down to the laundry to check we've not left anything there.'

'Righto, you do that. I've got a couple of letters to write – friends from my previous posting who I promised to keep updated with my progress.'

Calling it a formal dinner was a misnomer as it was anything but. No one had changed into their best blues and, as there was alcohol being served, the noise level was extraordinary. Fortunately, there were no speeches, as if anyone had stood up to talk, they wouldn't have been heard over the racket.

This was more an occasion for the girls to let their hair down, to exchange addresses, to congratulate each other on a successful course before they dispersed, quite possibly never to see each other again. After a quick headcount she realised the other group had eighteen in it so they'd lost two more than hers. The dreaded tap on the shoulder for those that failed to meet the standard was only too common. The officers for the RAF were trained at Cranwell and it took them a year or more, whereas they'd only had a little over three months.

Dutifully she made the rounds and exchanged handshakes and smiles with everyone before slipping away, leaving the others to continue the raucous celebrations. In peacetime the RAF cadets would have had their families watching their passing-out parade. Things were different now there was a war on and the WAAF hadn't really existed back then anyway.

They'd been told frequently by their lecturers and senior officers that training women to be officers was something extraordinary and they mustn't let the side down. They would be treated with the same respect as their male counterparts and those in the ranks would have to salute them. This probably wouldn't go down well with a lot of the men, but things were changing and they would just have to get used to it.

The next morning she completed her packing and hefted her kitbag onto her shoulder. The transport lorries were already outside and she was told she could put her belongings inside immediately. The mess was subdued, partly because a lot of the girls had hangovers, but also because they'd got to know each other well and saying goodbye to new friends was always difficult.

After breakfast they duly paraded, saluted the CO and that was it. Marion sat beside her on the slippery bench in the back of the transport, their feet firmly on their kitbags to stop them rolling away. They had travel warrants and most of them were catching a train going south.

'I don't want to sit in a compartment full of men smoking, Marion. I'd much rather sit on my bag in the passageway. I don't mind if you want to go inside. I'll be fine out there.'

'No, I'm not a smoker either, as you know. They should have non-smoking compartments. Shall we look for a *ladies only*? The porter said our train's already in but doesn't depart for another half an hour.'

'Then let's get on it now as I expect the other passengers might well be getting a cup of tea.'

There was only the one compartment set aside for ladies and they scrambled in, delighted they could sit in comparative peace. It wouldn't do to ask a man to stop smoking but she wouldn't hesitate to ask a woman to do so.

For once the train travelled directly to St Pancras. They emerged into the early afternoon sunlight eager to find something to eat. Charlotte looked around with interest. This was to be her home for the foreseeable future and despite the permanent smell of smoke, the boarded-up windows, the empty shops and the bombed-out shells of buildings she was excited to be there.

3

'We can go on the District and Metropolitan line from here to Aldgate East and then change and get another train to Westminster,' Marion suggested as she looked at the complicated map on the wall.

'It doesn't make sense to go so far out of our way. Why don't we get the Piccadilly line from here to Aldwych and then walk the rest of the way?' Charlotte suggested. 'We just have to cut down Waterloo Road and that leads us to the Embankment. Then we cross the Thames on Westminster Bridge and we're there.'

'Is this Sanctuary House hotel close to Westminster?'

'It certainly is – it's in Tothill Street. I'm sure we can manage to carry our bags from the underground to the hotel. Mind you, two years ago I could barely lift it let alone carry it half a mile.'

As it was the middle of the day the underground wasn't impossibly busy. Although this method of transport was efficient and inexpensive Charlotte had never enjoyed travelling this way and much preferred to catch a bus or trolley bus. Before the war it would have been a taxi but they were almost non-existent now.

She was relieved to emerge into the sunlight at Aldwych

station. It always surprised her how Londoners appeared unbothered by the destruction around them and continued to work, shop and enjoy themselves as if there was no danger living in the city.

Of course, the Blitz had stopped in May but there was the ever-present danger of a hit-and-run bomber evading the barrage balloons and the fighters and wreaking carnage somewhere. She was shocked at the damage in Victoria Street. It was a miracle that none of the government offices, Westminster Abbey or Westminster Cathedral had been bombed at the same time.

They paused at the entrance to Tothill Street to look at what was left of this section of Victoria Street. Both sides of the road had suffered equally. Many of the houses had been demolished, others were beyond repair, but the ones closest to where they were standing were just windowless, doors blown in, obviously uninhabitable at the moment.

'It must have been absolute hell living here when the bombs were dropping every night,' Marion said quietly. 'We heard the bombers, sometimes saw dogfights overhead, but where I was stationed was remarkably unscathed. What about you?'

'I was on the Suffolk coast and bombs were dropped regularly on the base but, thank God, there weren't many fatalities. Hitler seems to be concentrating on other cities at the moment, which is good for us, not so great for them.'

It occurred to her as she led the way into the foyer of The Sanctuary that it might have been wiser to book before turning up.

'Good afternoon, ma'am, do you have a reservation?' The concierge was glancing down at his book as he spoke.

'We don't, but my friends and I stayed here a couple of times last year. I'd like a twin room for a week and then a single room somewhere for myself as I'm now posted to the War Office.'

As soon as she mentioned she wished to stay there permanently he smiled. 'I have a room on the third floor. It is a twin but somewhat smaller than the others here so I'd be happy to let you have it after your friend departs.'

In other words, Charlotte realised, if the two of them were prepared to be somewhat cramped for the next week then she would actually be better placed when Marion left.

'That sounds perfectly fine to me. What do you think?'

Marion nodded. 'I don't mind if it's rather small with the two of us in it.'

'I assume the cost of this room will reflect its inadequacies?'

The man smiled. 'You will be charged as if it's a single, ma'am. Will you be wanting full board?'

'Obviously we want breakfast every morning but our plans are flexible at the moment. I assume it's in order to reserve a table for lunch or dinner on the day itself?'

He nodded. 'It's more expensive doing it that way but perfectly acceptable. Will you be dining in tonight?'

'Yes, definitely.'

There was no lift and no bellboy to carry their luggage, but this didn't put either of them off. 'Golly, it's a good thing we're fit. Being up in the gods like this will give us an excellent view of the city if nothing else,' Marion said as they reached the designated floor.

'Look, there are only four other rooms up here and we've got a bathroom and WC. I wonder if this is where the boarders live and the other floors are for itinerant visitors.'

Charlotte had the key and unlocked the door. She looked around with pleasure.

'I thought it would be much smaller than this. There's ample room to move around as long as we don't bang our heads on the eaves.'

'A couple of men wouldn't be so comfortable here – but it's perfect for us. Do you mind if I open the window?' Marion dumped her bag on the floor, flipped across the catch and heaved. The window shot up, depositing a cloud of pigeon droppings on her head.

'Good grief! How absolutely disgusting,' Marion said as she shook her head vigorously trying to dislodge the debris.

Charlotte couldn't answer as she was laughing, tears streaming down her cheeks, unable to offer any assistance at all. Eventually the remaining pigeon droppings were removed from the windowsill and the floor, and order was restored.

'It's a good thing there are bars on the window or I might have gone out head first.'

'I'm never sure if these bars were put there to keep people safe or to keep people in,' Charlotte said as she wiped her eyes.

Marion peered through the obstructions. 'It's three floors down, no fire escape, so I don't think anybody was being imprisoned. Maybe these rooms were originally part of the nursery and it was to stop little ones falling out.'

'Anyway, now the excitement's over, let's unpack,' Charlotte said. 'What luxury to be able to hang our belongings on hangers in a real wooden wardrobe. But even better, we're going to be sleeping on an actual mattress with smooth cotton sheets and blankets.'

'I'm going to make the most of it for the next seven nights. I expect I'll be back to three biscuits next week – although I'm not sure if officers have the same basic equipment as we've had these past two years. I do know I won't have to share.'

They were dab hands at unpacking and packing at speed and in less than half an hour the room was immaculate, everything where it should be, and they were ready to make their way downstairs. They jumped when a car backfired, the sound carrying to them through the open window. Then there was a second loud bang.

'Someone needs to get their car serviced,' Marion said with a smile. 'Come on, let's not waste a minute of our leave.'

'I'm absolutely starving. Shall we go in search of some sustenance before we do anything else?' Charlotte had their key in hand ready to hand in to the concierge at the desk. Strangely, the desk was deserted so she dropped the key with a clatter on the counter. 'I wonder where everybody is?'

'Haven't the foggiest,' her friend replied.

'There used to be a decent café not far from here. Basic food, but well cooked. Shall we see if we can get a bite of lunch there or do you want to go somewhere smarter?'

'I'm happy with egg and chips if it's available, Charlotte, and you know this area better than I.'

Outside they were surprised to see the hotel manager and two waiters staring towards a house a few doors down on the other side of the road. It explained why the foyer was empty.

The two of them were about to cross the road when the clang of a police car approaching at speed made them step back hurriedly. It roared past and moments later a second, plain black car, driven by a young woman in an Auxiliary Territorial Service uniform, followed.

The two vehicles screeched to a halt outside the smart house. 'I wonder what's going on,' Charlotte said. 'I'm curious. Shall we saunter down there?'

'They've stopped on the other side of the road. My word, the police are armed. Maybe it would be best if we went in the other direction.'

The concierge overheard the conversation and turned to them. 'I shouldn't go down there, ma'am. We heard shots fired a few moments ago. Something bad has happened.'

'Golly, it doesn't look like the sort of place where someone would fire a gun,' Marion said.

'We heard shots when we were upstairs,' Charlotte told him. 'We certainly won't go that way now.'

As she was talking, the ATS driver jumped out of the driver's side and opened the rear door of the black car. Her eyes widened as she watched a man unfold from the interior. He was well over six foot tall, with broad shoulders and dark hair cut in a military fashion. She couldn't see his face but she could see he was leaning heavily on a cane.

Two other plain-clothes men joined him on the pavement – they too were armed.

The stick the handsome man was using explained why he wasn't in uniform, but working as a member of the Criminal Investigation Department. From the deference accorded him by the uniformed men and his driver he must be an inspector at the very least. For some reason she wanted him to turn so she could get a good look at him. Was he scarred? Did he wear glasses? Exactly how old was he?

From his bearing she decided he must be no older than thirty – his hair was thick and no sign of grey in it, which was another indication of his age. Then he turned and looked straight at her. She blinked, her cheeks coloured, but she couldn't look away.

Dan stared at the attractive WAAF on the other side of the road. 'Dyson,' he said to one of the constables, 'get statements from that lot over there. They might well have heard or seen something pertinent.'

'Yes, sir, I'll do it straightaway.'

Dan almost ground his teeth. If a senior officer gave an order it should be carried out immediately. Was Dyson hoping to impress by saying he intended to do as he was told now and not after he'd had a fag and a cup of tea? God, how he missed the discipline of the army. He'd barely survived Dunkirk and had this bloody leg to remind him every day how lucky he'd been.

There'd been no further shots after the first two, no one had fled the scene, so either the gunman was dead or still in there waiting to shoot whoever stepped in first. The person who'd dialled 999 had said they'd heard screaming before the gun went off. Dan didn't trust his sergeant, Jones, which wasn't ideal. Also, the fact that he was under the command of someone ten years his junior made the man surly and almost insubordinate. Too bad – if the man had been good enough then he would have been promoted himself.

He gestured to the two plain-clothes men to take the back entrance and he approached the front. The three other uniformed men were only too happy to tuck in behind him. They weren't armed with anything more lethal than a truncheon so he didn't want them going in first.

He was a trained soldier, a marksman, and having a gun in *his* hand was safe. The other two had had no training in the use of weapons – they'd just been handed a revolver each and left to get on with it. God knows what would happen if they had to actually use them.

He approached the front door sideways, making his body the smallest target possible. There was a remote possibility whoever was inside might be standing behind the door, waiting for him to knock.

The stick was a damned nuisance but essential when walking – he propped it against the wall so he had both hands free. He reached over and turned the knob. It moved. The door wasn't locked. He took a steadying breath and pushed gently. Police were supposed to announce themselves before entering the property but he thought if he did so he might get his brains blown out.

He inched forward, keeping his back pressed against the door as it slowly swung inwards. He also needed the support as without his cane to lean on his duff leg was likely to collapse under him. He gave his eyes a few moments to adjust to the darkness of the hallway in front of him.

Not a sound – not even a moan. He sniffed and caught the distinctive aroma of death. He was pretty certain there was no one alive in this house. He was about to reach back for his cane but someone put it in his hand.

'We're looking for bodies, Jackson. I think we'll find the cadavers in the room to the right. It might be best if I went first.'

Jackson was a new recruit and was already looking a bit

green about the gills. Probably best not to let him vomit over the crime scene.

'Find the back door and let the others in.'

The constable dashed past him, obviously relieved he didn't have to view any bodies today. Dan thought his own weapon was redundant, but it was better to err on the side of caution so he kept it, safety catch off, in his hand.

He pushed open the sitting room door. There was no need to send for a medic – both the man and the woman were quite definitely deceased. He spoke over his shoulder to the other constable lurking behind him. 'This is a crime scene, but it's a murder-suicide. We need the police surgeon and the mortuary van. No need for fingerprinting or the forensic chaps to be fetched.'

The murderer had the gun in his mouth and the back of his head was blown off. His wife had been shot through the heart. God knows what drove a man to commit such a heinous crime and then kill himself. Better than facing the hangman's noose he supposed. Just another reason to avoid matrimony, in his opinion.

The uniformed branch could have cleared this up without the help of CID. He made his revolver safe and dropped it back in his coat pocket. He closed the door on the gruesome scene and turned to face his sergeant and detective constable.

'We need the photographer, but after that the bodies can be taken to the morgue. There'll have to be a post-mortem but it's a formality. Put your weapons away – no need for them here today.

'Inspector Chalmers, do you want us to remain here or can we return to Scotland Yard?' His sergeant never called him sir.

'Leave a PC at the door. I don't care which one. I'm already late for a post-mortem I wanted to attend.'

Charlotte gave her statement to the young constable who diligently wrote down every word she said in his little blue notebook. He then asked exactly the same questions of Marion and got identical answers. This procedure took more than a quarter of an hour and was a complete waste of time. Satisfied he'd discovered everything he was going to from the witnesses, the young man went into the hotel, presumably in search of the concierge and the waiter.

'This is a respectable street. The house the gunshots came from must belong to moderately wealthy people. I doubt it was a burglary,' Charlotte continued, 'not in broad daylight.'

'I expect we'll find out what happened this evening. Let's not waste any more time,' her friend said. 'At some point today I want to stroll around Westminster, visit the cathedral and the abbey and also wander into Piccadilly.'

'I thought we were going to the café for some lunch first?' She didn't hear Marion's response as the limping detective exited the house and moved, with remarkable agility for a man with a stick, to his waiting vehicle. For some reason she was intrigued by this policeman and rather wished that he'd been the one to interview her.

The car was moving before they were and she smiled wryly. 'Sorry, what did you say?'

'I said I'd changed my mind about your little café. Why not find somewhere smarter?'

*

They spent an enjoyable afternoon walking around the West End. Despite the fact that there was little to buy in the shops and even when there was, they didn't have enough points to purchase anything. They did find a small, very expensive restaurant and had a delicious omelette made with real eggs, which had actual cheese inside.

Marion insisted on walking along with her arm through hers and, although she found this degree of intimacy a little uncomfortable, it reminded her of her days at boarding school. It was quite common for girls to hug and kiss each other – not that she was one of those who did – and quite often the older girls shared a bed, which she thought unhygienic and rather odd.

However, she didn't want to spoil a delightful afternoon by removing her arm so smiled and carried on as if she was quite happy to be linked to her friend like this. She had embraced both Jane and Nancy more than once but couldn't recall ever walking as she was doing now with Marion.

The streets became busier as bowler-hatted businessmen in pinstriped trousers and black jackets poured out of their offices and headed for the stations to endure the long commute to their suburban homes. When they turned into Tothill Street she noticed there was no longer a police presence outside the house across the road.

'Good heavens, I would have thought they would still be dusting for fingerprints, taking photographs and so on. It's as if there hasn't been any excitement here today,' Charlotte said.

'Do you know, I've never seen a detective before. They don't have them everywhere. I think that the CID are located at Scotland Yard and then get sent all over the place to solve major crimes.'

'I'd not thought about it before. Did you notice the senior detective? I wonder if he was injured at Dunkirk?'

'The man with the cane? I suppose he did look like a soldier. I wouldn't want to get on the wrong side of him, would you?'

4

Attending a post-mortem wasn't something Dan enjoyed but sometimes, if you wanted to know more about the body and didn't want to wait until the coroner's report was written, then you had no option. Today was one of those days.

'DCI Daniel Chalmers,' he announced to the uniformed man on the door and was nodded through. Unfortunately, the pathologist had already completed his work and only the technician was there in his gumboots and rubber apron cleaning down the surfaces.

Dan swore under his breath and turned to retrace his steps. Walking anywhere was painful and having had to trek through the morgue unnecessarily just added to his frustration. As he was passing the second room where these grisly examinations took place a movement caught his eye. He paused to look. To his bewilderment he saw two mortuary attendants attempting to remove the corpse of a stout, middle-aged woman, fully-clothed, from the table.

His mouth curved. Somehow the cadaver had become frozen to the metal top and despite their best efforts they couldn't detach her. He watched as the men propped the tabletop against the wall, the body still firmly stuck to it, creating a macabre sculpture.

Fascinated, he remained where he was, watching in the shadows, intrigued to know how they would solve this problem. A few moments later the attendants returned with chisels and began to chip away at the ice.

He didn't remain to see the completion of their endeavours but watching them had amused him and very little did that nowadays. His car, driven by a nervous but efficient ATS woman was, as always, waiting for him.

Being a wounded veteran gave him a slight advantage over the other inspectors as he was the only one to have a chauffeured car at his disposal. Much to his father's fury Dan had refused to go to the Royal Military College at Sandhurst and follow the family tradition. Instead, after completing his degree at Oxford, he'd joined the police force.

By the time war had been declared he was already a sergeant – the youngest in the Met so he was told – and had just made the move into plain clothes. He'd taken the inspectors' exam and passed it easily but had had no time to take up his promotion. There'd been no need for his parent to harangue him to join up as Dan had immediately volunteered. Officer training was no longer a two-year process and he was commissioned within a few months and sent out to join his regiment in France as a lieutenant.

When Hitler's troops had broken through the Maginot Line and overwhelmed the Allies and the British forces, he'd been in the thick of it. In the chaos of the rapid retreat to Dunkirk he'd fought a rear-guard action, making sure that not only the active but also the wounded made their way to the beaches.

He'd caught a piece of shrapnel in his calf but had continued to lead his men. He'd been a lucky devil to have been picked up by small boat and taken to Blighty. It was nothing short of a miracle that so many had been evacuated over those few days last year.

Whilst in hospital he heard his father had died. It was no loss at all to him. He'd never got on with his father and hadn't seen him since he'd left for university. His mother had died when he was a boy and he scarcely remembered her.

He'd almost lost his leg and, but for the excellence of the army surgeons, would have done so. They patched him up and he'd been honourably discharged as unfit for further duty. The Met had welcomed him back – they were woefully short of experienced CID officers – and he was immediately given his present post as a detective inspector.

On returning to his cramped and cluttered office he was surprised to find the neatly typed reports from the interviews that the two constables had conducted with the witnesses were already on his desk. Not that these were needed but crimes, even ones that were so cut and dried as this, had to be entered in the book and all pertinent information filed.

Idly he read through the first statement. One of the WAAF was called Charlotte Fenimore and she'd put her address as The Sanctuary Hotel. Fenimore was a name he'd never forget. Major Fenimore had fought alongside him in the hideous retreat. The poor man had died in his arms. It was an unusual name so it was possible this young woman was related. Which of the two girls was Charlotte? The taller, darker girl had a familial resemblance to the major.

There was nothing much going on here at the moment

and some impulse made him decide to go in search of Miss Fenimore and see if she was indeed related to, or even the younger sister of the brave man he'd known for such a short time, but never forgotten.

This WAAF was an officer – the lowest rank – but nevertheless a person of moderate importance in the female side of things in the RAF. He had a quick look at this second report – the other WAAF was also an officer – the fact that they were both on leave could well mean they'd been recently promoted.

The ATS girl scrambled out of the driver's seat and saluted smartly. 'Where to, sir? Any more grisly murders to attend?'

'The Sanctuary Hotel. I'm going to dine there. Come back for me at nine o'clock.'

Having to be driven so short a distance just reinforced his irritation at being unable to walk as other men could. He knew he was abrupt with his driver and she didn't deserve to be the recipient of his ill humour.

Having lived through the horror of his own parents' unhappy marriage he'd decided long ago never to become trapped himself. Anyway – no woman would wish to become entangled with a cripple like him.

The foyer of the hotel was mercifully empty when he entered. He'd dined here several times as it was convenient for Scotland Yard. The head waiter greeted him like an old friend.

'Good evening, DI Chalmers, I have your usual table free.'

'Good. Before I eat I'm looking for someone. Do you have two WAAF officers eating here tonight?'

The man didn't even bother to look down at his list.

'Officers Fenimore and Russell have booked a table for seven o'clock. They should be here momentarily.'

'Thank you. I'll wait for them in the bar.'

'There's no need, sir, they are just approaching the dining room now.'

Dan found turning difficult and this was when he needed to rely on his stick the most. Walking straight was a doddle. The two girls were approaching him and the dark girl he thought might be related to the major saw him first.

He smiled and moved as smoothly as he could towards them. 'Good evening. I'm sorry to intrude but do you think I could have a few moments of your time, ASO Fenimore?'

The other WAAF frowned, nodded, and strode away. The girl he wished to speak to returned his smile. 'Of course, I'm always happy to help the police in any way I can. However, you have the advantage of me.'

'I'm sorry, I'm DI Daniel Chalmers. Would you mind coming into the snug with me? It's easier for me to be seated.' This wasn't really true as he was perfectly comfortable standing up but he didn't want to upset her in public if the man he'd known was indeed her brother.

He didn't offer to buy her a drink. Once they were comfortable he asked his question. 'Are you by any chance related to Major Giles Fenimore?'

Her eyes widened slightly and she nodded. 'Yes, I have a brother called Giles. He is quite a bit older than me and we've never been close.'

Bloody hell! She obviously didn't know the major was dead. 'I served with him in France. I'm sorry to be the one to tell you, but he died a hero in my arms at Dunkirk.'

*

For a moment Charlotte couldn't process what the inspector had just told her. Then for a second she couldn't breathe. Giles had been dead for eighteen months and she hadn't known.

'Thank you for coming to tell me. How did you know no one had informed me?'

'I didn't. I actually came to introduce myself and tell you how much I admired your brother, that he was a courageous and magnificent soldier.'

'I'm sure he was. But he was a thoroughly unpleasant brother and although I wish he hadn't died his demise means nothing to me personally.' DI Chalmers was looking at her through narrowed eyes and she hastily explained her callous remark. 'He bullied me horribly when I was a child. My mother, whom I loved dearly, sent me away to school when I was eight. I have another brother, Jasper, who is equally obnoxious. Is he dead too?'

If she'd expected to shock him by her revelation she would have been disappointed. He sat back and raised an eyebrow, which made her want to kick him.

'Were you a particularly annoying younger sister?'

For a moment she was rendered speechless by his remark but then she laughed. 'I was. I ignored everything I was told and did exactly as I pleased.' Her smile slipped as she continued. 'That doesn't excuse my brother from what he did to me.'

He snapped his fingers and a waiter appeared as if by magic at his shoulder. 'Two brandies – make them doubles.'

'I didn't know him for long. We only met as we were

fighting our way through France. I'm sorry to revive painful memories. I apologise for making light of what you told me.'

The drinks appeared and her companion pushed a glass into her hand. She put it down. 'Thank you, Inspector, but I don't drink spirits. Please excuse me, I don't wish to keep my friend waiting any longer. Thank you for taking the time to come and see me.' She stood and then smiled sadly. 'I might seem callous to you, but I hated him, so why should I pretend his death saddens me?'

She was on her feet and moving smoothly towards the exit before he had time to react. On entering the dining room she saw where Marion was sitting and hurried over to join her. 'I'm so sorry, I didn't know we were going to be ambushed by that man. It would seem that my oldest brother died in his arms at Dunkirk.'

'Golly, how awful! You don't look particularly upset by the news.'

'I'm not. He was like a stranger to me and a particularly nasty one at that. It's a matter of complete indifference to me whether he's alive or dead. I have another brother, not quite as appalling as the one who died, and I've no idea whether he's alive or dead either. The fact that the war office didn't inform me means I wasn't listed as next of kin. My parents are dead too.'

Marion leaned across and placed her hands over hers. 'You poor old thing, how horrid for you. I've still got two sisters, two sets of grandparents and my parents, all living happily in Surrey.'

'I'm surprised that you didn't want to spend your leave with them.' Charlotte spoke without thinking and was puzzled by the reaction she got.

'I'd much rather spend time with you, old girl. I've become rather attached to you over the past few months and am hoping that you feel the same.'

This was an odd way to talk about their friendship but Charlotte just smiled and gently removed her hands. 'I never thought I'd have another close friend, but I consider you to be one now. Have you looked at the menu? Is there anything worth having on it tonight?'

Marion was staring over her shoulder and Charlotte swivelled on her chair and saw the grim police inspector approaching their table. Surely not? Hadn't she made it abundantly clear that their conversation and brief acquaintance was over? She braced herself to rebuff him a second time but he swung past, totally ignoring her, and sat at a table on the far side of them.

She wasn't sure if she was offended or amused – but she was certainly relieved he had as little inclination to speak to her as she had to speak to him.

There was no choice, but the steak and kidney pie was excellent. More kidney than was usual but then offal wasn't rationed and beef was. The apple crumble and real crème anglaise were even better. They ordered coffee but this was a bitter disappointment – bitter being exactly what it was.

'I don't know how they have the cheek to sell this as if it's real coffee,' Marion said after her first swallow. 'I think it's that horrible acorn and chicory concoction, don't you?'

'I'm not going to drink it. Doing so would ruin a perfectly splendid meal. The head waiter's coming this way and I intend to make it abundantly clear I don't want this abomination added to our bill.'

They retreated to their eyrie in the attic and retired early to talk for hours about nothing much at all in the way that close friends often did. Tomorrow they were going to see Nancy in Chelmsford – it would be an unannounced visit but she was sure her friend would be delighted to see her.

In the last letter she'd had from Nancy she'd been told that Billy, now five, was happily at school and Betty, three and a half, was proving a devoted older sister to the baby. Lottie had only been a couple of weeks old the last time she'd seen her and would now be five months.

It was doubtful that David, Dr David Denny, Nancy's lovely husband, would be there as he led a busy life as a junior consultant surgeon at the Royal Free here in London. She'd told Marion that Billy and Betty were adopted, having been orphaned whilst evacuated at their house. She certainly had no intention of revealing that the baby wasn't David's but the daughter of Nancy's first love who'd been killed a week before their wedding just over a year ago.

Dan ate his solitary dinner, scarcely noticing what he put in his mouth, lost in thought. Being an excellent soldier, a courageous man under fire, didn't necessarily make you a decent bloke. He'd little time for sentimentality, and no objection to a disobedient child being occasionally lightly spanked by a parent, but what that girl had said had touched a chord.

He was an orphan, had no siblings, no relatives alive. His grandparents on both sides had been dead before he was old enough to remember them. His mother had been vague woman, flapping about the place, complaining bitterly about everything and taking no interest whatsoever in her only child. Father had been a forceful man, a fourth-generation soldier who had fought in the first lot and had a chest full of medals to prove it. His only interest in his son had been to bring him up to be a fifth-generation officer and gentleman.

If Dan hadn't inherited a decent annuity from his grandfather then he wouldn't have been able to defy Pa and go to Oxford and then become a policeman. If he was honest then he'd been better at being an officer in the army than he was at his present role as a detective inspector.

He glanced at his watch. His car would be arriving in ten minutes so he'd better get the bill. He glanced across and saw the table ASO Fenimore and her friend had been sitting at was now empty. The WAAF was taller than average, attractive but not beautiful. Her hair was dark, he wasn't sure about her eye colour, and her features were strong and uncompromising like her character.

He was used to having his orders obeyed. Her comprehensive dismissal of his attempt to take charge had initially annoyed him but now, after a decent meal and two large brandies, he was more relaxed about things. In fact, he rather hoped that when he next dined here she would be around and he could get to know her better.

It was standing room only on the train from Liverpool Street the next day, but she and Marion were quite happy to be sandwiched in the corridor with the other service people who couldn't find seats in the compartments. There were more brown jobs – as soldiers were called by the RAF – than any other service as Colchester, a stop further down the line, had a large army barracks.

'It's only a short walk from the station, Marion. I hope I can remember the way as I've only been there a couple of times.'

'Do you think we should have brought a gift of some sort?'

'No, not necessary. Nancy will just be delighted that we've come.'

They were still fifty yards from the walled front garden when Polly, the family dog, started barking. She increased her pace, delighted that this friendly canine was as pleased to see her as she was to be arriving. Only as she rang the bell that was set into the wall by the gate did she become aware that Marion wasn't as enthusiastic about the racket the dog was making as she was.

'I really don't like animals, Charlotte. That dog sounds quite dangerous.'

'Don't be silly – that's a friendly bark.' Charlotte put her hand on the gate and spoke to the excited animal on the other side. 'Just be patient, Polly, someone will let us in soon.'

The barking stopped and was replaced by scrabbling feet on the wood and inpatient yelps and whines. Someone was coming. The gate swung open and the dog erupted from behind it, landing square on her chest and sending her tumbling backwards. She lay on the ground attempting to stop the dog from slathering all over her face.

'Get off, you silly thing. Let me get up.'

'Charlotte, I don't believe it. Why didn't you tell me you were coming?' Nancy leaned over and grabbed Polly's collar and pulled her back. 'Naughty girl, you shouldn't knock people over. One day you'll do someone a mischief.'

5

Nancy helped Charlotte to her feet and once she was upright, they embraced. 'I'm sorry to arrive unannounced, but Marion and I have got a week's leave before we're reposted. I'm going to be working in London so hopefully can see you more often.' She turned to introduce her friend. 'This is Marion, we've become good chums over the past few months.'

'I'm so glad you both came. David's here – he's got a couple of days off. He's taken Billy and Betty for a walk but he'll be back soon. Come in – the kettle's on.'

Charlotte couldn't believe the change in Lottie. The baby was sitting in her wooden high chair, waving a rattle and laughing and pointing at her as she came in.

'Can I pick her up? Isn't she absolutely spiffing?'

'I shouldn't – Jenny's about to change her. Lottie's just filled her nappy.'

Marion visibly recoiled. 'I'm sorry, Nancy. I'm not fond of babies or dogs. Do you mind if I sit outside in one of those deckchairs whilst you two catch up?'

'Help yourself. I'll give you a shout when the tea's made.' Nancy raised an eyebrow at Charlotte and she shrugged.

'She was keen to come but I wouldn't have brought her

if I'd known she was going to be so unsociable. I'm really sorry, Nancy.'

'Some women aren't keen on little ones or dogs. I'll put Polly in the back garden when David gets back and the baby will go down for a nap. Jenny's fetching the laundry from the line but will do it on her return.'

David returned a few minutes later and stopped to talk to Marion but the children rushed in and threw themselves at Charlotte.

'Billy's had to stay home cos he's got nits, Auntie Charlotte,' Betty said gleefully.

'I haven't got them now. Daddy killed them all and then combed the dead ones out of my hair,' her brother said with a grin.

'I don't care if you have got them. I'm just pleased to see you both. I can't believe how much you've grown in the last few months. Are you loving school, Billy?'

'It's all right. I can read and write and do my sums already so it's a bit boring.'

The children vanished into another part of the house to fetch various pictures and toys to bring back to show her.

David arrived and strode across and Charlotte hugged him fiercely. He was such a lovely man, perfect for her friend, and he looked so much happier than he had done before he and Nancy had got married in June.

'I didn't expect to see you as well. I'm sorry...'

'Don't apologise, Charlotte; I'm delighted you came. I see you've been promoted and are now an officer.'

'A very lowly one, but I'm hoping to get rapid promotion. Is Marion coming in?'

'Not until she's sure my baby daughter and my dog have

been removed.' He kissed his wife, snapped his fingers at Polly and she followed him to the back door. 'Out you go, dog, and don't pester the gardeners.'

Jenny, the young girl who was the live-in helper, returned from putting the baby down in her cot upstairs and immediately picked up the mug of tea poured out for Marion.

'I'll take this out, shall I?'

'Yes, thanks. Will you tell Marion the coast's clear and she can come in and join us?' Nancy said as she dashed about the kitchen like a miniature whirlwind. 'I hope you're both staying for lunch? I'm doing a lovely omelette with vegetables from the garden.'

Charlotte had a feeling that Marion might refuse this offer so she accepted immediately. Why on earth had her friend insisted on coming if she was going to hide outside?

'Just the ticket – but we don't want to intrude on your time with David. I don't suppose you get a lot of it.'

He answered as he pulled out a chair and sat at the large scrubbed, wooden table. 'Better lately. This new friend of yours, have you known her long?'

'Since June – we did the officer training together and have become quite close.'

'I think it's possible she's jealous. She's obviously fond of you and resents the fact that you've come here to spend time with Nancy.'

'It's a bit more than that, love, if you know what I mean,' Nancy said to him with a wink.

Charlotte was completely mystified by this remark and the wink, but David nodded. He was about to explain when Marion followed Jenny into the kitchen. She thought they might have overheard the conversation. Before her new friend could speak Charlotte turned to her.

'We're staying for lunch. I've not seen my friends since June and want to catch up.'

'That's very kind of you to invite me as well, Nancy, but it's not fair to have your dog shut out because I'm frightened of her. Charlotte, I'm going back to London. Enjoy your visit.'

'Really, you don't have to go.'

Marion just smiled and marched out without another word, leaving a strange silence behind her. This was a side of Marion she'd not seen before and one she didn't appreciate.

'Nancy, what were you and David referring to?'

They exchanged glances and then he answered. 'We both think that your new friend is rather hoping to be more than a friend, if you get my drift.'

She frowned and thought about it. Then the pieces fell into place. 'Oh my God, Marion is someone who prefers women to men. I should have realised but it just never occurred to me. How awfully embarrassing – I've obviously not given her any indication that I reciprocated feelings of that sort.'

'It's very difficult for both men and women who feel like this to be obliged to live differently from everyone else. The local constabulary regularly round up any men they find loitering in public toilets. Personally, I think what anyone wishes to do in the privacy of their own bedroom is entirely their own business.'

At the mention of the word bedroom Charlotte jumped to her feet. 'We're sharing a room – she's always putting her arm around me, wanting to hold my hand and so on but it never occurred to me why she was doing it. I'd better go after her. I can't let her continue to believe I'm on the same wavelength as her.'

'I think you might well find that she's checked out by the time you get back,' David said. 'No point in rushing off and having an embarrassing conversation. Let the poor girl keep her dignity and leave.'

Over lunch they talked about Jane and Oscar. 'Is she now having a baby as she'd hoped?'

'No, she didn't catch on but they're seeing a bit more of each other as Jane has wangled a posting closer to him,' Nancy told her.

'I'm really looking forward to working in London from next week. I'm going to be living at The Sanctuary. I haven't told you about the excitement outside yesterday.'

Nancy was horrified that a gun had been fired so close to her best friend. 'Stay away from that CID bloke, Charlotte. He doesn't sound too friendly.'

'It was kind of him to take the trouble to tell me about my brother but I wish he hadn't. I should be sad that he's died but I'm not. Does that make me unfeeling?'

'Why should you grieve for someone you didn't love just because he's your brother? No need to pretend with us or anyone else who loves you.'

David nodded his agreement and got up to make coffee. 'In your honour I'm using the last of the gift Jane brought Nancy when Lottie was born.'

'Let me do it. I don't want to be waited on.' Charlotte got up and joined him at the sideboard. The children wanted to go in the garden and Jenny went out with them. Nancy dashed off to fetch the baby down.

'Charlotte,' David said, 'I'm glad we've got a few moments alone together. I met that Chalmers chap when he came to speak to a victim I was treating for stab wounds. He's dangerous – has a reputation for ruthlessness and my patient was terrified of him.'

'Thank you for the warning, but I doubt I'll see him again.'

Dan spent a relatively quiet day doing paperwork and reading the coroner's report for the PM he'd missed yesterday. He decided to eat at The Sanctuary again and told his driver to collect him there at nine o'clock as before.

He was just adjusting his grip on his stick and standing outside the door of the hotel when someone exiting at speed collided with him. Instinctively he gripped the arms of the young woman to try and steady himself but she too was unbalanced and together they crashed to the pavement.

By the time he'd untangled himself the concierge and another guest had burst through the door and were offering their assistance. He was relatively unscathed but the young lady was worryingly still.

Instead of taking the offered arm to help him to his feet, clumsily he knelt beside the WAAF. She had hit her head on the pavement and already there was an alarming amount of gore spreading around it.

'Quickly, I need a clean cloth folded into a pad. Someone dial for an ambulance.' He ripped off his tie and when the concierge handed him what he wanted he gently pressed the folded napkin against the injury and kept it in place with his tie. Then he checked the girl's pulse – steady enough to indicate she wasn't critically injured.

Only then did he recognise her as being ASO Fenimore's companion – the disapproving one. Her kitbag had gone flying at the collision and her belongings were scattered across the pavement. Now he accepted the help he needed to get to his feet and was grateful when a passing pedestrian handed him his cane.

'Can somebody collect her things and put them back? She'll be put on a charge if she loses anything.'

Willing hands soon had everything restored – probably incorrectly folded and not in the right order but at least nothing was missing. There was now a cushion under the comatose girl's head and a tartan rug over her. At least it kept her safe from the lewd stares of the workmen who'd gathered to watch on the other side of the road.

What damned bad luck to have caused, albeit inadvertently, an injury to someone he knew. The clang of the ambulance bell heralded its rapid arrival. The ambulance drivers were not medically trained and he almost certainly was more competent to deal with this emergency than they were. He'd dealt with many desperately injured soldiers under his command at Dunkirk and the basic course he'd taken during training at Sandhurst had proved invaluable.

He briefly informed the stretcher bearers – they were little more than that – what had happened and what he believed was wrong with the WAAF.

They made no attempt to interfere with his rudimentary first aid and deftly transferred the unconscious girl to the canvas stretcher. Moments later she was safely installed in the rear of the ambulance and being transported to St Thomas's which was close to Westminster Bridge.

The small crowd dispersed and he made his way into the hotel for a much-needed drink. He was somewhat dishevelled and diners weren't allowed into the dining room without a tie and his was now on its way to the hospital.

The concierge, Bates, met him with a smile. 'If you would care to accompany me, sir, I can help you restore your appearance and also supply you with the item of clothing that you're now missing.'

'Thank you. From your expression I'm much in need of a tidy-up.'

He viewed himself in the mirror of the staff bathroom that he'd been taken to. There were smudges of blood on his face; his hands were covered in it and there were also smears on his shirt. He used a wet flannel to restore his hands and face and wiped the worst from his clothes afterwards.

His mouth quirked as he slipped the borrowed tie under his collar. God knows where Bates had found this abomination – it was purple and green checks, but served the purpose. He hoped he didn't see anyone from Scotland Yard whilst wearing it or he'd be sniggered at behind his back for the next week.

He prided himself on his sartorial elegance. He decided once he'd been released from the convalescent home and was ready to work that he might be a cripple but he was going to be the best dressed one in London. Having inherited a decent fortune from his parents he was in the enviable position of being able to indulge his whim. The suit and shirt he was wearing were, naturally, bespoke from Savile Row, his shoes handmade from Hobbs.

Satisfied he could do no more he shouldered his way out through the swinging doors that led to the staff area of the hotel and emerged into the foyer. He was ushered like a visiting dignitary into the dining room and given the best table.

'There will be no charge for your dinner or drinks tonight, DCI Chalmers – it's the least we can do in the circumstances. I thought you'd like to know that ASO Russell has regained consciousness and is suffering from a severe concussion but nothing life-threatening.'

'Thank you. How the devil did you know that?'

Bates smiled. 'I rang the hospital myself and made enquiries. ASO Fenimore has yet to return but I can assure you that I shall make it my personal business to inform her of her friend's unfortunate accident.'

Dan was just enjoying the last delicious mouthful of apple pie and custard when he glanced up and saw the Fenimore girl hurrying towards him. He dropped his cutlery and reached for his stick in order to stand up.

'No, please stay where you are, Detective Inspector Chalmers. I just wanted to thank you for helping Marion. I'm glad that you weren't hurt as well in the collision.'

'Please, will you join me for coffee? I promise I won't try and force a cognac on you.'

She nodded and pulled out the chair before a hovering waiter could do it for her. 'I hope the coffee is better than the nasty ersatz drink we got last night.' She stopped and smiled. 'I'm sorry, that was hardly tactful when you have so kindly offered to buy me some.'

'They wouldn't dare serve me with anything but the real stuff.'

'I suppose you want to know why Marion was rushing off in such a hurry.'

He couldn't tell her that he had absolutely no interest in the reasons her friend had been leaving but he was prepared to listen if it meant this attractive young lady remained with him for a while longer.

'I am curious. I assumed she'd been recalled from leave, had an emergency posting.'

'No, I wish it had been. There was a misunderstanding and she thought it better to leave immediately.' The young woman didn't seem inclined to elaborate and he'd no intention of enquiring further.

Charlotte tried not to look at his extraordinary tie but her eyes kept moving in that direction. She couldn't help herself and had to ask why he was wearing it as it was so out of character. 'Your tie?'

He grinned, making him look less austere and more approachable. 'I know, hideous isn't it? I used mine to hold a pad of cloth against the cut in your friend's head. Bates, the concierge, kindly loaned me this one, for without it I couldn't have eaten here tonight.'

She leaned over and touched the dark marks on his once immaculate suit. 'Are those bloodstains?'

'I'm afraid so. She lost a lot of blood but that's not surprising as head wounds bleed copiously. She's going to be absolutely fine – I wish I could say the same for my suit.'

She sat back and drank the rest of her delicious coffee. 'Aren't such things an occupational hazard?'

'Good God, I'm a detective inspector not a medic. Mostly I view bodies and there's no necessity for me to touch them.' He poured her another cup. 'This is hardly a suitable conversation over the dinner table. My name's Daniel – I'm called Dan – are you prepared to drop the formalities?'

'I'm Charlotte, but you already knew that I expect.'

His smile was warm, which made him look even more attractive. David had told her to be careful but he'd not met Dan. She was confident she was safe with him. 'Well, Charlotte, I've enjoyed our conversation but my car will be here in a minute. I seem to recall that you said this was your permanent residence in your statement. Is that correct?'

'Yes, I'll be working at Victory House from next Monday. I can't tell you how much I'm enjoying sleeping on a real bed with actual sheets.'

He chuckled, a deep rich sound. 'What the hell did you sleep on before?'

When she explained about the three biscuit mattresses, he shook his head in disbelief. 'No wonder you girls are so tough. Your accommodation sounds worse than that of a POW.' Slowly he pushed his chair back, gripped the edge of the table with one hand and his cane with the other and rose smoothly to his feet.

'I dine here several times a week – would you care to join me tomorrow night?'

She didn't hesitate. 'I'd love to. I'll go and see Marion tomorrow even though it might be a bit tricky after what happened yesterday.' Her cheeks flushed as she realised that she might have to explain her statement.

'Don't look so embarrassed – I think I know exactly why she took off in such a hurry.' He didn't elaborate and she'd no intention of asking him as then she'd have to discuss something she'd rather forget.

Although he was obliged to use a cane, his limp wasn't too bad. He was a head taller than her so must be well over six foot – as she'd estimated when she first saw him – as she was five foot six inches in her socks. She said good night in the foyer. The blackouts were in place at nine o'clock. The nights were already drawing in and lights were necessary inside a building.

She already had her key so headed straight for the stairs. He was an interesting man, a bit abrupt, plain-speaking, but highly intelligent. When she knew him better perhaps she'd ask him how he came by his injury.

David was wrong to say that she should avoid him. Dan might well be feared by the underworld, the criminals, but she was confident she, and any other woman, would be perfectly safe in his company.

6

Dan startled his driver by smiling at her as he got into the car. She drove him expertly through the dark streets without running over any pedestrians – which had been a major problem in London at the start of the blackout – and pulled up outside his home. He'd sold the family house in Mayfair and rented an apartment in Kensington as stairs were no longer something he wished to negotiate every day.

The doorman touched his cap and smiled. 'All quiet, Inspector. Let's hope we get none of those blighters over ruining our evening.'

'No bomber's moon tonight, Sid, and the Luftwaffe are all but done. Good night.'

He'd chosen this particular apartment block because it had a lift, was fully serviced, and was close enough to shops if he should care to visit them. He didn't employ a full-time housekeeper as there was no necessity – he was rarely home long enough to do anything but change his clothes and sleep.

However, a maid service was included in the rent as was the laundering, pressing and polishing of his clothes and footwear. What had made this particular apartment so attractive to him was the fact that they had an excellent chef working in the bowels of the building and provided an excellent room service, which he preferred to use rather than cook for himself.

For the first time since his accident he didn't feel like an unwanted human reject. Charlotte was a lovely young woman; she'd seen him hobbling about the place and didn't seem put off by his injury. Was it possible, despite everything, that sometime in the future he might be considered a fully functioning and acceptable male by a member of the opposite sex?

He completed his ablutions, as always, before retiring. He was frequently called out in the middle of the night and had no intention of appearing anything but clean-shaven and immaculate whatever the hour. A suit, a crisp, freshly laundered shirt and a blue silk tie were neatly arranged on the wooden stand at the end of his bed.

He slept in fresh underwear, which made dressing a matter of minutes. He was roused after a few hours' sleep by the harsh jangling of the telephone and reached out with one hand to pick up the receiver.

'Chalmers speaking.'

'There's been a double homicide down at the docks, sir. You're needed. Nasty business. Your car's on its way.'

Dan rolled out of bed, snatched up his stick and with the ease of much practice was dressed, and on his way out, in less than five minutes. The lift clanked and grumbled, the sound loud in the darkness. There was always somebody on duty at the desk and the man was alert and, despite the fact there were no lights, had obviously seen the silhouette of his car pull up outside and was already heading for the door.

The spacious foyer was dark. There were no blackouts

at the windows and residents came and went at night by the pinprick of light from their trusty torches. He slipped the man half a crown and stepped into the night. There was no bomber's moon tonight and thank God London was being ignored by the remnants of the Luftwaffe. The poor bastards elsewhere were getting the brunt of the bombing now.

He gave the address to the driver – not a girl he recognised. This was always irritating but he supposed his regular girl had to sleep sometime. The streets were deserted, which meant travelling at speed was relatively safe, and he arrived at the Royal Albert Dock a little over half an hour from when he'd received the phone call. He was impressed with this driver's navigational skills. Driving from Kensington to the docks in the dark with almost no headlights was something very few men could do as well as she had.

There was no time to speak to her but he would make a point of actually asking her name and thanking her when eventually he returned to the car.

The PC who'd been on call at Scotland Yard had omitted to give him two pieces of vital information. The first being that both the bodies were foreign sailors and the second was that his own sergeant, Jones, was already there. There was no sign of any witnesses or uniformed men, just Jones and his shadow, DC Smith.

'For God's sake, what the hell's going on? Who reported this? Why aren't people being interviewed?'

'Cut and dried, Detective Inspector Chalmers – no need for you to have been called at all. The two of them got into a fight and killed each other,' Jones said with a supercilious sneer.

Dan barely restrained the impulse to knock the idiot's teeth into the back of his throat. He ignored Jones and turned to Smith. 'I want half a dozen uniformed men here – now – and the photographer and police surgeon.' The man hesitated for a second too long. 'Get a move on, you snivelling bastard. I'll not have insubordination from you.'

The man took off at a run without even a second glance at Jones, which was fortunate for him. Dan then turned his attention to the bodies, still ignoring his sergeant. He would be dealt with later. He'd had as much as he was going to take from this man and he intended to have him removed from CID immediately and posted somewhere, as far away as could be arranged, from Scotland Yard.

Impatiently he pulled off the cover on his torch that kept the light to a miserable thread and shone the full beam down on the two men. If an Air Raid Precautions warden yelled at him to put the light out, he'd ignore it. The blackout wasn't needed tonight as there were no enemy aircraft within miles.

It was immediately obvious that both men had been stabbed and certainly they both had a knife in their hands. What the idiot sergeant had failed to understand was that the chances of both men killing each other simultaneously with a knife was remote to say the least. If one of the bodies had been several yards away indicating this man had crawled, injured, before expiring then the sergeant's interpretation could possibly have been right.

Therefore, they were looking for a third man, the actual murderer – possibly of both cadavers. Valuable time had been wasted and whoever had perpetrated this crime was long gone, almost certainly back onto one of the ships presently docked here. He could hear the water lapping against the boards. It would be high tide in an hour or two.

There was the sudden sound of activity on one of the ships. Sailors shouting, the rumble of ship's engines, pounding feet as ropes were untied and tossed aboard. He watched, frustrated, as the vessel slowly left its berth. Any chance he had of solving this crime tonight was literally vanishing before his eyes. Merchant vessels rarely travelled singly; they would be escorted in a convoy by the Royal Navy and a squadron of fighters.

He had the name of the ship in question. It was the *Dromore Castle*. All he had to do was send word to the customs officers at the other docks and they would notify the Yard when it arrived. He doubted that it was heading out to sea. A possible reason for its sudden departure was that it contained the murderer of at least one of these two men.

Dockers would be arriving as soon as it was light. The remaining ships berthed here were ready to continue loading whatever cargo they were going to transport. There were many factories producing vital war supplies in London and these goods would be transported to wherever they were needed. These small ships would creep down the coast of Britain in the hope that the German subs didn't dare to come in so close.

The nightwatchman had been the one to call in the murder. 'It was like this, guv: I never heard nothing untoward when I did me rounds at ten o'clock. There weren't no shouting and it were a right shock to see the two blokes dead on the ground when I went out later.'

'Do you recognise either of them?' Dan asked. Another

black mark for Sergeant Jones as it hadn't occurred to him that if these two men had killed each other then they would still have their ID cards and wallets on their persons.

'No, I ain't seen neither of them before. Will you blokes be here long? They'll want to get started in a couple of hours.'

'Should be done by then. Thank you for your cooperation.'

Charlotte headed for St Thomas's the following afternoon. She'd managed to find a somewhat ancient box of Rowntree's Dairy Box hidden on a shelf behind items of stationery in a newsagent around the corner. She purchased it with the last of her points. Seeing Marion, knowing what she did now, was going to be awkward. She was determined to overcome her embarrassment and try and put her friend at ease.

She wasn't appalled or shocked, more sad for someone who found themselves unable to live as others did. At no time at all had Marion made any improper advances and, although Charlotte felt they could no longer be friends, she wished things to end on a positive note.

Visiting was between two o'clock and three o'clock so she'd timed it exactly right. She enquired at the desk in the entrance hall and was directed to the ward in which Marion was presently housed. The hospital was immaculate – smelled of carbolic soap and boiled cabbage. The nurses who walked briskly past her, their starched aprons crackling as they went, smiled, acknowledging her because she too was in uniform.

There were already several other visitors in the women's

medical ward. She glanced down the rows of beds, all immaculate, no creases to be seen in any of the blue bedspreads. The occupants of the beds were mostly sitting up and taking an interest. This couldn't be a ward for seriously ill patients, which was encouraging.

Marion was at the far end and her head was bandaged, her face pale, but she smiled when she saw Charlotte approaching.

'I hoped you'd come. I'm so sorry to have rushed off like that. What an idiot to have knocked both the inspector and myself to the ground. Was he hurt in the fall?'

'No, he's absolutely fine.' Charlotte handed over the chocolates, which were well received. There was a single wooden chair set beside the bed for a visitor and she didn't like to move it closer in case the officious staff nurse rushed over and reprimanded her.

'I think you rushed off because you overheard the conversation I was having with Nancy and David. Obviously, I must have misled you somehow. I'm really sorry but I don't think we can be friends anymore in the circumstances.'

'You've nothing to apologise for, Charlotte. Wishful thinking on my part – nothing you did. I'm so glad we spent the last few months together. I'll always think of you fondly and thank you for coming.'

'I wanted to be sure that you were all right. How long are you going to be in hospital, do you know?'

'The consultant said it will be for another few days. I could go straight from hospital to my new posting if I knew where it was to be.'

'I'll go to Victory House and tell them what's happened.

I'm sure they'll send you a travel warrant and the necessary details.'

There wasn't much else to say after this and an awkward silence settled between them. Charlotte got to her feet. 'Goodbye, Marion. It was nice knowing you. I hope you get on well wherever you're going.'

She was glad to have something concrete to do. If only life wasn't so complicated sometimes. She'd just extracted herself from a potentially embarrassing situation with Marion and had begun to worry that becoming involved with Dan might well be equally complicated.

This wasn't going to deter her from seeing him. He was the first man who'd stirred anything remotely romantic inside her very practical head. He was everything a sensible girl would steer well clear of. He was acerbic, injured, worked in a dangerous and difficult profession and she doubted they had anything in common. That said, there was something about this tall, handsome man that attracted her – something besides his looks – and she'd no idea what.

As expected, it took her an hour to find the correct person at Victory House to deal with the information about Marion. She would be working here herself next week and hoped that next time she came, the people she spoke to would be more amenable. Somehow, wandering around London on her own no longer seemed so appealing.

There was a Boots chemist not far from the hotel she was staying in and she made her way to the back of the shop to the library section. She found three books that looked promising – an Agatha Christie, a Jane Austen called *Sense and Sensibility* and some sort of Gothic romance. She paid her one shilling and sixpence and left, happy with her selection.

For the first time she wished she had a lovely gown to wear for her first ever dinner engagement. When she unlocked the door to her room she stopped, eyes wide. The second, unwanted, single bed had vanished to be replaced by a comfortable armchair. There was a small table beside it upon which sat a charming lamp.

She wasn't sure whether to rush downstairs and thank the concierge or take this opportunity to use the bathroom, which was empty at the moment. She decided on the latter and was in the process of collecting her wash bag and towel when there was a knock on the door.

Outside was a smiling boot boy – he couldn't be more than ten years old – wearing a uniform two sizes too big for him. Even more surprising was the fact that he was clutching a wireless in his arms.

'This is for you, miss. I were told to bring it up.' These were obviously carefully rehearsed words and she smiled.

'That's so kind. Would you like me to take it or can you bring it in and put it on the chest of drawers for me?'

'I'll do it, ta ever so. Me ma works in the kitchens like and I'm working here on an evening when she's got a shift.' He grinned and put the wireless where she wanted it with no difficulty. 'Mind you, miss, I ain't getting paid. I've to rely on tips.'

'Then I'm sure you'll do very well.' She'd already removed a shilling from her purse and dropped it into his outstretched hand. 'Thank you, young man, and please thank the management for making my room so much more comfortable.'

The boy dropped the coin into his pocket and went away whistling. She couldn't resist plugging in the radio and then, after waiting for it to warm up, she twiddled the knobs. All she got were screeches and whines so she abandoned it for the moment. She'd have another go when she got back from the bathroom.

She spent longer putting her hair up than usual and also added a smudge of red lipstick and a light dusting of face powder. Against all the regulations she was wearing her only pair of silk stockings instead of the beige lisle ones, which were WAAF-issue.

Eventually she'd mastered the tuning and volume on the wireless and had been listening to a jolly band playing American tunes for the past half an hour. She glanced at her watch – exactly five minutes to seven – time to go.

She paused at the door before switching off the central light to admire what was to be her home for the foreseeable future. There were no pictures on the walls at the moment and she was going to go to a couple of second-hand shops tomorrow and see what she could find to brighten them up. Her prized possessions were two photographs. One of Jane and Oscar on their wedding day and another of Nancy, David and their three children.

Walking slowly down the three flights of stairs was almost impossible as she had an unexpected desire to skip. Tonight she was stepping into new territory. She wasn't exactly scared, more excited and eager to discover what all the fuss was about. Other girls had talked about enjoying their social life, praising their current beau, but hadn't been bothered when the relationship ended as there was always another partner waiting in the wings.

This was her first foray into that strange world as she'd never had the slightest inclination to spend time alone with any man until she'd met the attractive, damaged policeman a few days ago.

Dan could legitimately have returned to his apartment to get some much-needed sleep but he was determined to set in motion the removal of the sergeant who'd been a constant irritation to him this past year. Jones had made a dozen errors, was almost certainly taking backhanders from various criminals in their patch, but this was the first time he had behaved in a way that merited being removed from his privileged position as a member of CID.

Whilst convalescing Dan had taught himself to type correctly, unlike most of the constables who laboriously used two fingers to compile their reports. This was a document he didn't want anyone else to see.

He sent a uniformed PC to get him a mug of tea as well as anything available in the canteen. Whilst waiting for his breakfast he removed a notebook from the locked desk drawer. In this he'd written every misdemeanour, every insolent remark, every disobeying of orders by Jones.

Once completed he put the carbon copy back into his desk drawer alongside the notebook and locked it again. Then he carefully typed the name of the person to whom this indictment was going. Sheer willpower and nervous energy was keeping him awake – as a soldier he'd frequently gone thirty-six hours without sleep and he was confident he could do so again if necessary.

The letter was handed to a trustworthy constable to be

delivered immediately and then Dan turned his attention to the murders. He'd already made several telephone calls but the ship he sought had failed to dock. The hold must have been loaded the previous night. Maybe their early departure was a coincidence.

He headed for the coroner's office in the hope that he might find some answers there. He didn't, as the PMs wouldn't be done until the next day. He didn't expect to hear anything today from the chief superintendent so decided to catch up on his sleep. He kept a camp bed, fully assembled, propped up against the wall of his office for such an eventuality.

Like most military men he'd learned to sleep when the opportunity arose. With some difficulty he lowered himself, stretched out his legs and, with a sigh of satisfaction, fell asleep immediately.

7

Charlotte hadn't brought a handbag with her as she wasn't going anywhere apart from the hotel dining room. Neither did she have to hand in her key for the same reason. She'd expected Dan to be waiting in the foyer to greet her, as it was exactly the time they were to meet.

He wasn't there – maybe he was in the bar buying drinks or perhaps already at the table. After a quick inspection it was clear he was late. She wasn't sure what the etiquette was in the circumstances; should she return upstairs and come down again in twenty minutes or sit in the small lounge until he arrived?

She wasn't annoyed, or worried that he'd changed his mind. He was a busy policeman and could very well be delayed by an urgent matter relating to a case he was handling. She was sure if he couldn't come then he'd ring the hotel.

The time ticked slowly by and at forty-five minutes past seven he'd failed to appear and sent no message either. By that point her equanimity had evaporated and she couldn't believe how upset she was, which was quite ridiculous as she scarcely knew the man.

Her stomach rumbled and she almost marched into the

dining room on her own, but decided against it. She hadn't actually booked a table and could hardly ask to sit at the one he'd booked as it would just make her look pathetic.

Sadly, she made her way upstairs, hungry and upset that the promised dinner wasn't forthcoming. She'd just carefully unrolled her precious stockings and was standing in bare feet when there was a knock. The loud band music playing on her new wireless had drowned out any warning of the approach.

Hastily she stuffed the hosiery under the pillow on her bed, turned off the music, and then went to answer the door. Standing outside, his face grey, looking as if he was about to collapse, was her errant dinner date. Without hesitation she stepped aside and took his arm. 'Come and sit down, Dan – you don't look at all well. Why on earth did you come up here yourself?'

He didn't speak for a moment, obviously catching his breath after the unnecessary, and what must have been very painful, climb up the three flights of stairs. Gently she guided him to her armchair and he flopped into it gratefully.

'Sod me, I had to come. I'm so sorry I didn't ring. I was called out last night and then fell asleep after work and only woke up twenty minutes ago.'

Only then did she see that he wasn't as immaculately turned out as usual. Her smile was genuine. 'That's perfectly all right. I guessed it was something like that and that you hadn't stood me up. You really should have sent the boot boy up to fetch me.'

'I should have, you're quite correct. I fear it might be some time before I'm able to negotiate the stairs again.'

'Stay where you are. I'll put the wireless on for you.'

He turned and looked at the set sitting proudly on the dressing table. 'It arrived then. I thought you might like it. This one was standing idle in my spare bedroom so I had it sent over.'

She turned her back and fiddled with the knobs to hide her confusion. Did giving her such a valuable item have any significance? Surely accepting such a generous gift from a man she barely knew wasn't something she ought to do?

'Thank you, Dan, but I consider it a loan. As soon as I manage to locate one of my own then I'll return this to you. In the meantime, I'm going to enjoy having it to listen to in the evening.'

'As you wish. Keep it as long as you need.' He glanced at the bed. 'Do you mind if I stretch out on that for a bit? I need to get my leg straight and the weight off it.'

She handed him his cane and then grabbed his other arm. He needed every ounce of her strength to regain his feet and only just managed to stumble the few feet to the bed before toppling onto it. With some difficulty he managed to lift his legs onto the counterpane then, with what sounded more like a groan than a sigh, he sagged backwards.

His eyes were closed, there was still little colour in his face and she was concerned that he was having a relapse of some sort. She decided not to tell him where she was going but let him rest. If he'd been up all night and then worked all day after only a few hours' sleep, it was likely he'd not eaten either.

This time she hurtled down to the ground floor where the concierge was hovering anxiously. 'DI Chalmers made it as far as my bedroom but is now collapsed on my bed. I really don't think he's able to come down again under his own volition at the moment.'

'Of course, of course, exceptional circumstances require exceptional measures. He insisted he should come up and apologise in person although I tried to prevent him. I've taken the liberty of having something prepared on trays. Shall I have it sent up immediately?'

'Yes, he could be faint with hunger as well as from the pain of climbing the stairs with his injury. Do you think you could put a large brandy on the tray for him? I'd like a very weak shandy.'

'I'll see to it myself, ASO Fenimore.'

Charlotte was about to dash back up when she remembered she'd not thanked him for her furniture. 'By the way, I really appreciate the chair and so on. Will it be all right for me to put a couple of pictures on the walls?'

He beamed. 'Just tell me when you've found something you like and I'll have the handyman put them up for you. I expect you've realised that all our permanent residents are on your floor and all of them have a similar arrangement to yours.'

She could hear the lively music drifting down from her bedroom when she reached the second landing. In future she must have it on more quietly and not leave her door open if she wasn't to annoy her neighbours. She had yet to meet any of them but no doubt they were working somewhere similar to her, like the War Office.

Dan was still stretched out on the bed but his colour was better. His eyes flickered open as she stood above him and for the first time she noticed that he had long black lashes and his eyes reminded her of the heather on the moors in Scotland.

'You look a bit better. Do you think you could sit up? Our dinner's arriving on trays at any moment. I think as long as we leave the door open our breach of protocol is not going to be mentioned.'

His gurgle of laughter touched a chord inside. He pushed himself up on his elbows. 'Not only was I appallingly late but I've now also taken possession of your bed. Our reputations will be in shreds, Charlotte. I'll have to make an honest woman of you.'

The words spoken in jest still sent a shiver of something she didn't recognise down her spine. 'I don't have time for any of that antiquated nonsense, DI Chalmers. I'm quite certain that no one thinks we're doing anything we shouldn't.'

His smile this time was dangerous and there was a glint in his eye. He sat up smoothly and swung his legs to the floor. 'One of us can use that table to eat from, the other will have to sit here.'

She giggled – not something she'd ever done before. 'As you're the one already in possession of the bed, obviously I'll take the armchair and the table.'

As the door was wide open they heard the approach of the trays as they rattled towards the room. She jumped to her feet and looked for her handbag so she could get out some coins for the tip.

'Absolutely not. I invited you for dinner so any expense is mine.'

She raised an eyebrow. 'I'll do it and you can reimburse me if you insist.'

★

Dan nodded as by the time he'd rummaged in his pocket for the necessary cash the waiters would be hovering expectantly. He hadn't realised how hungry he was until the mouth-watering aroma of what he hoped was liver and onion gravy wafted towards him. It didn't matter to him if it was offal – he was a carnivore and would happily abstain from all fruit and vegetables apart from potatoes.

The bed he was sitting on was a narrow single, which meant he could keep his feet on the floor and still have his back against the wall. This would make eating his meal a good deal easier. A waiter he recognised carefully put the wooden tray across Dan's knees. He was about to thank him but the man winked inappropriately.

The other man put his burden down on the small table and, once the necessary monetary exchange had taken place, turned from Charlotte and leered.

Fortunately for both waiters he was encumbered by his meal so couldn't get to his feet quickly enough to wipe the smirks from their faces. His enjoyment in the occasion vanished. This whole bloody fiasco was entirely his fault and now he'd set tongues wagging and there would be talk and innuendos about his relationship with this lovely, innocent young woman.

'Please, Dan, ignore them. I don't need protecting from their gossip. If the concierge is okay about us being here then that's all that matters.' She smiled and his anger vanished as quickly as it had appeared. 'If I get a reputation for being a floozy then I'll be evicted. Now *that* would make me very cross indeed.'

He lifted the lid covering his dinner. He'd been right. Two slices of perfectly cooked lamb's liver smothered with onion gravy and accompanied by a mound of mashed potato. 'I notice there's no dessert on the tray – just our drinks. Did you think I needed a restorative?' He nodded towards the brandy.

'You obviously don't now. You can share my shandy if you like. I'll tip some into my tooth mug and you can have the glass.'

The wireless was playing some sort of orchestral music, unobtrusive and the perfect background to a meal. Charlotte was enjoying her food as much as he was. Halfway through they were interrupted by the arrival of the hotel manager.

Dan froze, a forkful of food suspended in front of his mouth. He couldn't remember the fellow's name, but if he'd come up himself there must be something seriously wrong. What the hell would he do if Charlotte did get thrown out of her digs?

The manager paused in the doorway. 'I must apologise for interrupting your dinner, Detective Inspector Chalmers, Assistant Section Officer Fenimore. I've come in person to apologise for the inexcusable rudeness of the two waiters who brought your meal. They have both been dismissed for insolence and inappropriate behaviour.'

To his astonishment Charlotte laughed. 'Good heavens, I can't imagine what they might have said after they left here to warrant such a harsh punishment. The extent of their rudeness was to wink and smile suggestively. I only gave them threepence each, which I thought was sufficient to express our disapproval.'

'I overheard them talking about the situation in a highly unacceptable manner. I won't tolerate such a breach of rules by any member of staff. Both of you are valued customers and, although having a gentleman friend in your bedroom would normally be frowned upon, as it was the suggestion of the concierge it has my full support.'

'I can assure you under normal circumstances we would be dining downstairs. However, as you're here, could you please convey our thanks and compliments to the chef for this delicious meal. Also, whatever's available for dessert would be gratefully received.' She put her tray aside and stood up gracefully.

The manager positively glowed under her warm gaze. 'Of course, and there will be no charge at all this evening. I believe we have actual coffee – would you like a jug brought up with your dessert?'

When he'd gone Dan resumed eating despite the fact that the gravy had now congealed. She was amused by his wishing to clear his plate. He wiped his mouth on his napkin and nodded happily. 'There's a war on, my dear, and any sort of waste is unacceptable. Did you know that it's actually a crime to feed the birds?'

'You're making that up. Are you telling me that someone would arrest me if I threw out a piece of burnt toast?'

'Well, I certainly wouldn't but there might be some officious, uniformed PC who would take delight in doing so. Waste not want not and...'

'Make do and mend,' she said solemnly.

'Dig for victory,' he followed up. He was actually enjoying this silly exchange of current slogans.

'I can't think of any others. I wonder what delight we'll get for pudding. After several years of boarding school food and then two years of being in the WAAF, I'm far less fussy than one might expect.'

He put the tray beside him on the bed and drained the remainder of the shandy. 'I had a similar upbringing, then three years at Oxford reading law, followed by three years in the police force before I volunteered. Army rations were probably no better than what you were served but, after I was invalided out, I decided I would eat only the best available.'

'It's a constant surprise to me how hotels like these can still produce such excellent food when rationing is so strict. We have two guesses each as to what will be brought up to us next. Apple pie and custard is my first guess.'

'Rice pudding.'

'Oh, I hope not – it's the one thing I really can't eat. No, that's not true. Tapioca is even worse.'

'What's your second suggestion and what does the winner get?'

'Jam roly-poly and custard. The winner can decide where we go on our next date.' She'd spoken without thought and he saw her cheeks colour painfully when she realised what she'd said.

'Chocolate-flavoured blancmange and evaporated milk. If I win I thought we could go to the cinema. What do you want to do if it's your choice?'

'I was going to suggest the same thing so the winner can choose what we go to see.'

In fact, neither of them was correct and they had a strange concoction, which they were told was called an orange whip. It tasted all right but wasn't as good at any of their suggestions. The coffee made up for the disappointing pudding.

They were interrupted for a third time by a breathless boot boy who said Dan's car had arrived.

'I'd no idea it was so late. I have to go, Charlotte, but I've had a most enjoyable evening and can't wait to repeat the experience.'

'I was thinking about us going to the cinema, Dan. Do you have a definite day off? I take up my new position on Monday and I don't know if I'll be working fixed hours or permanently on duty.'

'To be honest I rarely take my designated free time. This means we've got three days before your leave is over and I'll try and get at least two of them off. There's only one matter outstanding and as soon as that's sorted then I'll insist that I'm allowed to take two of my owed leave days.'

Charlotte accompanied Dan downstairs. She'd brought the two trays, neatly stacked one on top of each other, plus the empty plates, cups and coffee jug. A waiter rushed up and took them from her with a grateful smile.

'I'll see you tomorrow night. Reserve a table for yourself just in case I'm delayed but otherwise we'll dine together. I'll know by then if I've managed to wangle a couple of free days.'

She stood a couple of feet away from him, making it clear to anyone who might be interested – and she had a horrible feeling that from now on their every move would be scrutinised – they were no more than friends.

'Good night, Dan, it's been an interesting evening.

Promise me that whatever happens you'll never attempt those stairs again.'

This could be taken in two ways: one, that she was concerned for his welfare or two, she wasn't interested in anything more than a friendship. She thought both were accurate at the moment.

The next morning she'd intended to dawdle over her breakfast but the chilly reception she received from those who served her made her uncomfortable. She really wished the manager hadn't sacked the two waiters as she was definitely *persona non grata* with the ones who were left. It would be such a shame if she had to look for somewhere else to live as this was in the ideal location, her room was lovely, and it wasn't ridiculously expensive either.

The September sun warmed her back and she decided to head for the East End. Despite the fact that this part of London had been bombed repeatedly she was certain she'd still find market stalls, second-hand shops and other places selling the sort of knick-knacks, pictures and ornaments she was looking for.

The underground didn't appeal to her and she wasn't exactly sure which bus to take so decided to walk along Victoria embankment. She was pretty sure eventually that would lead her to the sort of area she was looking for. She wouldn't have to go as far as Poplar – where Nancy's family lived – but somewhere around Liverpool Street, Bishopsgate, would no doubt have what she wanted.

After walking for a while she had the strange feeling that someone was following her. At first she dismissed this as ridiculous, but the unease persisted. The second time a man in a flat cap pulled down low so she couldn't see his face crossed the road behind her and she knew she was right.

She stopped and pretended to be looking in a taped-up shop window, hoping she might see the man more clearly and thus be able to give a description to Dan when she saw him. The follower didn't appear behind her and she didn't like to look over her shoulder.

She was approaching Blackfriars – even with there being almost no private traffic it was still a busy road. She waited with half a dozen other pedestrians for a gap in the traffic. As a double-decker bus approached she received a violent shove in the small of her back and was sent hurtling forward in the path of the massive vehicle.

8

Dan walked into Scotland Yard the following morning eager to see if his damning report had been acted on. He was halfway up the staircase that led to his office when Jones appeared at the top, his face twisted with hate.

'You stuck-up bastard. Think you know better than us just because you've been to a posh school and university. You'd better watch your back, mate – no one likes a snitch. I might not be working here anymore, but I've mates in CID and they're going to make your life a misery. You're going to regret what you've just done, I promise you.'

Jones was now level with Dan and he gripped the metal banister firmly with his free hand and raised his cane just in case he had to fend off a physical attack.

The sergeant barged into him and if he hadn't been prepared he would have gone head first down the stairs. Dan rammed the handle of his stick into his attacker's belly. The man reeled back, gagging, his arms flailing, and almost lost his balance.

'You're a disgrace to the Met, Jones, and we'll be better off without your pernicious presence here. Your threats are empty – you know as well as I do that any attempt to undermine my authority will end in that person's instant dismissal.'

His erstwhile sergeant spat in his face but didn't wait around to be thumped again. Although he could see no one, Dan was well aware what had happened had been watched by several men. The fact that nobody had stepped forward, offered support or condemnation, was a true indication of the state of things at the Yard.

After removing a handkerchief from his pocket he wiped the spittle from his face and then continued on his slow progress to the first floor, and thus to his office. He dropped the square of cotton into the waste bin as he walked past.

There was no need for him to go in search of the superintendent to discover exactly what had transpired. He'd scarcely had time to settle behind his desk before his commanding officer marched in. Chief Superintendent Bailey was a man of middle height, middle years and middle ability. The best men had volunteered, leaving the distinctly average behind to run things. He made a token gesture of standing up and as expected was waved back into his seat.

'If Jones was so corrupt, inefficient and generally useless why the devil didn't you do something about it before now?'

Dan assumed this was a rhetorical question so remained silent. His boss continued.

'This bloody place is going to hell in a hand cart. Did you know that two plain-clothes men on night duty were caught looting a jeweller's last year?'

This seemed an odd thing to be talking about right now. 'No, sir, I didn't. I only took up my position in January.'

'Somehow they managed to convince my predecessor that they weren't in fact looting but collecting the valuables in order to hand them in for safekeeping. Stuff and nonsense. Both of them should have been prosecuted.'

Suddenly the penny dropped. 'Jones and Smith by any chance?'

'Exactly so. I could have got rid of them months ago if you'd had the sense to involve me sooner. Never mind – good work, Chalmers. Nasty pair of buggers and we're well shot of them.'

'Have you sacked Smith as well? I didn't realise that. I met Jones a few minutes ago and he attempted to push me down the stairs.'

'He obviously failed. You might be lame but you're still stronger and fitter than most of my men. Who do you want to have as your sergeant?'

'I'll give it some thought. Jones told me to watch my back, that he has many friends still here prepared to make my life difficult. I want to be quite certain that whoever is promoted is one hundred per cent loyal to the force and not to him.'

'Sensible chap. Was there anything else whilst I'm here?'

'Yes, I'm taking two days' owed leave from tomorrow. DI Culley is quite capable of doing my job whilst I'm absent.'

'You do look distinctly jaded, Chalmers. Couple of days off will do you good. Probably better to be away from here until the dust settles.' He stopped at the door and turned back, his face grim. 'I suggest you keep your revolver with you in future. Jones and Smith have criminal connections, villains in the East End. I'm sure they've been taking backhanders from them for years. Have an armed DC with you at all times. Can't be too careful.'

The thought of having what amounted to a bodyguard

was the last thing he wanted. Jones might be a corrupt policeman but he wasn't insane and neither were the men he called his friends who were still members of the CID. He was in no physical danger; he was certain of that. What he needed to look out for was pettifogging interference in his investigations – lost reports, missing evidence and so on. These would be inconveniences but not anything to worry about.

There were no fresh homicides for him to deal with that afternoon so, paperwork completed satisfactorily, he left the Yard earlier than usual. He'd already rung the hotel to reserve a table for two at seven o'clock and asked them to pass the message on to Charlotte. There was ample time for him to get home, bathe, change and be on time for his date.

In the short drive to Kensington he thought back to the last time he'd been involved with a woman. It had been one Sarah Danby, and they'd been engaged to be married but she'd called it off when he became a policeman. An officer in the army was an acceptable profession for a husband but being a policeman wasn't.

There'd been a couple of brief liaisons with willing young women but nothing at all since he was injured, until now. He didn't want to screw this up. His driver had parked the car and, at his insistence and expense, was snatching a quick meal before returning to collect him at a quarter to seven.

To say the girl was surprised was an understatement. She'd been driving him every day for months and this was the first time he'd shown the slightest interest in her as a person. This didn't show him in a particularly good light and he vowed to do better in future.

When he walked through the doors of the hotel the

concierge beckoned him to the desk. 'Inspector, I rang the Yard but they said you'd left. ASO Fenimore has yet to return so hasn't received your message.'

'That's strange. Did she book a table for herself for a later time?'

'No – that is she booked it for seven o'clock. I do hope nothing untoward has occurred.'

Dan swallowed bile. The snarled warning he'd got from Jones was fresh in his memory. The perfect way to get revenge on him would be to harm Charlotte. Then the knot in his stomach relaxed. No one knew about this burgeoning relationship – she was probably just running late – this was what young women did.

The telephone behind the desk rang shrilly and a smartly dressed middle-aged woman appeared from the back office to answer it.

Everything happened so fast. Charlotte fell face first into the road in front of the approaching bus. Someone screamed. Brakes screeched. Then everything went dark. Was she dead? An overwhelming smell of petrol and oil made her gag.

'Stay where you are, miss, the bus is going to reverse. A bloody miracle you weren't killed.' This was a man's voice but she couldn't see him. She couldn't see anything as her eyes were firmly closed. Something was dripping into her hair. Her face and knees hurt but at least she was alive.

As her head cleared she understood that she was under the bus, lying between the wheels. People were shouting. She heard a police whistle, the clang of an ambulance and then the vehicle that could have killed her began to inch backwards.

As soon as she could breathe freely, see clearly, she rolled over and sat up. For a moment her head spun and she thought she was going to vomit.

A constable crouched down beside her. 'You stop where you are, miss. The ambulance is just coming. You need to be checked out at the hospital.'

'Thank you, but I'm perfectly fine apart from some minor abrasions. I'd be grateful if you'd help me to my feet.'

She held out her hand and he had no option but to take it. A small crowd had gathered and being the centre of attention was acutely embarrassing. She'd lost her hat, there was oil in her hair and all over her uniform, blood dripping from the cuts on her knees, but she was alive.

She agreed to climb into the ambulance because at least that got her away from the well-wishers and interested spectators.

'I don't reckon you suffered serious damage, miss, but better to be safe than sorry,' the ambulance man said as he slammed the doors at the rear of the vehicle. He continued to speak from the other side but she could hear him quite clearly. 'You've got a couple of nasty cuts on your face and you could need some stitches in that knee.'

The ambulance rocked and bumped, making it rather unpleasant to be a passenger. She couldn't help thinking how horrible it would be if she was actually seriously hurt and then bounced about like this. She wished one of the men had travelled inside with her, as being on her own in the gloomy interior gave her too much time to think back to how the accident had happened.

Someone had pushed her – there was no doubt about that. It was the man who'd been following her but she couldn't understand why anyone should wish to harm her. The only people she could think of who had a reason to dislike her were the two waiters who'd been dismissed. This hadn't been anything to do with her or Dan but there'd been a dreadful atmosphere in the dining room that morning.

She smiled at her fanciful thoughts. The waiters would soon find another job – there was a shortage of workers as all the able-bodied men were now conscripted. Both these waiters must have flat feet or something like that, otherwise they too would be in uniform.

There would be another job waiting for them – they wouldn't be unemployed for long. Even if they were it wasn't likely they would attempt to murder her to get their revenge. When she saw Dan tonight, she would tell him about the push. He would find the culprit and bring him to justice. It was almost certainly a case of mistaken identity – one WAAF looked very much like another from the back.

As she'd stumbled into the ambulance someone had put her squashed and bloodstained hat into her hand. Thank goodness she had a spare, as this one had gone for a Burton along with her lisle stockings.

It was bizarre being treated in the same hospital where she'd visited Marion the day before. A nurse cleaned her up and then a junior doctor put a couple of stitches in her right knee.

'There you are, ASO Fenimore. All tickety-boo. You look as though you've been in a prize fight but the bruising and so on will fade after a few days. When did you say you start your next posting?'

'Monday. Don't suggest that I ask for sick leave, as I'm not going to do so. Thank you for your able assistance. Am I free to leave now?'

'You are. Has someone come to collect you? I think it would be wise not to put any unnecessary weight on the knee I've just stitched.'

She frowned. 'Then let's hope I can find a taxi.' She'd been given a pair of crutches and thought she was competent to use them efficiently.

There were two ambulances pulling in as she stepped out into the evening sunshine. It was now just after a quarter to seven and whatever happened she wasn't going to have time to change even if she was actually at the hotel by seven.

There was a public telephone box across the road. She knew the number and asked the operator to connect her. A well-spoken woman picked up the receiver.

'Good evening, it's ASO Fenimore. I don't suppose that DI Chalmers has arrived so I could speak to him for a moment?'

'He has, he's standing right here. Inspector, ASO Fenimore is on the line for you.'

'Charlotte, is something wrong?'

'I had a bit of an accident. I'm outside St Thomas's and can't find a taxi. I'm sorry, I'm going to be really late.'

He said something extremely rude. 'Stay where you are. I'll get my driver to collect you.'

He hung up abruptly and didn't ask for any further details. She supposed he wanted to get off the line so he could contact his driver. She was still slightly flustered by his swearing – obviously she'd heard airmen using those sorts of words, but no one had ever said them to her.

In less than fifteen minutes his car arrived. She almost expected him to be inside but the car was empty. The driver opened the back door for her.

'Golly, you've been in the wars. The inspector was very upset – I've never heard him so angry.'

'Thank you for coming so promptly. I hate to be a nuisance but I'm really grateful I didn't have to hobble all the way to the hotel.'

'I should think not. What was the doctor thinking sending you out on crutches and as white as a sheet and with all those cuts and bruises on your face?'

'I'll be absolutely fine after a nice cup of tea and something to eat. I'm just a bit shocked. It's not every day you almost get run over by a double-decker bus.'

Dan waited outside for the car to arrive. He couldn't see Charlotte clearly in the back of the vehicle. As soon as it was stationary, he threw open the rear door. For a second he was immobile, too shocked to move. Her beautiful face was cut and bruised, there were dark shadows under her eyes and her skin was almost translucent. Her usually smart uniform was bloodstained and torn, and both knees were heavily bandaged.

'Jesus Christ! What in God's name happened to you?' He wanted to be able to pick her up, carry her in and take care of her but his sodding leg made that impossible. Instead, he leaned in and gently helped her wriggle across the leather seat. 'Give me your crutches, I'll hand them back to you once you're out.'

He propped them on the car, added his own stick, then

braced his good leg against the car and reached in and lifted her out. 'Don't try and talk, my dear, let's get inside first.'

She didn't argue and he was able to keep one arm around her waist as he escorted her slowly across the pavement. The doorman had the door open for them. She wasn't going to be able to get upstairs to her own room. What the hell was she going to do?

He turned to his driver. 'This is a no-go situation. I'm going to have to take her back to my apartment.'

'Very well, sir. Shall I go up and collect her things do you think?'

Charlotte interrupted. 'Excuse me, both of you, I might be slightly injured but I'm neither deaf nor stupid. I can't stay at your apartment, Dan, that's out of the question.'

She looked so outraged he smiled. 'Yes you can, because I'll stay here in your room.' As soon as he said the words, he realised how ridiculous the suggestion was. Now she returned his smile. 'I can't go up the stairs either. We're at an impasse, but we can hardly stand about here discussing it. Shall we go in and decide what's best to do whilst you have a hot drink and gather your thoughts?'

Their predicament had been observed by the hotel staff and the efficient woman who was acting as manager tonight came up with a sensible suggestion.

'Do you think you could manage one flight of stairs, sir?' He nodded. 'Then I have a room vacant on the first floor that you can use whilst Assistant Section Officer Fenimore stays at your apartment.'

His arm was still firmly around Charlotte's waist and he could feel her shaking. Shock was obviously taking a hold. 'Thank you, but we both need to sit down. We'll continue this conversation in the small lounge, if that's all right with you?'

Somehow, he got them both there safely. He settled her in the nearest chair, put her crutches out of the way so no one could fall over them – especially himself. 'My dear, would you like my driver to go upstairs and pack you a bag? Then I'll go with you to Kensington so I can collect what I need for the next couple of nights and also to show you where everything is. There's room service and laundry et cetera – you can get your uniform sorted out by them. It can go on my account.'

For a moment she looked blank then she managed a weak smile. 'Thank you, I really do want to lie down. I'm feeling rather shaky. Just tell your driver to pack what she thinks is sensible. I do hope I'm not going to be sick.'

He looked around and saw a suitable receptacle for such an eventuality. He carefully removed the aspidistra from the copper pot and handed it to her. She looked at the pot gratefully. The sooner he got her into bed at his apartment the better. Why the hell hadn't they kept her in overnight? How had she come to be in such a state? These answers would have to wait – first things first: a hot, sweet cup of tea would do them both good.

Then he returned to the foyer to speak to his driver. She'd had the common sense to wait knowing she would be needed.

'Get Charlotte's key from the desk. Her room's on the top floor. She said to bring whatever you think she needs.'

'Yes, sir.' The girl dashed off to do his bidding and he gestured to a lurking waiter. The man turned his back as if he hadn't seen him. His pent-up worry, and his anger at seeing the girl he'd come to consider under his protection in such a sorry state, made his temper fray.

In parade-ground voice he barked his order. 'You, I want a pot of tea with extra sugar brought to the small lounge immediately. Do I make myself quite clear?'

The man jumped as if stabbed in the arse with a bayonet, spun, nodded and fled. He wasn't the only one who'd reacted – he thought that probably everyone in the dining room and many of those upstairs had heard his command.

Certainly, the assistant manager had as she appeared at the double from her office. He smiled, shrugged and swung his way back into the lounge.

9

Charlotte was jerked from an uneasy doze when Dan snarled loudly at a waiter who'd obviously ignored him. Her stomach was more settled so the plant pot wasn't needed. She leaned over the side of the chair and put it on the carpet.

She could hear him talking to someone quietly – no doubt apologising for raising his voice – and then he joined her.

'You look a bit better. We'll have a cup of tea here and then I'll take you to my apartment. Did they give you any pain relief?'

'I've got a bottle of aspirin in my room so didn't need the hospital to provide more. Tea would be lovely though – and a few plain biscuits if they've got any.'

A waiter sidled in with a tray and put it down on the table beside her and backed out before she could speak to him. There was a plate piled high with Rich tea biscuits and these were exactly what she wanted.

He folded his long length into the seat opposite and, as he sipped his tea, he watched her carefully over the rim of the cup. He'd left the saucer on the tray.

'Tell me exactly what happened, my dear. I know there was something more to it than a simple fall.'

She'd intended not to discuss this until they were alone as she already guessed what his reaction would be. He listened carefully, asked several questions, perfectly polite and apparently calm, but his eyes were hard and his lips thinned. She understood now why David had told her to think carefully about getting involved with Dan.

He leaned forward and took her hands in his. For some reason she'd expected them to be smooth, like a gentleman's hands, as he certainly looked the part and his nails were well manicured. But where his skin touched hers it was hard, workmanlike, perhaps from his previous life as a soldier.

'Someone tried to kill you, Charlotte, there's no doubt about it. I know who's behind this and I give you my word they will regret what they tried to do. You're under my protection now. I guarantee that nothing similar will happen again.' His fingers tightened as he spoke to emphasise his words.

'I thought it might be something to do with those waiters but that's silly isn't it?'

'I'm afraid it's something to do with me. If I'd known that my being seen with you would put you in danger I'd never have asked you to spend time with me.'

He released her, sat back and refilled both their cups. She put down the half-eaten biscuit, no longer having the appetite for it. Should she ask him why her association with him would make someone who didn't know her wish to push her under a bus?

His driver appeared in the doorway, nodded and then vanished. 'Your belongings must be in the car, my dear, so it's time to go. Allow me to help you to your feet. I might be a useless cripple but I've still got strength in my arms.'

Referring to himself as useless was so extraordinary, so ridiculous, she spoke without thinking. 'You have a damaged leg, Dan – that doesn't make you anything but a hero. A doctor who works at the Royal Free told me that you're a dangerous man, that I should have nothing to do with you, that you're feared by the criminal element of London. I hardly think that would be the case if you weren't a strong, efficient CID officer.'

For some reason he ignored most of her outburst and focused on what David had said. 'Yet here you are – didn't his words of warning put you off?'

'Absolutely not. You might be dangerous to a villain but as far as I'm concerned, you're a gentleman and I'm absolutely safe in your company.'

If she hadn't already put down her cup she would have dropped it. His smile was blinding – his eyes pinned her to the seat like a butterfly on a board – and in that moment she knew it was quite likely he'd become someone rather special in her life.

He grasped her elbows and lifted her bodily from the chair. She was impressed and surprised that just by bracing his good leg against something solid he had the strength and stability to do this. He handed her the crutches.

'Can you manage or do you want some assistance? I got you in here safely and can get you out again just as easily.'

Tentatively she put the crutches in front of her and then swung her least injured leg forward. It was comparatively simple then to move her other one.

'I can do this, thank you, but please walk beside me just in case I lose my balance or something.'

The dining room was now busy, which meant no one was

looking in her direction. Moving the few yards from the lounge to the car was more difficult than she'd anticipated but somehow she gritted her teeth and made it without needing him to prop her up.

Dan got in the back with her. His driver slammed the door, dashed around to her side of the car and moved smoothly away, displaying her driving expertise.

'This is much more comfortable than the ambulance. I can't believe that being bounced about as I was would do a badly injured person any good at all.'

'I'm sure you're right. But if you're seriously ill or injured, I don't suppose you'd care or even notice.'

Having never suffered from travel sickness she was dismayed to be feeling very unwell after a few minutes. The thought of being sick in this immaculate car was enough to keep her swallowing madly and holding her breath, praying the journey would be over swiftly.

He put his trilby in her lap. 'Use that if you have to – I've got several others.'

The car pulled up just in time to prevent an embarrassing situation. He flung open the door on his side, letting in a wave of very welcome fresh air. She edged across the seat – not waiting for the driver to come round and let her out – and when he leaned in and picked her up she went willingly. He was a brave man as he didn't know if she was going to be ill all over him whilst he was holding her.

'Are you better now? Do you need my hat?'

She managed a small nod. 'Keep your hat on your head, Detective Inspector Chalmers; I'm perfectly fine now I'm out of the car.'

She scarcely had time to take in her grand surroundings

as a liveried doorman was out on the pavement already. Dan, for the second time today, had his arm firmly around her waist as she moved unsteadily into the spacious entrance hall.

The lift clanked and rattled but worked efficiently. She kept moving forward until she was inside his apartment.

When she woke, she was disorientated, not sure where she was. She lay still in the darkness for a few minutes trying to gather her thoughts. She ached all over, particularly her knees and face, but, thank God, she no longer felt sick or dizzy.

She wasn't sure if it was night or day as the blackouts were drawn. One thing she was very certain of was that if she didn't find the WC immediately there would be another kind of embarrassing accident. She sat up. Where were her clothes? Who had undressed her? She was wearing her WAAF-issue voluminous cotton nightgown and nothing else at all.

Dan was reluctant to leave Charlotte on her own in a place she wasn't familiar with, especially as she seemed unwell enough to have been kept in hospital. He'd helped Simmons remove Charlotte's outer garments but left the rest to her. The patient was now deeply asleep and worryingly pale.

'Private Simmons, would you be prepared to stay here with Charlotte? You'll be well compensated.'

His driver, a pretty girl with mouse brown hair and pale blue eyes, looked somewhat taken aback. 'I was going to suggest that I did so, sir, and will be more than happy to take care of your young lady. My digs aren't anything to write home about so it'll be a pleasure to be in the lap of luxury for a couple of nights.'

This was the longest speech she'd ever made – not that he'd ever given her the opportunity to talk. 'I really appreciate it. I'll stay here whilst you go back and get what you need. Do you have to report your actual whereabouts to anyone?'

She grinned. 'I have to take the car back for inspection and refuelling when necessary but otherwise nobody cares where I am, as long as I'm on police business.'

'Excellent. Will you be long collecting your belongings from your digs?'

'I don't need to go back there at all. I keep a change of clothes in a bag in the boot. All I've got to do is go and get them.'

Whilst she was gone he removed three freshly laundered shirts from his wardrobe. He carefully placed these in the bottom of his suitcase and then added clean underwear, socks, ties, handkerchiefs and his shaving gear.

He'd got used to having his own bathroom and didn't relish having to share one with strangers for the next three days. The thought of anybody seeing his mangled leg filled him with horror. He checked his appearance in the mirror and was satisfied he didn't need to shave or change his shirt – he still looked impeccable.

If his driver remained here during the day then he wouldn't be able to move about the city himself. He walked into his own bedroom, where he'd put Charlotte, and checked her pulse. Steady and regular, if a little faint, but he was confident she was sleeping and not comatose.

Hopefully by tomorrow morning the patient would be awake and safe to leave on her own, but tonight he would be less worried if there was someone in the apartment with her. The blackouts were already drawn and he carefully placed a torch next to the glass of water on the bedside table.

'I'll sleep in here, sir. I'll be comfortable on that sofa sort of thing by the window.'

Simmons was referring to the *chaise longue*. 'No, you'll sleep in the spare bedroom next door to this one. With both doors open you'll be able to hear if she calls out.'

It didn't take long to show his unexpected guest where everything was, what number to call for laundry service or if she needed anything to eat or drink. 'I'll have someone come up and collect Charlotte's uniform. They should have it cleaned and pressed and returned before she needs to wear it again.'

'I fetched everything she had. I've hung it up alongside your things. Hope you don't mind, but I couldn't leave it in the kitbag as it would be creased.'

For some reason the thought that Charlotte's clothes were now adjacent to his pleased him. It created a feeling of intimacy that wasn't really warranted in the circumstances.

He hefted his overnight bag in one hand and his driver returned him to the hotel. She was given instructions to ring at once if there was any change and not to come for him until Charlotte was awake and didn't need her help.

The man behind the desk was new to him but he was

polite, unlike the waiter from before. 'Here is your key, sir. You had a table booked for dinner and the kitchen will be closing soon. Do you wish to eat before you retire?'

As a soldier he'd soon learned the hard way to eat and sleep when the opportunity arose. 'I'll eat. It doesn't matter what it is. I'd like a jug of coffee if there is any; if not, a pot of tea.' He picked up his key. 'I need to be able to use the telephone in my bedroom. Will that be possible?'

'All calls have to go through the switchboard here but there will always be someone here to answer and connect you whatever time of the night it might be.'

Dan hadn't allowed himself to think about what had almost happened to Charlotte and exactly who was behind the attempt on her life. He thought it perfectly possible the two disgruntled waiters had been the ones questioned by his erstwhile sergeant and his henchman. The dismissed men would have been only too happy to supply information about a girl who was already important to him.

Would he have done anything differently if he'd known the repercussions involved? He thought for a moment and came to the unpalatable conclusion that he might well have allowed the corrupt CID men to continue in their jobs if he'd known that by dismissing them he would put Charlotte in danger.

Condoning Jones and Smith's corruption would make him almost as bad as they were. Therefore, he was glad the decision had been taken from him even if it meant the next week or so might be difficult for him and even more so for her.

He devoured everything that was put in front of him but, if he'd been asked, he wouldn't have been able to say what it was. He was eager to get upstairs and start making calls. He also had to inform the Yard of his whereabouts – he should have done that first. Then he smiled. There was no need for him to tell anyone what he was doing or where he was as he was on leave until the weekend.

It was fortuitous that this nasty business had started when he wasn't on duty, as he could now devote his entire time to finding the bastard and dealing with him personally. A surge of icy rage swept through him and the coffee cup he was holding cracked beneath his grip. The resulting mess and the fussing waiter gave him time to recover control of his emotions.

Upstairs he began to make his calls. The first was to a publican in the East End who wasn't exactly a hardened criminal but certainly not entirely on the straight and narrow. Dan had prevented this man's only son from being shot as a deserter. He'd arranged for a friend of his, a psychiatrist, to pronounce the young man as unfit for active service owing to mental instability. Freddie was happily working at the pub, keeping up the pretence of being slightly insane.

One word from Dan and the army would pounce on the boy and drag him back to be court-martialled. Having this connection had proved useful more than once and he had every intention of exploiting the favour owed and getting O'Reilly to do his sleuthing for him.

When he had the name of the would-be murderer he would deal with the man himself. He would extract the information he needed and then dispose of the bastard. Breaking his neck would be an absolute pleasure.

*

Charlotte woke up and remembered where she was and why she was there but it didn't help in this particular circumstance as she had no idea where she would find the bathroom.

'Just a minute, ma'am, I'll help you.' Dan's driver appeared in an equally unflattering and voluminous nightgown, no doubt issued by the army.

'I'll hop if you'll put your arm around me. I hope it's not far or I'm going to wet myself.'

'Got his own bog and everything, the inspector has. Very posh indeed. It's that door over there.'

Charlotte didn't have time to admire the bathroom on her way in – her need was too urgent. Afterwards as she was propped against the sink washing her hands she looked around. The tiles were French, she thought, or maybe Italian as they had a beautiful cobalt blue floral pattern on them. There was no bath in this bathroom but a magnificent free-standing shower tiled in the same exotic pattern.

'Are you all right in there, ma'am? Do you need any help?'

'I'm fine and coming out now. I can hop to the door easily enough by putting my hand against the wall.'

'I reckon you're a bit peckish, seeing as you didn't eat anything yesterday. The inspector said all I have to do is pick up that telephone receiver and ask for whatever you want to be fetched up. Sounds like blooming magic to me.'

'What's the time? I don't like to disturb them and it would probably cost twice as much to have food and drink brought up in the middle of the night.'

'It's just after midnight. Don't you worry about a few bob. The inspector's ever so rich. Go on then, what do you fancy?'

Half an hour later the two of them were drinking delicious cocoa made with real milk and plenty of sugar, as well as a selection of freshly made sandwiches.

'I shudder to think how much this is going to cost but it's absolutely delicious. I do believe that was real roast beef in one sandwich and actual cheese and pickle in the other.'

'Best midnight feast I've ever had. The only thing I miss about being seconded to the inspector, instead of being in the motor pool on a base somewhere, is the mess hall. Most nights I just get fish and chips as my digs only do breakfast and I have to fend for myself for lunch and supper.'

'Does he know that you don't get full board?'

'To tell you the truth, ma'am, until recently he didn't even know my name.'

Charlotte smiled. 'That doesn't surprise me in the slightest. I'm sure he hasn't ignored you deliberately – I just don't think he sees anything apart from his work.'

10

Dan didn't turn in until the small hours but, when he finally clambered into bed he'd found the information he needed. O'Reilly had already heard about what had happened and knew exactly who the little bastard was and had sent out two of his men to capture the culprit. He would hold him at his pub until Dan arrived to interrogate him.

Charlotte was safe enough whilst she remained at his apartment but as soon as she returned to the hotel, and took up her position at Victory House, it would be easy for a determined assassin to get at her. This meant it was imperative he dealt with the situation in the next four days.

He'd also decided it was better if his driver didn't accompany him and hang about in the less salubrious parts of London he intended to visit today. Therefore, he called in another favour – this time from a fellow officer who, like him, had been injured at Dunkirk. However, Charles now had a desk job and had been happy to loan him his car and driver for the next couple of days.

Dan was up, shaved and ready to start the day at six o'clock despite the fact he'd only had four hours' sleep. His first task was to ring home and speak to Simmons.

'Is that you, sir?' Simmons asked nervously.

'It is indeed. How is Charlotte this morning?'

'She's asleep but she woke up to use the bog and we had a midnight feast. I reckon she's over the worst, apart from being a bit stiff and that. Are you wanting me to come for you right now?'

'No, I've made other arrangements for today. Your duties for the time being are to keep Charlotte company. Feel free to take some exercise, get some fresh air, as I'm sure the patient won't require constant supervision.'

'The car's in the yard round the back, sir, as it was a bit conspicuous out front.'

'Well done, Simmons, I should have thought of that myself. Please convey my best wishes to Charlotte and tell her that I'll come and see her sometime today.'

He hung up and then checked he had spare ammunition in his coat pocket and that his revolver was loaded and ready to fire. He didn't expect to use it but the part of East End he was visiting later was a dangerous place, so it was wise to be prepared.

Breakfast was a meal he usually ignored but, as it was included in the price of his room, he decided to see what was on offer. The all-pervading aroma of kippers filled the dining room. He backed away hastily – fish of any sort made him gag.

The car wasn't due for another half an hour and there was little point in returning to his room. It wasn't raining and there'd been no overnight bombing, so the air was fresh outside. He'd lean against the wall of the hotel and enjoy half an hour of solitude and peace.

If he smoked this would be the perfect time for a cigarette

but he'd never adopted the habit. He preferred a double whisky to help him to unwind. He was pleasantly relaxed, enjoying the early morning sunshine, when the concierge appeared at his side.

'Sir, there's an urgent telephone call for you.'

'Thank you, it's a good thing my driver's late.' There'd been no need to explain why he was lurking about outside – what he did was his own damn business and nobody else's.

The receiver was handed to him. He moved as far as the flex attaching it to the telephone itself would allow, before putting it to his ear. 'Chalmers speaking.'

'Thank God, some bugger's gone and shot the man what we were holding for you. God knows how they knew he was being held here,' O'Reilly whispered.

'Are you hurt? Are the perpetrators still on the premises?'

'They bleedin' well are. I dialled 999 and I can hear the ambulance and your lot coming down the street. Stay away, mate, not safe here for you.' The line went dead.

This was bad news – the worst possible. He'd now dragged O'Reilly and his family into danger. He leaned against the reception counter trying to marshal his thoughts into some sort of order. He'd always known that Jones and Smith were corrupt but until now he'd not known they were so deeply connected to the criminal world.

This was no longer something he could deal with by himself. A murder had been committed and, instead of going to Whitechapel, he'd now head straight for the Yard and make a full report about what had happened yesterday and both his and Charlotte's involvement in it.

He rather thought that he would be wise to accept the

protection of an armed DC. There was more to this than revenge; he wanted to discuss his theory with the chief super. He leaned over the counter and waggled the receiver at the girl sitting at the switchboard. She nodded and waited to hear to whom he wanted to be connected.

This time he rang the desk in the foyer of his apartment block, not his own apartment. 'DI Chalmers speaking. ASO Fenimore and my driver Private Simmons are in my apartment at the moment. Under no circumstances allow anyone apart from staff to go up there. This is a matter of the utmost importance.'

'Yes, sir.'

'Keep an eye out for anyone hanging around who shouldn't be there and immediately alert the Yard. Can you transfer my call to my apartment?'

This time Charlotte answered. 'Dan, how lovely to speak to you. I can only apologise again for turning you out of your beautiful apartment.'

He ignored her pleasantry. 'Listen, you're in extreme danger. I'm sending an armed constable to stand outside the apartment. Tell Simmons to forget going out for a walk. You must both remain inside with the door locked and only open it to receive food and so on sent up from downstairs.'

'You're frightening me. What's going on?'

'I would have told you yesterday but you were too unwell.' He gave her a succinct explanation and she listened without comment.

'I accept that those corrupt policemen must be behind the attacks but what I don't understand is why the need for revenge on you would involve killing the man who tried to kill me.'

'I don't either but I intend to find out. Stay indoors and I'll come and see you when I can. I can't tell you how sorry I am that I've dragged you into this.'

'It's not your fault. Please, Dan, be careful. These sound like ruthless and dangerous men and until you know exactly what's going on, you're blundering around in the dark.'

'Blundering certainly, my dear, but it's broad daylight in case you haven't put the blackouts up.'

His feeble attempt at a joke was well received; her laughter was exactly what he needed to focus his mind. For the first time in his life he had something worthwhile to fight for. Of course, he'd fought for King and Country like everyone else in the Armed Forces, but now he had someone of his own to protect.

It was extraordinary that he'd only met Charlotte a few days ago and already he knew he'd happily die for her if necessary. His mouth curved – he was just being overdramatic. Then all desire to smile faded. Thousands of men had already died to protect those they loved, which made his silent vow only too real.

Dan's warning made Charlotte's situation even worse. In four days' time she was supposed to be taking up a new position, an important one, and she honestly didn't think she was going to be fit enough to do it.

'I've got two black eyes, cuts and grazes everywhere and my hair's full of engine oil. I'd really like to wash it but don't know how I can do it and still keep my bandages dry.'

'They gave you some fresh dressings, didn't they?' Violet

Simmons was proving to be an entertaining and intelligent companion – she reminded her of Nancy although Violet came from Romford not Poplar.

'I'm not sure. If they did, they would be in my haversack.'

A few minutes later the dressings were found and she was sitting on the stool in the bathroom – a shower room really – whilst the bandages were being carefully unrolled to use again.

'Do you mind awfully staying in here whilst I shower and wash my hair? I really don't want to do myself any more damage and I'm still a bit wobbly on the old pins.'

'I expect it's the same in the WAAF as it is in the ATS – communal showers and medical inspections just wearing our knickers.'

'Absolutely. I went to boarding school and absolutely no privacy there either. I'm not sure if we should take off the actual dressings or let them get wet and then remove them.'

'They'll be easier to take off wet. You stop there a minute and I'll get the shower running. There's a second bathroom – for guests and such I suppose – with a proper bath and a bog. We just had a galvanised tin bath in front of the range in the kitchen and an outside privy. Think I've died and gone to heaven being here.'

It was absolute bliss standing under the stream of hot water, especially as there could be no feelings of guilt about using more than the regulation five inches of water. She stepped out a new woman. She was handed a large soft towel and couldn't help thinking as she enveloped herself in it that the material might well have been against Dan's naked flesh too.

A flicker of something she now recognised as desire almost made her legs give way. How could Marion have thought her interested in women in that way?

An hour later her knees were redressed and bandaged and she was back in her warm and voluminous nightgown. The two of them were sitting at the dining room table eating a very tasty vegetable stew. It might have been a meat stew but there certainly wasn't any meat in the tureen that had been sent up to them.

'If we carry on eating like this then I'm going to be too fat to get into my uniform on Monday,' she said with a smile after eating every scrap of her helping of spotted dick and custard.

'Smashing isn't it? The inspector must have pots of cash to live somewhere like this as he certainly couldn't afford it on policeman's money.'

'I couldn't help noticing when I happened to glance into the wardrobe that all his suits have been made in Savile Row, his shirts are made to measure, as well as his shoes. I wonder why a man who obviously doesn't have to work for a living chooses to be a detective?'

They really shouldn't be discussing Dan like this as Violet worked for him and he certainly wouldn't want her to know his personal business. Too late – the words were spoken. Spending time with Marion had made her more relaxed about chatting, less reserved in her manner.

'He's bloody good at his job – I can tell you that much. I might be invisible to him but I watch everything. I reckon he's one of the few honest cops in the CID. They have a rotten reputation you know – I could tell you some stories but from your expression you don't want to hear them.'

'Actually, I'd love to know more about him but I'm not comfortable discussing him like this. We've only just started seeing each other and I think he should be the one to tell me about his life.'

'Fair enough. One thing I can say is that since he met you, he actually smiles sometimes.'

Charlotte glanced down at her nightie. 'I'm going to get dressed. He said he's coming to see us sometime today and he can't come in with me wearing this.'

'I shouldn't bother with stockings and suspenders. Pity you WAAFs don't wear slacks. When I was working in the motor pool I wore overalls – much more comfortable.'

'It depends what part of the service we work in. My friend Nancy was in catering and she had different-coloured overalls depending on what she was doing. Unfortunately, I have to wear a skirt and stockings.'

She decided that there was no need to put on her tie or her jacket – just underwear, shirt and skirt would be sufficient. The apartment was wonderfully warm and the radiators in all the rooms were hot enough to dry clothes on.

'Quick, Charlotte, you need to see this,' Violet called urgently from the sitting room.

She grabbed the crutches and was at her side in moments. There was no need to ask what she was supposed to be looking at. They were two rough-looking characters loitering across the road. 'Did they see you, Violet?'

'No, I'm sure they didn't. Keep an eye on them whilst I tell the bobby who should be outside the door by now.' Neither of them had bothered to check if he'd arrived as he hadn't been there when their lunch had come up an hour ago.

Her companion was halfway to the door when someone knocked. Charlotte shook her head and beckoned Violet back. 'Don't open it. We've not ordered anything and Dan told us to keep the door locked,' she whispered.

'Let's go into your bedroom and lock that door as well.'

Moving silently on crutches would be difficult especially on the slippery parquet floor. It would be quicker to hop holding on to Violet's arm. Her heart was hammering, her palms clammy. She really didn't like being frightened.

She collapsed on the bed, relieved they were both now safe inside two solid, locked doors. The telephone – she could ring downstairs and speak to the man behind the desk. The line was dead. However much she rattled the bar it remained inert. Her heart was thundering, her mouth dry and she was appalled at how scared she was. Before meeting Dan her life had been so safe and straightforward.

'Whoever's trying to get to me must be in the building. Thank God we didn't open the apartment door.'

'We can't tell the inspector what's happening either. We don't even know if the armed policeman actually arrived, do we?' Violet clambered onto the bed and they huddled together, shivering, trying to give each other much-needed courage.

'One thing I do know, Violet, I'm not sure now that I want to be involved with the inspector. He might be charming, attractive and all that, but he's turned my life into a nightmare. I'm all right with bombs and so on – somehow that's impersonal. However, being hunted like a fox by actual men who want to kill me is absolutely terrifying.'

'I don't blame you. If I was you, I'd find somewhere else

to live – don't go back to the hotel. I brought all your things with me just in case.'

'Then that's what I'll do. Please, don't tell him what I'm planning to do. It's better for both of us that he doesn't know where I am.' Was she being a coward to give up on him so easily? David had warned her and she should have listened to him: Dan was a dangerous person to be around.

Dan didn't ask permission from his superior to set things in motion – better to apologise for overstepping than be refused permission to have armed policemen guarding Charlotte. The two men he wanted for this job were still busy from this morning's murder. He spoke to the inspector in charge of that investigation and found out that the men would be released as soon as they'd finished taking witness statements. This meant Charlotte would be unguarded until later today – this shouldn't be a problem as she was perfectly safe inside the apartment. Once this was in place he went in search of the chief super.

He marched in without asking the vigilant policewoman, who was acting as receptionist and secretary, for permission.

'We need to talk,' he announced boldly. He hooked out a chair and sat down – again without being invited to. He explained what had occurred and what he wanted to do about it.

'Good God, man, you should have informed me yesterday. I know about the murder at the Anchor and Hope. We have the two suspects behind bars. I suggest you take over the interrogation as you have a personal involvement in this.'

'Doesn't it strike you as extraordinary that just the dismissal of two bent cops has caused this?'

'Now you mention it, Chalmers, it does seem excessive.'

'I can think of only one logical explanation. Jones has to be more deeply embedded in the criminal underworld than either of us realised. Do we know anything about his family connections?'

The secretary was sent to root out the files and returned with commendable speed to put two manila folders on the desk between them. He picked up the one with Jones's name and his boss opened the other one.

There was nothing that raised alarm bells until he reached the information about Jones's wife. He swore loudly. 'This explains it. He's married to the daughter of the villain I've been trying to put away ever since I joined CID. The slippery bastard always has an alibi – his minions are prepared to lie for him.

'And on three occasions evidence linking him to a crime mysteriously vanished so the cases were dismissed.'

'With Jones as his son-in-law he would always be one step ahead of any investigation or raid that we put in place. I wonder how deep this infiltration has gone. I'm going to suspend the two other DCs he worked with until you've completed a full investigation into their probity.'

'So, by dismissing Jones and Smith I upset the entire Bentley clan and cut Reggie Bentley off from what must have been an invaluable source of information.'

'Now will you agree to have an armed DC with you?'

'Absolutely. I'd like to have Wainwright. I trust him. He's just passed his sergeant's exam so he might well be the perfect replacement. I'll know better once I've worked with him.'

'ASO Fenimore has nothing to do with any of this. It's sheer bad luck for her that the two of you met as you did. I'd keep her as far away from you as possible until this matter's settled.'

'Unfortunately, sir, she's presently staying in my apartment as she couldn't manage the stairs at the hotel. I'm at the hotel until she's well enough to return. My driver's keeping her company.'

'My, my, that won't do, young man. Most irregular. I suggest you find her somewhere safe to move to and then sever the connection. The poor girl, from what you've told me, is about to take up an important position. I don't want anyone from there making a formal complaint about Scotland Yard.'

'I scarcely know the girl. Obviously, I had no option but to offer her my apartment as she was only injured because of her tenuous association with me. As far as I'm concerned, she's just another member of the public in need of our protection.'

He'd raised his voice slightly to ensure that the girl outside the door overheard. He wanted this disinformation spread around the Yard as quickly as possible. The only way he could keep Charlotte safe was to act as if she meant nothing to him – even though the reverse was true.

II

Dan decided to leave the interrogation of the murder suspects to the man in charge of that investigation. He'd spoken to him so was confident that if any information could be extracted to help with his own case, then it would be passed on to him immediately.

As the man who'd attempted to push Charlotte under a bus had been executed by his employers there was no need for him to pursue that line of enquiry. What he'd really like to do was speak to his informants, but until he had more information about what was going on, he would be better remaining at the Yard where he was safe.

He spent the morning going through old case files; anything to do with Reggie Bentley and his extended family was fetched from the archives. By the time he'd completed a cursory search he'd confirmed his first suspicions.

Jones had been in CID for many years and every case that involved Bentley wriggling out of prosecution had his name down as the investigating officer. Why hadn't he seen the pattern before – why hadn't anybody else?

His discovery explained why Jones had been so angry at being dismissed, but he still couldn't see where first attempting to murder Charlotte, and then killing the man who'd tried to do it, fitted into the grand scheme of things.

The only feasible explanation was that the man had acted of his own volition. Bentley didn't allow any of his minions to step out of line. It hadn't been a sudden impulse, as Charlotte had said she'd seen the man following her for some time before he actually pushed her under the bus.

His stomach gurgled loudly and he checked his watch. Good God – almost two o'clock. He'd had no breakfast and had now missed his lunch too. He decided he'd return to his apartment and have something sent up from their kitchen. It was essential that he talked to Charlotte but he was reluctant to discuss anything of a personal nature whilst his driver was on the premises.

There was no need to "sever the connection" as the chief super had suggested, although he was resigned to the fact she'd be much safer having nothing to do with him. Then he smiled. If he was right about the man shot dead this morning then there was no need to stop seeing her, as the danger was over.

He was overthinking this – making it more complicated than it actually was. Reggie Bentley was nobody's fool and he would get the full weight of the Yard falling on his head if he actually killed either Charlotte or himself. Therefore, he was in no more danger now than he ever was. He couldn't be one hundred per cent certain until he knew more about the murder victim but he was now more optimistic than he'd been last night.

His borrowed driver saluted smartly and drove him the short distance to Kensington. 'Get yourself some lunch somewhere – I'll be about an hour. He tossed the man half a crown and the bespectacled private grinned.

'Thanks, guv, just the ticket. Do I leave the car here or can I take it to find my lunch?'

'As you please.'

He walked in to find chaos in the normally calm and well organised foyer. The two DCs he'd sent were involved in a lively conversation with a man in overalls and the concierge.

'What the devil's going on here?' At his snapped question the four of them fell silent and turned to look at him. He knew what was coming next. All would attempt to explain their point of view simultaneously.

He nodded authoritatively at DC Brown. 'You, explain what's going on here. Make it brief.'

'The telephone lines are down, sir. This man here has come to fix them. I was stationed outside your apartment and knocked to tell the young ladies what was going on but they haven't answered. It's been over two hours.'

'That explains why you're here but not what the fuss is about.'

'I'm trying to get a pass key from this person but he's refusing to give me one.'

Dan snapped his fingers and the concierge instantly dropped the necessary key into his hand. 'When will the lines be restored?'

The overalled man shook his head and sucked the end of his pencil. 'Not sure about that, guv. Got a mate out in the street checking the box. Another one's at the exchange. Until we locate the fault, we can't fix it, see?'

'Right. Do your best. I need to be in constant contact with Scotland Yard so the sooner the better.' He gestured to the two DCs. 'Stay down here – I'll have my driver return you to your normal duties later. Emergency is over.' Then he gave his order for sandwiches and coffee – if it was available – otherwise tea, and headed for the lift.

His men hadn't disputed his assessment of the situation and he hoped he hadn't got it wrong. He'd been in the force for four years altogether and not done so yet.

He opened the door and then yelled from where he was. He didn't want to alarm the girls further. 'I'm coming in. There's a fault on the line. Nothing to worry about – everything is absolutely tickety-boo.'

He'd used his best parade-ground voice knowing it would carry even into his bedroom where he guessed the two of them were hiding. The two bedrooms and a second bathroom opened off the central entrance hall on the right. The sitting room, kitchen and dining room were on the left. There was the definite sound of a key being turned and then the door was flung open.

He'd expected Charlotte to be the first to emerge and was both frustrated and surprised when Simmons stepped out.

'Blimey, sir, we thought someone was trying to break in. There were a couple of dodgy-looking geezers lurking on the other side of the road and we put two and two together and made five.'

He noticed there was a tray piled high with dirty crockery on the floor by the door, so at least the girls had eaten before their self-imposed incarceration.

'Is Charlotte unwell?'

'She's in the bog – she'll be along in a minute,' the girl said cheerfully.

'There's no need for you to be here now, Simmons, unless

Charlotte can't manage on her own. The man who tried to kill her is no longer a problem and the case is solved.' He thought it better not to mention the man had been shot by his employer.

His sandwiches and coffee arrived before Charlotte did and he had a nasty suspicion the girl was avoiding him.

'Help yourself to coffee. I ordered enough for all three of us as well as those biscuits.' He left his driver happily munching and headed for the bedroom. The door was still firmly shut. It seemed odd knocking on the door of his own room but he had no option.

'Charlotte, we need to talk. Open the door.' He didn't say please, didn't give her an option, and his firm approach had the desired effect. She was used to following orders after all.

'You'd better come in. I was just packing my things. I don't need the crutches so there's no need for me to be here and you can have your home back.'

'You were told not to walk on that leg for a few days and it's only been a day since the accident.'

'I know that. I'm not stupid. I also don't want to be in your debt any longer. I barely know you and I think it better if we don't see each other again. I'd never have agreed to have dinner with you if I'd known someone was going to try and kill me because they thought I was your girlfriend.'

Charlotte hadn't meant to blurt her feelings out and wished she'd been a little less abrupt when she saw the dismay on his face. He smiled sadly.

'I understand completely, my dear, and think you've made the right decision. My work's dangerous and I'd never forgive myself if anything happened to you because we were friends. It's perfectly safe for you to go back to the hotel. The man who tried to kill you acted independently and he's been dealt with. Are you quite sure you'll be able to manage three flights of stairs?'

He'd accepted her decision without argument, with resignation really, and she wished they'd met under different circumstances.

'On second thought, maybe it would be better to stay here one more day. I intended to find somewhere else to live but if you're quite sure it's safe then I'd much rather remain at The Sanctuary.'

'I don't think you need Simmons here but I'm happy to leave her if you're enjoying her company.'

'I am – she's great fun. Did you know that her digs don't provide full board? She's been living on fish and chips.'

'Of course I didn't know that. I'll find her somewhere better. She can stay here until you leave. There's coffee and biscuits in the dining room if you'd like some. I haven't eaten since last night and have also got sandwiches – I might be persuaded to let you have one of those if you ask nicely.'

He was making this much easier than she'd anticipated. He really was such a charming man and it was a shame things couldn't go any further. She was sad when he left, knowing she was unlikely to spend time with him again. Once she took up her new post she'd be so busy she wouldn't have time to worry about what might have been.

The following evening she was safely reinstalled in her room under the eaves and delighted to be back. She suspected that

Dan would no longer eat there in the evenings, which was a shame as he'd said it was his favourite place.

Her right knee was now almost healed and didn't require a dressing. The left knee, the one with the stitches in it, was sore but she was able to put weight on it without too much discomfort. There was now no need for the bandages, which meant she could put on her stockings and appear correctly dressed.

As she sat listening to *It's That Man Again* – better known as *ITMA* – that night she wondered if she should really insist that Dan took back his wireless. Having it made all the difference, made a hotel room into something more homely. She still had to find herself a couple of pictures for the walls, but there was no urgency.

She decided for the next few nights she would have room service despite the fact that it was an extravagance she couldn't really afford. It wasn't just because the stairs were uncomfortable for her to go up and down, it was also because she didn't want to risk bumping into Dan. It wouldn't take much to persuade her to reconsider her decision and that would be bad for both of them.

Charlotte removed the stitches herself on Sunday morning as the cut had healed and they were pulling. There was no need, she decided, to traipse up to the hospital in order to get a nurse to do it. The bruises under her eyes were now fading and with a little discreetly applied powder she hoped nobody would notice when she turned up at her new posting at eight o'clock tomorrow morning.

There'd been no further contact from Dan and she wasn't sure if she was disappointed or relieved. Anyway, romance was something she'd avoided so far and was certain she

could do without it for the foreseeable future as she had her
duty to perform.

Immaculate in her freshly cleaned and pressed uniform,
hat on correctly, stocking seams straight, buttons and shoes
polished to a high shine, she was ready to make her way
to Victory House. It was quite likely she would bump into
Marion but she thought that wouldn't be a problem now
the dust had settled.

One of the requirements for this new duty was that she
could drive and she was keen to know why she needed this
skill. She set off briskly down Tothill Street, turned left
into Victoria Street and headed for Whitehall. Having been
to this building when she first volunteered three years ago
she would have had no difficulty finding her way even if she
hadn't been there on Marion's behalf the other day.

How different her third visit was to the first. This time
she was an officer, immaculately turned out, confident and
knew what she was doing unlike the nervous gaggle of new
recruits milling about waiting to be herded somewhere or
other. Now these would be conscripts, not volunteers, as all
young women had to do war work of some sort.

All she knew was that the department she was to join
was headed by a Wing Commander Sanderson. Now she
had to discover his whereabouts. It would have helped if
she'd known what department she was joining but it was
something to do with logistics so maybe this was her first
test. If she was going to be in charge of moving either people
or goods from place to place then she should be able to find
her own way to these offices.

In the end she asked and was directed up the stairs. Here
all the personnel were bustling about, obviously frantically

busy with whatever they did. She was saluted three times, which was a novelty, and she had to do the same to a senior officer.

The offices she was looking for were at the far end of the first floor. She could hear the noise of typewriters clacking, telephones ringing and the constant murmur of voices. This was obviously a big department and she was likely to be a very small cog in it.

She marched in, head high, and headed for the far end where there seemed to be more NCOs than other ranks. One or two looked up and smiled but mostly she was ignored. There were a dozen desks all occupied by typists, secretaries and clerks. Most of the personnel were female but there was a sprinkling of RAF amongst them – mostly older men – presumably too ancient to serve in an active capacity.

With some relief she saw the name of the man who headed this large, busy, department. There didn't seem to be a secretary sitting at a desk outside.

She was dithering about deciding what to do when a man spoke behind her.

'Go in – no need to knock. There's nobody in the office to answer you anyway as we're both out here.'

She spun and saluted smartly. Wing Commander Sanderson vaguely flapped his hand in the right direction and smiled. 'None of that nonsense with me, my girl; keep it for the corridors. Come in. Things have got rather disorganised since my last assistant was dismissed from the service because she was pregnant.'

'No chance of that happening to me, I can assure you, sir.' She'd spoken without thinking and could have offended him but he laughed.

'Jolly good show. You young girls do things my generation wouldn't have dared to do. There's a war on – nobody knows when the next bomb's going to drop on our heads so no judgement from me on that score.'

The man she was to work directly for was in his forties or fifties – it was hard to tell. He had thick, wavy grey hair, twinkling blue eyes and looked fit as a fiddle. She liked him already. She was about to stand aside to allow him to go in first but he waved her in front of him. Ladies first, but senior officers should also precede juniors.

What was to be her personal workplace was a large room dominated by a massive, scruffy wooden desk piled high with dozens of folders, and an in-tray that was overflowing and an out-tray that was empty. There was a small side room and her heart sunk. This was presumably where she was to work and it was little bigger than a shoebox.

'That's where the old files are stored,' her boss said cheerfully. He saw her bemused expression and chuckled.

'Being an observant young lady I'm sure you've noticed there are two chairs at this desk, one on either side. Underneath the mess there are also two telephones. I'm hoping you can restore my workspace from chaos to calm.'

To add credence to his story the conversation was interrupted by the strident ring of one of the invisible telephones. Inspiration struck and Charlotte looked for the flexes rather than the receivers. When she found these she just had to pull and both telephones emerged, scattering papers in all directions. Triumphantly she picked up the one that was ringing.

'Good morning, Wing Commander Sanderson' office.'

'I need the old bugger down here at the double.' The plummy voice neglected to identify himself and hung up.

'An anonymous gentleman who referred to you as an old bugger wishes you to go immediately to see him. I'm hoping you know who this might be.'

'Brigadier Carstairs. He is in the office at the end of the hall. Make sense of all this whilst I'm gone.' He gestured vaguely at the strewn papers, nodded jovially and vanished at remarkable speed for a man of his years. This was all very peculiar. There were dozens of secretarial staff outside in the main room so why on earth hadn't he got one of those to keep his office in order?

Seeing someone twenty years older than Dan moving about so freely reminded her how hard it must be for him to be incapacitated. She pushed the thought aside – their relationship was over and she had a job to do.

Dan made a point of not visiting The Sanctuary for his evening meal and instead used room service when he returned home. Reggie's men, the ones who had been caught red-handed at the scene of the crime, pleaded guilty and no doubt would go before the beak in a week or two and then shortly afterwards be executed.

Too many men and women had died and were dying because of the war and it seemed unnecessary to add to the number by hanging anyone found guilty of murder. He'd never thought twice about the death penalty but now was coming to the idea that life imprisonment might be a better deterrent.

Wainwright was now his sergeant and so far the

arrangement was working out splendidly. The young man was short-sighted and deaf in one ear, which had made him ineligible for conscription. Dan had his own office and Wainwright had a desk outside the door. There was a painfully young, inexperienced WPC sitting on an adjacent desk upon which was the telephone and typewriter.

Dan was supposed to use the telephone to summon either of them but it was easier to bang on the floor with his stick. Then the girl, he thought her name might be Davidson, would stand up and he'd either beckon her or shake his head. Then his sergeant would come in instead of her. The system was working well.

There'd been no bombs dropped recently, no new homicides for him to investigate, so the three of them were working together trying to find evidence that would bring not only Bentley, but also Jones and Smith, to justice. Keeping busy was the perfect way to keep his mind from drifting towards Charlotte and what might have been.

He was roused from his work by a sudden commotion outside. He was about to go and investigate when the door flew open and both his sergeant and the WPC rushed in.

'We think we've found it, sir – the link you're looking for,' Wainwright said as he advanced with a handful of papers closely followed by the girl who was also smiling.

'Show me. I could do with some good news. All I've got here are examples of police incompetence and corruption.'

'Look, either Jones or Smith visited the evidence room. Then a few days later a case was dismissed against Bentley owing to lack of proof. This can't be a coincidence.'

'I don't believe in coincidences. Well done both of you.' He quickly glanced down the papers. 'Did you notice that the signature of the man signing these sheets is the same each time?

'Bloody hell, it's indecipherable,' Wainwright exclaimed. 'Do you think that was done deliberately?'

'I'm certain of it. We've got at least one other corrupt policeman in Bentley's pay working here. He's a very dangerous man. For God's sake don't talk about any of this.' He sat back in his chair closing his eyes for a moment, trying to come up with what would be a valid reason for Wainwright to visit the locked room downstairs in the basement.

'We need to arrest someone selling luxury items on the black market or recover some stolen property. That way you'll have a legitimate reason to go down there and not arouse any suspicion. I think there are no more than three possible suspects. Davidson, can you surreptitiously get me any information you have on those men?'

'I can do that, Inspector. For the first time since I started working here, I feel as if I'm doing something worthwhile. Thank you for agreeing to have me as part of your team – nobody else wanted a WPC anywhere near their department. We're only employed to take care of *women's matters* and I want to do proper police work.'

'I'm glad to have you.'

12

Charlotte viewed the chaos on the desk with disapproval. The fact that his previous assistant had left to have a baby was no excuse for allowing things to accumulate in this fashion. This was supposed to be the logistics department – how on earth could it run efficiently if the head of the department didn't know where anything was?

She decided to sort things out by date initially and then take it from there. Soon she had the chaos of paper into some semblance of order. She was relieved that most of the documents were just confirmations that someone had been moved to the correct place. These she moved to a shelf in the small storeroom to be dealt with later.

There were dozens of requests for mechanics and other WAAF occupations, barrage balloon operatives, catering assistants, orderlies and so on but none of them referred to aircrew – presumably these were dealt with somewhere else.

She realised now that this particular logistics office dealt solely with people and not equipment. That was somewhat easier than having to juggle both. The requests that hadn't been dealt with in some cases were over a week old and had been at the bottom of the wing commander's bulging in-tray. These would obviously have to be allocated first.

Hopefully, by the time her boss returned she'd have made satisfactory inroads into the mess. However, it was going to take her the rest of the day to bring order to this chaos. At least she could see the surface of his desk and he had space to work. She'd sharpened all his pencils, filled up the two fountain pens from the ink bottle hidden in the back of his desk drawer and had positioned a clean notepad and blotting paper directly in front of his chair.

The telephones were visible and usable, which was fortuitous as she'd answered three calls already. She'd done her best to placate the irate callers who were demanding to know when their request for extra personnel was going to be dealt with.

She was just starting to file the papers that had been dealt with when the door flew open and the Wing Commander erupted into the room. She was going to have to get used to him rushing about the place like a lunatic.

He didn't comment on her hard work, didn't seem to notice, and headed straight for his desk. He glared at the messages. 'It's all very well people demanding this and that but I've only got one pair of hands.'

She thought it wasn't sensible to point out that he had dozens of pairs of hands in the main office who could have dealt with all this backlog.

'You'll see, sir, that I've prioritised the requests by date. I don't know exactly what I'm going to be doing here. Am I your secretary?'

If she had announced she was a devil worshipper he couldn't have been more shocked. 'Secretary? Whatever gave you that idea?' He stopped and smiled. 'It's not always like this, Fenimore. Once you've got things in here organised again you can delegate the paperwork. Plenty of clerks and secretaries out there.'

'There are, sir, and forgive me for stating the obvious but if you'd got one or two of them to stand in until I arrived there wouldn't have been this muddle.'

'Very true. Too late to repine. I prefer to work with someone I can trust, someone intelligent. Now, sit down and I'll tell you exactly what you'll be doing here.'

She did as requested and listened eagerly as he outlined her duties. 'I now understand why you wanted someone who could drive. Are you really saying that bases request personnel that they don't need and don't have the accommodation for?'

'I certainly am. We don't want to upset anyone, tread on any important toes, but war is expensive and we can't afford to waste money. Therefore, your job is to investigate anything that might seem like a bogus request.'

'I'm sorry if I'm being dense, sir, but how will I know this? There are hundreds and hundreds of bases all over the country.'

'Indeed there are. No doubt, being an observant young lady, you've already noticed the maps displayed all around the walls. Every base is marked and the information about it is in the appropriate folder underneath the map. Your job is to check each suspicious request against the information and if you see anything odd bring it to my attention.'

Things began to fall into place. If a small, non-operative, RAF base requested a dozen extra catering staff then this needed looking into. 'What about requests for spare parts, equipment food and so on?'

'Parts and so on? Good heavens, that's another department altogether. We just deal with personnel of various sorts.'

'And if I find something that doesn't add up – what do I do next? Will the people involved be court-martialled?'

'You'd be surprised to know, Fenimore, that quite often it's a genuine error and the people involved are reluctant to own up to their mistakes. No, we try and smooth things over without calling in the RAF police.'

'Well, that's a relief as I'd hate to be involved with sending people to prison or whatever the equivalent is in the RAF.' There was another pertinent question she needed answering. 'Does every request for trained personnel come across your desk?'

'No, no, anything straightforward is dealt with by the efficient staff outside. Anything that raises a red flag is passed on to us. You'd be amazed to know that not all members of the RAF are scrupulously honest.'

'I expect we have a mix of all sorts as in every service, sir. There's something I don't understand about all this. Why would having extra personnel that aren't needed be of any benefit to these bases?'

'Ah, my explanation was incomplete. The wages for these extra WAAF or RAF bods is paid directly to the base adjutant. The surplus staff are sent elsewhere without going through the required channels and then their names reappear. There are hundreds of thousands of people involved in both services. We are only talking about a few hundred and they can be lost in the system. It's our job to find them and stop the dishonesty.'

'So I travel to these places and look for myself? I suppose it's not clear if the request is genuine or not in some circumstances.'

Abruptly he changed the subject and gestured towards

the fading bruises on her face. She explained how she'd come by them.

'Well, my girl, I'm glad they didn't succeed. Crime is rife in the capital, especially in the East End of London, and the depleted police force is struggling to keep pace with it.'

Her stomach gurgled loudly and he chuckled. 'Get yourself some lunch. Bring me back a sandwich and a pot of tea. You've done splendid work so far and I can see that I've been sent the perfect candidate.'

The excellent canteen had very little left to buy as it was now long past lunchtime.

'Wing Commander Sanderson has asked me to take him back a sandwich of some sort and a pot of tea,' she told the girl behind the counter. 'But you don't seem to have anything left.'

'Never you mind, ducks, I'll make him a lovely sarnie, nice bit of piccalilli and spam, just what he likes. I've got a rock cake you can have, if you'd like it?'

'Thank you so much, that would be spiffing. I was too nervous to eat any breakfast this morning.'

'Here you are then, I'll bring the tray over when it's done.'

Charlotte was about to get out some coins but the girl shook her head. 'No, this'll go on his bill. He'd have my guts for garters if I charged you.'

She took her tea and bun to an empty table, not sure now if she'd made the right decision to accept this posting and not get retrained to be a plotter or filterer. This didn't seem like honourable war work – she wasn't helping to fight the Germans or helping the British aircrew stay safe as she'd been doing before.

Asking to be reassigned the moment she arrived wouldn't

look good on her record, however, and would make further promotion unlikely. Then she smiled. She was now in a similar line of work to Dan – was this fate giving her a nudge? Things had changed in the past few months and she rather thought that she had too.

Marion had developed romantic feelings for her, she'd got involved with Dan, someone had tried to push her under a bus and now she was working for an eccentric wing commander doing a job she wasn't entirely comfortable with. However, she was going to see how it worked out before she made any decisions about asking for a transfer.

She was still somewhat undecided about Dan. He'd almost lost his life fighting for King and Country and he deserved a chance at happiness – but she just wasn't sure she was the girl to give it to him.

Dan was aware that digging the dirt on fellow officers would cause them to close ranks. It still puzzled him that anybody could have thought murdering Charlotte would be of any benefit to Reggie Bentley. The reverse would be true, if anything. Hopefully, all would become clear when he unearthed the relevant information.

Knowing that at least two other members of this division were corrupt made him determined to get the proof necessary to bring them to justice. He was well aware that his colleagues sometimes bent the rules, that interrogation could be heavy-handed, but there was nothing he could do about that. What he wanted to do was stop the flow of information to Bentley and bring his organisation down.

The upper ranks of the police force had an inner circle

of men who were members of the Freemasons, who turned a blind eye when fellow members transgressed. He'd been invited to join but declined politely. He had no time for such nonsense but was well aware that being on the outside of the circle put him at risk.

Had Jones and Smith got away with their corruption for so long because they were both members of this club? Bailey, the chief superintendent, had been the one to invite him to join so he knew he was a lodge leader or something equally ridiculous. What about those three men he suspected of colluding with his erstwhile sergeant? Would it be possible to discover if they too were Masons?

This was an added inconvenience to an already difficult investigation. What he needed was a straightforward homicide or major crime to be getting on with at the same time as the one he didn't want to become common knowledge.

The telephone on his desk rang and he picked it up. 'Chalmers speaking.'

'Wainwright here, sir. One of my snouts has just given me some tasty info. You remember the spate of burglaries and looting in the West End last month?'

'It wasn't my case, but I do recall some bigwigs made a fuss because their homes were targets. What about it?'

'This informant has told me where the stolen goods are presently being stored. It cost me a fiver but I reckon it's worth it. Can you meet me there?'

Dan memorised the address, snatched up his coat, hat and stick and headed out. 'Davidson, prevaricate if anyone wants to know where I am. This is the opportunity we've been looking for.'

'Yes, sir. If anyone enquires, where shall I say you've gone?'

'Use your imagination. Would you find a list of the property stolen during the spate of break-ins last month in the West End?'

He'd checked the time before he left his office and with any luck the stolen goods would be in his custody before the blackout. The days were noticeably drawing in, but that was only to be expected at the beginning of October. Crime flourished in the darkness and winters were always busier for CID than the summer.

Recently he'd changed his pattern and now travelled in the front seat next to Simmons rather than sitting in the rear seat as if being driven by a chauffeur. This new arrangement suited them both and it was certainly easier for him to enter and exit from the front.

'Wait here, Simmons, hopefully this won't take long.'

Wainwright was looking inconspicuous, smoking a cigarette, his collar turned up and his hat pulled down low over his brow. Unfortunately, because of his stick Dan was easily recognisable. He gestured to his sergeant to go into the premises – strictly speaking he should have got a warrant first but he doubted there'd be any complaints as so many VIPs would get their valuables back.

The place they were illegally entering was part of a row of old buildings once used as stables but now housed a miscellany of unwanted debris and dilapidated furniture. These sad items were presumably rescued from bombed houses and being kept in the hope the owners would one day find somewhere else to live.

'I've already broken the lock, sir, and whilst I've been here I've not seen anyone hanging about taking an interest.'

'Good to know. I'll stay in the doorway. I'm useless in the dark and better off holding my revolver in case of armed interruption.'

Wainwright nodded and switched on his torch. 'I know exactly where the stash is. It won't take long to recover it.'

He was correct and in less than five minutes he'd returned with a bulging sack and a broad grin. 'Bloody hell, a king's ransom here. Someone's going to be very upset when they discover we've recovered the stolen property.'

Less than an hour after leaving the Yard they were back. Wainwright carried the goods like a trophy and Dan was sure word would rapidly spread that a substantial amount of ill-gotten gains had been recovered.

Davidson joined the two of them in his office and firmly closed the door. The necessary list of items was waiting. His sergeant unceremoniously tipped the contents of the sack onto the desk.

'Now, that's an impressive haul,' he said. 'It'll be easier to check things off if we sort it first.' There was a kaleidoscope of jewellery, watches, silverware and other less identifiable objects. Not surprising that the owners had kicked up a fuss. 'I'll do the silverware; Davidson, you do the jewellery. Wainwright, you do everything else. Just put it in piles. No time to gawp at such wealth, you two, not for the likes of us.'

By the time every piece had been listed and then checked against the original list it was late. Perfect for the next part of their plan.

'I can't come with you to the evidence room. That would arouse suspicion as I've never done so before. The two of you must accomplish this together. Offer to check in everything yourself, tell whoever's on duty that you'll put it in the boxes and label them. They'll be eager to knock off and will be happy to let you get on with it. With any luck you'll be left unsupervised and have ample time to find what we're looking for.'

They both knew that to progress the case against Jones and Smith they had to find verification of tampering. Written proof that items that had been placed in safekeeping had actually been removed. The incidences had been far enough apart for no one to have linked them – he certainly hadn't. If the things that had gone missing had been logged in the book and not been logged out then either they were somewhere in the wrong box, or had been removed deliberately. He was confident that the two of them would find the answers.

For him to remain in his office so late might just draw unwanted attention to what was going on in the evidence room. Therefore, it would be better for him to leave. Wainwright and Davidson could tell him tomorrow what they found out.

It had been ten days since he'd eaten at The Sanctuary and he thought that was long enough to allow him to return there without causing either himself or Charlotte any undue embarrassment.

Charlotte's new duties kept her busy and she was beginning to enjoy her new role as investigator into possible malfeasance. So far she'd not had to go in person and, thankfully, every incident had been easily cleared up over the telephone. In fact, all of them had been clerical errors and in only one case had the extra personnel actually been sent to that particular base.

There was, however, one that needed her to visit the base itself. It had proven impossible to speak to the adjutant and she was quite certain twenty WAAF had been sent there for general duties three months ago when there were only two dozen airmen on the base. It wasn't an active airfield, just a storage depot, and the only aircraft that visited were those delivering and collecting various items stored in the disused hangars.

Her boss had said there was no urgency to make the long drive and that she should arrange to go the following week.

'It will take you a day to get there, at least one day to unravel what's going on, and a day to come back. That means spending two nights away. Are you comfortable travelling across the country by yourself?'

'Perfectly, thank you. I'm looking forward to it. After all, it's why I'm here, isn't it?'

'Yes, yes, it is. Keep receipts and you'll be reimbursed for any expenses on your return. Do you have enough to pay your way or shall I raid the petty cash for you?'

'I can manage.'

She'd booked a table in the dining room at the hotel for the first time since she and Dan had parted company. She'd been eating at the café around the corner most nights to avoid the risk of bumping into him. There'd been ample time to think about the reasons why she'd decided to not see him anymore and she'd written a list with the pros and cons of becoming better acquainted. The plus side had far outweighed the negative and she'd come to the conclusion she ought to see him again at least. He was the first man she'd taken the slightest interest in and this might be why she was finding it so hard to move on.

There was barely time to rush up to her bedroom, have a quick wash, and dash downstairs in order to be on time. Tables were in demand and it was frowned upon if you were late. As she was a permanent resident, she hoped being ten minutes tardy would be overlooked. Thankfully, the ill will caused by the dismissal of the two waiters had dissipated and her breakfast was always served with a smile.

The first person she saw as she jumped the last few steps was Dan. He was just turning away from the head waiter looking dissatisfied. 'Dan, I was hoping to bump into you again. I've got a table – would you care to join me?'

13

Dan couldn't believe his luck. 'Charlotte, thank you. I'd be delighted to join you.'

'I'm a bit late but I'm sure now there's two of us they won't complain.'

Once they were comfortably settled at a table tucked away in a corner, which suited him perfectly, he had time to look at her properly. 'The bruises have gone, no sign of any scarring. Thank goodness for that.' He nodded towards her knees, which were hidden under the tablecloth. 'What about the stitches?'

'I took them out myself ages ago. No scars there either.'

'You look well. Obviously your new posting is one you're enjoying.'

She leaned back in her chair and scrutinised him carefully. 'I wish I could say the same for you. You look exhausted. Have you taken a day off since I saw you last?'

He shrugged. 'Been too busy. Anyway, little point in having a day off if I've got nothing to do with it apart from listening to the wireless and reading the newspaper. I've not taken any time off for weeks.'

'Part of my new job is investigating false accounting at RAF bases all over the country. I've got to drive to the wilds of Norfolk on Monday. I don't suppose you'd care to come with me? With all the road signs removed I'm going to get hopelessly lost without an excellent navigator.'

He choked on his beer. By the time he'd stopped coughing he'd recovered his composure enough to answer. 'I thought we weren't seeing each other anymore?'

'I regret saying that. I like you, Dan. I want to get to know you better.' Then a painful wash of colour flooded her cheeks as she understood why he'd been so surprised. 'Good heavens, I'm not suggesting we sleep together. Separate bedrooms of course. I should have made that clear from the offset.'

'In which case I'd love to come. I'll take three days off. Tell me exactly what it is you've got to do?'

He carefully kept the lively conversation away from any discussion of his own work. He'd like to be able to share his worries, his plans, but he'd been given a second chance with this lovely girl and he wasn't going to screw it up again. From now on he'd make sure he kept his private life separate from his police work.

The problem with this was that he'd not deliberately involved her last time and still she'd been in danger. Was he putting her at risk by renewing their acquaintanceship?

The evening passed too quickly and he was shocked to see Simmons lurking in the doorway, waiting for him to say his good nights so she could drive him home and then clock off herself.

'I've enjoyed myself, Charlotte. Do you eat here every night?' He spoke as he stood up and reached for his cane.

'Yes, they always fit me in if I want to eat here. I've come to an arrangement with the hotel that I'll have whatever's likely to be left over and don't choose from the menu. This means that I get my meals at a very reasonable rate.'

'In which case, I'd like to join you when I'm free. Is this the table you always have?'

'Yes, it's one nobody wants as it's rather close to the kitchen doors. There are three other tables in similar positions and they too are used by the other permanent guests. I can request a better table but then I don't get my special deal.'

'I'm hoping that we could dine together a couple of times a week. I notice no bill has been presented – I assume this is being put on your tab. You must allow me to pay my way.'

'No, I invited you. You can pay for some meals when we go to Norfolk next week.' She walked with him and when she saw Simmons she rushed forward smiling. 'I'm so glad to see you, Violet. How are you?'

Dan continued walking, leaving the two girls to talk for a few minutes. He was glad he'd done so when Wainwright appeared at his side. 'Sorry to startle you, sir, but we need to talk and we can't do it at the Yard.'

'Right, I understand. Come with me to Kensington. I've managed to get some real coffee and would be happy to share it with you. Do you mind finding your way back to your digs from there? I can't ask Simmons to hang around as she's been on duty all day.'

'That's all right. I'm lodging with an aunt just over Lambeth Bridge in Black Prince Road. No more than a couple of miles and I'm happy to walk.'

'Good God, get a cab. I'd no idea you lived so far away. I'll get the concierge to find one for you.'

Simmons came out full of apologies for keeping them

waiting. 'I like Charlotte ever so much, sir, and I'm going to come back and listen to her wireless for a bit if that's all right with you.'

This time he got in the back of the car with Wainwright. 'Your personal life is nothing to do with me, Simmons. However, I'm happy that the two of you are friends.'

Wainwright was surprised there were no blackouts in the reception area of the apartment block. 'The bloke behind the counter has to sit in darkness – can't see that's a good idea.'

'This way whoever's on duty can see residents coming and going, can call us when our drivers are here and so on.'

Dan quickly explained to Frank, the man on duty tonight, that he wanted a cab in an hour and a half and then led the way into cramped lift.

Neither of them spoke until they were safely inside. 'Hats and coats in the closet by the door, Wainwright. We might as well sit in the kitchen then we can talk whilst I make the coffee.'

His sergeant took care of the outside garments and he swung his way to the cabinets. There was a small table with two bentwood chairs where they could sit and talk in relative comfort.

'Impressive apartment, sir. Mind you, we all knew you were a toff.' Dan raised an eyebrow and his sergeant laughed. 'You couldn't afford to dress the way you do on a copper's wages.'

'I'm glad my sartorial elegance hasn't gone unnoticed. Now – sit down and tell me what you and Davidson have discovered that couldn't wait until the morning.'

*

Charlotte had been disappointed that there hadn't been time for coffee with Dan but meeting Violet made up for that.

'My friend, DI Chalmers's driver, is coming back to see me. I'm not sure about the rules for permanent guests – am I allowed to invite Private Simmons to my room for tea and to listen to the wireless?'

The duty manager, an elderly man with a bristly moustache and kind eyes, smiled. 'Of course you can, ASO Fenimore. I'll have tea sent up when the young lady arrives. It's just gentleman callers that are frowned upon.'

'Goodness, I know that. Thank you very much – that would be splendid. She's just running the inspector home and will then come straight back.'

She'd managed to buy two pretty prints of the river in bygone days and she'd been able to hang them herself from the picture rail. They made her room seem cosier. Every night that she returned to clean sheets, real blankets and a soft pillow she was grateful she was no longer living in the WAAF's quarters sleeping on the horribly uncomfortable biscuits.

In her rush to be downstairs in time for her reservation she'd not noticed the two letters propped prominently on the bureau. She picked them up knowing that one would be from Nancy and the other from Jane.

She'd written them both long letters about her exploits, the embarrassing hospital visit with Marion, as well as her near-death experience. She'd not as of yet updated them on her change of heart about Dan or given them any information about her new posting.

Violet had said she would park the car in its usual place behind Scotland Yard and then walk the short distance to the hotel. Her lodgings were now near Horseferry Road so calling in here was more or less on her way home anyway.

She opened the letter from Nancy first:

Dear Charlotte,

What an exciting life you're having. The most exciting thing to happen to my family recently is that Lottie has got her first tooth. Billy is getting on well at school and is a credit to us. Betty misses him dreadfully and keeps trying to escape and follow him.

Oh, I forgot, Polly is having puppies any day. We've no idea how this happened as she's never out on her own and we've not seen any sign of a visiting dog in our garden.

David reckons the big lurcher that lives across the river swam over and did the deed! Heaven knows what we going to do with them as nobody wants puppies because they don't have any spare food to feed them with. Jethro, one of the gardeners, has said he'll drown them in a bucket for me – but I won't let him do that.

I like the sound of your Dan – I hope you reconsider and see him again as he sounds perfect for you. I don't like hearing about you almost being run over by a bus – you've got to be more careful.

Now you've got a car at your disposal maybe you can nip down and see us again soon? I miss being busy, doing my bit for the war effort, but am so happy married to David and he does more than enough working in London what with the bombs and all that.

I almost forgot – one of my brothers got arrested for stealing and was up before the beak. Because he's not quite right in the head they let him off with a stern talking-to and I expect my pa gave him a good seeing-to with his belt.

Write back soon – lots of love from all of us here,
Nancy

Charlotte read the letter again smiling whilst she did so. For the first time she felt a flutter of excitement that maybe one day she too could have a happy domestic life like Nancy's. Early days yet, but she knew enough about men to know Dan found her as attractive as she found him, which was always a good start in any relationship. Not that she had any experience – but she'd heard enough gossip from the girls she'd billeted with over the years.

She hadn't told either Jane or Nancy that her near miss with a bus had been a deliberate attempt on someone's part to kill her. There was no need to worry them unnecessarily. Eagerly she slit the second envelope and pulled out the other letter.

Dear Charlotte,

Forgive me for starting with my own news before I comment on yours. Oscar and I are expecting a baby next spring – the middle of March – and we couldn't be more excited.

Of course, I'm sad that I'm going to have to resign from the WAAF but the Queen B has agreed I can stay until I begin to show as my work is so important. This means I'll have to leave before Christmas I expect.

I know what you're thinking – not a good time to bring a baby into the world but we both want a family and Oscar wanted me to have his baby in case anything happened to him.

His life is a lot quieter now. He's patrolling the channel and the estuary protecting the merchant shipping from overhead attack and this is still a highly dangerous occupation.

I'm going to live with his parents until the end of the war. Even though I'm now quite close to my own mother neither of us wanted to live under the same roof again – too many bad memories.

Oscar and I can decide where we want to live when he's demobbed. I still think there might be a chance that he wants to get ordained like his father and then I'll be a vicar's wife. Imagine that!

Now to you and your news. Almost being squashed by a double-decker bus isn't good – not like you to be so careless. Is there more to this than you've told me?

I don't think I've heard the last of this Detective Inspector Dan Chalmers. Write to me soon – I love hearing from you and Nancy, as Oscar rarely has time to write to me.

All my love,

Jane

So – Jane had succeeded in getting pregnant during the six weeks she'd spent with Oscar in the summer. No – that couldn't be right as if she'd got pregnant in May the baby

would be due in February. Her husband was a Spitfire pilot –
the bravest of the brave – and they must somewhere have
wangled a twenty-four pass in June. Good for them – she
rather liked the idea of being a godmother to another baby.

She just had time to put the letters away in her stationery
folder before she heard the rattle of crockery. Her friend
must be approaching the open door of her bedroom.

'Come in, Violet, I bet they were pleased you offered to
bring the tea up.'

Her friend beamed. 'You bet they were. We got a couple of
custard creams and a slice of cake to share on the strength
of it. I said I'd take it down again when I go.'

Charlotte didn't feel it was right to discuss her work even
though it wasn't hush-hush like it had been before. Violet
had no such reservations about discussing everything she
knew about Dan and his team.

'There's a few bent coppers at the Yard – more than a
few, I reckon – and my inspector, his sergeant and the WPC
are trying to ferret them out.'

'That won't make them very popular.'

'Too right. They don't think I know anything. Being the
driver it's as if I'm invisible. But I hear things – I don't tell
no one, mind you – but you're different. You're walking
out with him so it's all right to tell you, isn't it?'

Charlotte was tempted to encourage her guest to reveal
whatever she'd learned but decided against it. If Dan
wanted her to know about his investigations then he'd tell
her himself. This evening he'd dodged questions about his
current work and to hear from someone else what he'd
deliberately not told her wouldn't be right.

'No, that would be a betrayal of confidence. You're not

just his driver, you're also part of his team and must keep any secrets to yourself in the same way that the others do.'

'Fair enough. This room's a bit of all right, isn't it? You've made it ever so comfy. I wish I had a wireless in my room. Shall we see what's on?'

They were delighted to find the Tommy Dorsey band performing a concert somewhere, which was being broadcast live. Soon they were up and dancing and both were sad when the evening ended.

'That was fun, Charlotte. I had ever such a good time. I'd better take this tray down or the kitchen will be closed.'

'We must do it again. I hope we didn't disturb the other guests on this floor with our jumping about. It's awfully late – I didn't realise how quickly the time had gone.'

The bulbs in the passageways were so dim one could hardly see and she hoped Violet didn't trip over something and drop the tray on the way down. She offered to accompany her with her torch but this was politely refused.

'At least we know he wasn't called out tonight because he'd have rung here to find me. Do you know the only reason I got such a good billet this time is because he insisted they put in a telephone so he could contact me? My landlady's cock-a-hoop as she's the only one in the road with their own telephone – think she's ever so posh.'

Dan poured the boiling water on the coffee and stirred it vigorously. He'd already placed the two mugs, the sugar and the milk on the table. 'Now, I'm impatient to hear what happened in the evidence room tonight.'

'It worked out exactly as you thought it would, sir.

Sergeant Reynolds – he looks about hundred and twenty and as if he was dragged out of retirement in order to work again – was only too happy to knock off and leave us to it.'

'I know exactly who you mean. He was a good cop in his day but should be home tending his allotment, or sitting with his feet up, not spending hours in the basement guarding the evidence room.'

'It took us about an hour to book everything in and put it on the shelf. Then we found the boxes relating to the relevant incidents and the missing items were still missing. The records showed that nobody had taken them out officially so we decided to look through ancient boxes, those that are never going to be looked in again this century, and see if the things might have been shoved in there.'

'Go on, man, the suspense is killing me.'

'We found three of the things but not the other two. We've made a note of the numbers on the boxes that we found them in and then put everything back exactly as it was. Joan, that is WPC Davidson, even found some dust from a corner and sprinkled it over the boxes we'd looked in so they look exactly like the others adjacent to them.'

'This calls for more than coffee. I've got some whisky left – would you care for some?'

Spirits of any kind were in short supply unless you got it on the black market or could pay the prices at the Ritz or the Savoy. His sergeant was only too happy to accept the offer.

'How are we going to proceed now, sir? We've proved that someone tampered with the evidence but we can't pin it on either Jones or Smith, even though we know it was one or other of them.'

'Until I know who else is involved in this, I can't do anything. That being said, I'm delighted with the results as they've justified my suspicions. Now we have to wait until I can charge that bastard Bentley with something else and watch to see who tries to interfere with my case.'

'My informant, the one who led us to the stolen property, said he'd let me know if he hears anything interesting.'

'Recovering the stolen goods is going to upset Bentley – they'd been hidden long enough for him to start having them fenced. It's not as if the man's short of funds, but he'll be seething and on the lookout for another way to replace what, no doubt, he thinks was rightfully his,' Dan said with a smile.

The telephone jangled loudly in the hall and without being asked Wainwright hurried out to answer it. From the end of the conversation Dan could hear it wasn't anything urgent.

'The taxi's here. It's half an hour earlier than we asked, but I'm just grateful not to have to walk.'

'By the way, I'm going to take three days' leave from Monday next week. You're more than ready to stand in for me.'

'Good for you, sir – you never take your days off. Doing anything nice?'

'None of your damn business, Wainwright. Good night, and thank you.'

14

Charlotte collected the designated car with some trepidation. Being able to drive and actually doing it were not the same thing. The hotel had made her a wicker hamper of sandwiches and so on for the journey and also included a thermos of tea. Dan would be impressed.

As she no longer bothered to take either her tin hat or gas mask with her, she only had her haversack with her overnight necessities to carry as well as the picnic basket. On her way home last night she'd put the necessary maps and paperwork in the back of the car that she was to use. This was a smart, black Austin Eleven with leather seats – it even had a heater, not that she thought they would need it as she'd no intention of driving at night. What she'd wanted to do was give it a test run, but that was out of the question.

A WAAF from the motor pool was waiting to greet her that morning. The girl saluted smartly and Charlotte returned the gesture. 'Good morning, ma'am, a lovely day for a drive. I filled the tank and there's a can in the back in case you run out before you reach the base. Is there anything you want to know?'

'No, I'm familiar with this car although it's a newer

model than the one I drove. I'll return it safely to you on Wednesday night.'

The girl opened the rear door so the picnic basket could be placed on the seat. Charlotte wasn't going to wait to have the driver's door opened in the same way so scrambled in with more haste than dignity.

The bit she'd been dreading was having to reverse the vehicle so she could exit through the archway into the street beyond. To her relief this manoeuvre wasn't necessary as the car was facing in the correct direction. She nodded her thanks and the girl grinned and stepped back.

The engine fired immediately without the necessity of enriching the petrol by using the choke, so she released the handbrake, engaged the gears with commendable smoothness, and drove out like a professional.

She was picking Dan up outside his apartment in Kensington and she'd familiarised herself with the route last night. He was waiting – looking handsome, happy, and incredibly smart – outside the door. She glided to a halt and he tossed his bag, coat and hat onto the rear seat and joined her in the front.

'This is an impressive vehicle, Charlotte; let's hope you can return it in the same condition.'

She laughed. 'Are you suggesting that I'm a rotten driver and likely to crash into the nearest haystack or ditch?'

'Not at all. It's a long drive and the roads in Norfolk are narrow and nowadays are full of RAF traffic. Just a matter of luck if we avoid being involved in some sort of minor collision.'

'Well, that's really cheered me up. Not only am I likely to get lost, as I've no confidence in your ability to navigate, but I'm also likely to be hit by a marauding RAF vehicle no doubt full of drunken pilots.'

He reached over the back of his seat with no difficulty and flicked through the pile of maps before extracting the one he wanted. 'Can you find your way out of London?'

'I memorised the route. I was stationed near Felixstowe for a year and am familiar with that area. It's once we pass there that I'm going to need your assistance. The place we're going is just the other side of Great Yarmouth.'

'I'll do my best, my dear, but it'll be a miracle if we get there without having to stop and ask for directions half a dozen times.'

There was no further conversation as she wanted to concentrate. Driving through the city was comparatively easy as long as you knew where you were going because civilians no longer had access to petrol and the only vehicles on the road were official ones.

Soon they were bowling along in the Essex countryside and she rolled the window down to let in the October sunshine. 'Autumn and spring are my favourite seasons. The trees look their best then. I expect you've noticed I've got a picnic on the back seat. I thought we could find a spot along the coast. We can't go down on the beach but we could sit on a cliff somewhere and enjoy the breeze and the view.'

'I thought I was taking you out to lunch.'

'We've got three days, Dan, plenty of time. I haven't booked our overnight accommodation but I doubt the hotels and guesthouses will be busy.'

'I've been thinking about that, Charlotte. Would you have any objection if I flash my warrant card and say I'm on official business? Then they'll think that you're my driver.'

Her gloved hands clenched on the wheel. She bit back her initial angry remark. It wouldn't be helpful to fall out with him at the start of the three days. She was trying to think of some way to tell him how annoyed she was without offending him when he reached out and touched her arm.

'Sorry, that was heavy-handed of me. We're going to a rural area where standards and opinions are quite different from those in the capital. Think about it. Do you think your wing commander would be happy to know that I've come with you?'

'I don't suppose he'd care, but you're right, I didn't tell him. I overreacted. We don't want to give people the wrong idea so yes, let's pretend I'm your driver.'

His rich, deep baritone chuckle filled the car. 'Well, you are, so it's not a pretence. I know for a fact that the occasional CID officer has been sent to Norfolk so I don't think anyone will raise an eyebrow if we play it that way.'

'I really didn't think this through, did I? I just thought when I knew I had to spend three days in the wilds of Norfolk that I'd like to have you with me, to be able to get to know you away from work and everything else.'

'I'm delighted that you did. It's exactly what I need. To be out of contact from my work, and in such charming company for three days.' He sighed and shifted a little in his seat. She looked at him anxiously and he smiled wryly. 'Sorry, bloody leg. Nothing to worry about.'

Later, when they had been driving for three hours and had passed Colchester some time earlier, she recognised the countryside as being close to Felixstowe. 'Start looking for somewhere we can stop and have a picnic. I've decided I don't want to eat on a cliff. Preferably not a field full of cows. I'd be happy with horses – I really miss being able to ride.'

'I didn't know you rode. I'd gathered from your diction that, like me, you come from the upper classes. Would you like to know something about my past?'

'Yes, that would be perfect. Then I'll tell you about mine.'

She wasn't surprised to discover that he too had been estranged from his family – he had the appearance of a man who preferred to be on his own. When she'd finished a brief résumé of her past he nodded as if unsurprised.

'We have a lot in common, don't you think? We've both taken our own paths despite the disapproval of our families. I suppose your remaining brother inherits the ancestral home?'

'He doesn't – the bank does. It was mortgaged to the hilt. What about yours?'

'I handed it over to the RAF to use as a hospital for pilots recovering from burns. God knows what I'll do with it when they leave at the end of the war. Donate it to the nation, perhaps.'

'I doubt they'll want it as they'll be too busy building homes for those who have lost theirs in the Blitz and also for returning servicemen. What about the National Trust?'

'I'd forgotten about them. I'm sure they'll be happy to have it especially as there are two working farms on the estate that will more than pay for the upkeep of the building. I expect people will want to go somewhere for a day out when this damned war's over.'

'Being near St Albans there are bound to be charabancs of eager visitors coming from the city for a day out in the country. I take it you have a private income.' She wished the words unsaid as soon as she'd spoken as one didn't ask about someone's wealth – it just wasn't done.

He didn't take offence. 'I've got more than enough to live on and don't have to work – I just prefer to.'

'I've nothing at all from my family to fall back on. I have to manage on the meagre pittance I get from the WAAF.'

She almost swerved into the ditch when he grabbed her arm and shouted in her ear. 'There, the perfect place and you can park right off the road.'

Dan cracked his elbow painfully on the door as the car screeched to a halt. It was entirely his own fault for yelling and he braced himself for a well-deserved reprimand.

'For heaven's sake, Dan, don't do that. We could have ended up in the ditch. Remember, I'm not an experienced driver.'

'Now you tell me. I apologise for yelling but you have to admit it was worth the small risk of an accident to be able to have our lunch in such a perfect place,' he joked.

She reversed carefully to the correct side of the road and then continued backwards until she was neatly positioned in the narrow lane.

'Look, horses in the field just as you asked. Also, a perfect patch of grass next to the gate to sit on, which is out of sight of the road.'

She was already out of the car and exclaiming in delight. She turned and her smile made him feel young and whole again. 'I forgive you. This is absolutely what I was hoping for. We can feed the crusts to the horses and there's nobody here to arrest us for doing so.'

'I think you're forgetting, Assistant Section Officer Fenimore, that I'm a policeman. I believe it would be my duty to arrest you for breaking the law.'

She snatched off her hat and threw it at him and he caught it easily with one hand. As long as he was balancing against something solid there was no danger he'd fall over even if he wasn't leaning on his stick.

'Arrest me if you dare, Detective Inspector Chalmers. I'm shocked that someone as superior as yourself has been reduced to being the Crust Police.'

She handed him the picnic basket and she brought the rug and the thermos. There was no need to lock the car as they could see it, but it was invisible to anyone driving past.

Sitting on the ground was going to be tricky, as getting up again would require her assistance. He was reluctant to show her just how crippled he was when they were getting on so well. She didn't look at him as if he was half a man and he didn't want to see the change in her expression when he had to ask for help.

'Don't sit on the blanket, Dan – I've got a deckchair in the car. Can you manage better with that?'

'Perfect. Thank you for thinking of it.'

She returned and set it up for him and soon they were drinking piping-hot tea and munching through a delicious array of sandwiches all with recognisable fillings. There were also a couple of sausage rolls with actual sausage meat in them, two hard-boiled eggs with a twist of salt in a bit of greaseproof paper, as well as two large, crisp apples.

The horses were enormous, Shires by the look of it, and they ambled over to hang their massive heads over the fence and see what goodies they might be offered.

'Did you ride before your accident?'

'I did, but never hunted. I've not tried it since.'

'I'm sure you could manage even with your damaged leg. When this war's over you must try again. Imagine being able to gallop over the fields – what a feeling that would be.'

'As long as you come with me then I'm prepared to give it a go. Shall we give them the leftovers?'

They'd both made sure that the crusts they'd saved were just bread and he noticed she too had left a lot of apple on the core. They'd sat and talked for an hour and the more time he spent with her the better he liked her. She was twenty-three years old and completely inexperienced when it came to men. He couldn't understand how this could be true as she'd lived on RAF bases. Airmen were never slow to take advantage of a pretty girl.

She offered her hand and he took it. For the first time since he'd been crippled, he didn't resent being offered assistance. Why the hell she wasn't repulsed by his injury he'd no idea but it made him feel good again about himself.

They leaned against the fence fussing the horses and feeding them the leftovers. They were standing so close together it seemed natural for him to put his arm around her shoulders whilst the massive animals crunched happily on the apple cores.

To his delight she leaned into him. A surge of something he recognised as happiness almost overwhelmed him. How could this beautiful, intelligent, wonderful girl even look twice at a wreck of a man like him?

'I suppose we should make a move,' he said but remained exactly where he was.

She turned slightly within his embrace and looked up at

him. Their faces were inches apart. What happened next was inevitable – he pressed his lips to hers. Not a passionate kiss; he didn't want to alarm her.

It was brief but pleasurable. He smiled down at her. Her cheeks were slightly flushed, her lips parted and she'd never looked more desirable.

'That was unexpected, Dan, but I enjoyed it. I suppose that means things have moved on between us and now I'm your girlfriend.' She didn't sound too sure and he hurried to reassure her.

'I hope so. I wouldn't have kissed you if I didn't think you were ready to move things on a little. I knew the moment I saw you across the street the day of that murder-suicide that you were going to be someone special in my life.'

Her eyes widened. 'Golly, how extraordinary! I noticed you too but, if I'm honest, it didn't occur to me that one day we'd be together. I just saw a tall, handsome man doing his job.'

'How old do you think I am?'

She looked at him closely. 'About thirty, possibly a few years older than that.'

'I'm twenty-seven, only four years your senior.'

'I wouldn't care if you were forty-four – age has nothing to do with it. It's how a couple get on that matters.'

A wave of despair made him step away. Could he ask her to become closer to him, one day to possibly be his wife, when he was so horribly disfigured? Was this a mistake? Was it better to stop it now before they both got hurt?

'I'll bring the deckchair; can you bring the rest?'

She ignored his suggestion and took his hand in hers, making it impossible for him to retreat as he wanted to.

'I don't care about your leg. I know that's what's worrying you. It might be different if I'd known you when you were uninjured but I'm going into this relationship fully aware that you're not as fit as you'd like to be. It makes no difference to me and it shouldn't make any difference to you.'

'Darling girl, it's all very well saying that now. You haven't seen the damage. I can't run – sometimes I can scarcely walk. Why would you want to saddle yourself with a man like me when you could have someone so much better?'

'I've had more than enough opportunity to have *someone better* as you put it but, until I met you, I didn't want anyone at all. If you're so worried I'll be revolted and run away screaming then drop your trousers now and show me.'

Her suggestion was so outrageous and so obviously not meant to be taken literally that he laughed. 'Right, we can't be seen here so I should think it's safe enough.' He shrugged off his jacket and was about to flick down his braces when she too started to laugh.

'All right, there's no need to show me at this exact minute. Good heavens, I don't think an unmarried girl should see a gentleman's legs until their wedding night.'

They gathered up the remnants of their picnic and stowed it neatly on the back seat. The deckchair fitted perfectly into the boot. He couldn't remember when life had looked so promising – not even when he was at university had he felt so alive, so optimistic, and it was all down to the young woman sitting beside him in the car.

Charlotte wasn't given to bursting into song but today she wished she had the voice of a nightingale and could sing one of the latest songs 'There'll Be Bluebirds Over the White Cliffs of Dover' would be perfect and suited her mood.

'Can you sing, Dan? Something else I don't know about you.'

'Voice like a foghorn, sweetheart, and completely tone deaf.'

'That makes two of us – another thing we have in common. The base I have to investigate is fifteen miles from Great Yarmouth so I thought we might have a better chance of finding somewhere decent to stay there, rather than travel closer. There's a small village a couple of miles from the base but that's all.'

'We should be there long before dark, despite having spent two hours eating lunch.'

'Consider this your annual vacation – you don't have to do anything apart from relax and enjoy yourself. I'm the one who's got to work.'

'Indeed you do, but not until tomorrow, so today we're both on holiday. We've been remarkably lucky with the weather today – that picnic wouldn't have been half so enjoyable eaten in the car.'

'That's true – I can't remember having had such a splendid time before. The kitchen staff at the hotel were so generous. It's even better than being at boarding school and I quite enjoyed that – I hated being at home.'

His prowess as a navigator was unnecessary as the coast road ran directly to Great Yarmouth and even she couldn't get lost. They'd been driving for an hour when he shifted as if uncomfortable. She glanced sideways and saw his eyes were closed and he was gritting his teeth. He was obviously in serious pain.

Without hesitation she pulled into the side of the road, regardless of the fact that if a lorry wanted to pass at this particular point then they might find it difficult.

'Why have we stopped?'

'Would it help if you got out and walked around for a bit? I can't bear to see you in so much discomfort.'

'Yes, it would help, but I'm not going to do it. Look, Charlotte, if this is going to work between us you've got to accept how things are and not try and mollycoddle me. I've learned to live with the pain. There's nothing else I can do.'

She bit her lip and nodded. 'Of course, I'm sorry. This is new to me. I'll get the hang of it, please don't be cross with me.'

He reached out and took her hand – she'd not bothered to put her driving gloves back on – and raised it to his mouth. The touch of his lips made her glow all over.

'I didn't mean to be so abrupt, darling. I'm not used to having someone care about me – it's I who must adapt, not you.'

15

Dan rather wished he'd agreed to get out and stretch his leg, not been so stoic, as by the time they reached the seaside town of Great Yarmouth every bump in the road was agony. To his surprise she unexpectedly pulled over by a row of dismal and dilapidated shops.

'Don't argue, Dan, get out and walk up and down until you've eased the kinks out of your leg. I don't suppose the shops have much in them but you can always have a look and see if you can find some chocolate or a packet of biscuits.'

In the time it took him to reach over the back for his coat, hat and cane, she'd nipped around the car and was opening the door as if she was truly his driver – or chauffeur – depending on how you looked at it.

She saluted smartly and winked. 'I'll return as instructed in half an hour, sir.'

'Thank you, Fenimore. As you were.' He'd almost returned her salute but remembered in time he was no longer entitled to do so.

She slammed his door shut then was back in the car and driving away before he had time to put on his hat. As expected, there was nothing worth buying especially as what was available was kept for locals with their ration books behind the counter.

Walking was excruciating for the first hundred yards but after that the pain eased and he was able to move more freely. The wind from the sea was bracing to say the least and several degrees colder than it had been when they'd stopped for lunch. He glanced at the sky, vast expanses of it, and there were heavy black clouds rolling in.

He buttoned his coat up to the neck and wished he'd had the foresight to bring a scarf. He was more than ready to return to the car when Charlotte returned on cue. This time she didn't get out but left him to get in under his own volition.

'I found the perfect place. I've booked two rooms for two nights and also for dinner tonight. I'm hoping we might get a meal on the base tomorrow.'

She didn't ask him how he was, which was a relief as he had no wish to discuss his infirmity any more than he had to. The hotel, a large Victorian edifice overlooking the windswept beach, had a car park at the back and she parked expertly.

'Will anyone come out for our bags?'

'No, we have to take them ourselves. They're horribly short-staffed and those they do have are as old as Methuselah. I didn't choose it for the service or comfort but because it made me smile. You'll see why when we get inside.'

Fortunately, there were only a couple of steps to negotiate and he followed her into a cavernous foyer in which their voices echoed. There were small clusters of tables and chairs marooned in a sea of parquet flooring at which were seated a handful of miserable-looking, elderly guests.

What in God's name could have possessed Charlotte to bring him here? He didn't find the spectacle at all amusing. On the far side of the depressing space was an enormous mahogany desk polished to a high shine. Behind it stood a decrepit personage in black tailcoat.

She led the way across, unaware of his reaction, presumably still thinking the whole thing a bit of a hoot – as someone like her would say.

'This is DI Chalmers. I've already signed in for both of us. I've come to collect our keys.'

This was shouted at the poor old bloke who nodded and smiled. Without speaking he handed her the keys attached to equally shiny mahogany fobs.

'The lift's over there. It just about works – it's like something from a Gothic novel.'

The lift operator was an equally ancient man, in a faded burgundy livery. She held up the keys and he nodded and a few moments later the lift lurched into action. Their rooms were on the first floor and after the alarming experience he thought maybe he'd attempt the stairs in future.

'My room's at this end of the corridor and yours is at the other. The lift is the same distance from both of them. It's like stepping back in time, isn't it?' She turned with a bright smile, which slowly faded as she noticed his expression.

'There has to have been something better than this. Give me the key – I'll find my own way. Did you think being amongst people in a worse state than me would somehow make me feel better? If you did – you failed.'

She stared at him as if seeing him for the first time and he realised he'd made a catastrophic error reacting as he had.

'I chose this hotel because they desperately need the

booking, because it's clean and comfortable and one of the guests said the food, despite arriving a bit colder than it should be, is delicious. I also thought you would find the old-fashioned formality sweet, the incredibly old staff as endearing and amusing as I did. I obviously completely misjudged both you and the situation.'

She tossed him his key, turned and marched, parade-ground stiff, to the far end of the long passageway. He could follow her, try and apologise, explain why he'd reacted so badly, but thought he'd leave it until she'd had time to calm down and he'd had time to think of a way to put things right.

His room was old-fashioned but spotless. There was even a private bathroom – but no shower so he'd have to make do with a strip wash. He poured himself a glass of water from the crystal glass jug on the bedside table and swallowed two of his painkillers.

There was a leather folder on the bureau with the mealtimes. They were set times – presumably if you didn't come you didn't eat. He checked his watch – two hours before he needed to go down to dine. Plenty of time to rehearse his grovelling apology.

He flopped onto the bed not bothering to remove his shoes as putting them back on was a struggle. He reviewed what had just happened and tried to work out why he'd been so dismissive and rude. He could think of no exonerating excuse apart from the fact he was in appalling pain and had been for some time.

The medication he carried with him was morphine-based and, as always, it worked wonderfully but also knocked him out completely. He woke with a jolt in an unfamiliar room in total darkness.

★

Charlotte stormed into her bedroom and hurled her haversack across the room. She paced up and down for several minutes until she regained her temper. What was wrong with the man? They'd been getting on so well and she thought they understood each other. How wrong had she been?

They weren't compatible at all – it had been the sunshine, the delicious picnic, the romance of the moment that had made her think they might be able to make a go of it. He was basically a bad-tempered man totally lacking a sense of humour. He'd allowed his unfortunate injury to turn him into someone who, on further reflection, she really didn't want to get closer to.

She kicked off her shoes and flung herself onto the bed. This trip had started so well. He'd kissed her, put his arm around her, and she'd really enjoyed it. He called her darling, sweetheart, and she'd loved those endearments too.

They were, obviously, from similar backgrounds, which gave them something in common but that was as far as it went. She'd blithely said his injured leg wasn't a problem, that she found him attractive – this was true. He was everything she could hope to have in a future lover. Even thinking these words made her hot all over.

However, what she couldn't deal with were his mercurial changes of mood. His grim outlook on life, the fact that he thought everyone was treating him differently because of his leg. That she couldn't live with, didn't want to. When eventually she got married it would be to someone she could laugh with, share memories with, say whatever she liked to without fear and she'd never have that with him. She'd be constantly walking on eggshells wondering if she was going to trigger an angry response.

What was she going to do about the situation? She was supposed to be a young woman with high moral principles and although she'd not condemned Nancy's behaviour, she had been slightly shocked. Jane hadn't pre-empted her marriage vows and Charlotte had always thought she'd not do so herself.

But being with Dan when she found him almost irresistible physically would inevitably mean she went to bed with him. She didn't want to do that and for the second time that day bitterly regretted her impulsive decision to invite him to accompany her. She might be considered an adult, had held down a responsible job for two years, but when it came to affairs of the heart she was as innocent as a child.

This was a disaster of her own making and the only way she could extricate herself was to abandon him at the hotel and continue to the base on her own. He was a resourceful man and could find his own way back to London. Doing this would be so appalling that any hope of a reconciliation would be out of the question. This would be better for both of them as if she spent any more time with him they would quite likely become lovers and then get married.

The prospect of spending the rest of her life with someone so embittered, someone so irascible and unstable was enough to convince her she'd made the right decision. He would make a wretched father – any child would have to be careful not to upset him and that was no way for a little one to grow up. They should have the unconditional love that David gave his brood. Oscar would do the same for his baby when it arrived.

She got up, reclaimed her shoes, collected her key and bag and was about to head downstairs. Dan wouldn't be down until seven o'clock when dinner was served, which gave her ample time to escape. Then she decided to write him a letter – he deserved that at least.

Dear Dan,

When you get this, I will be miles away. I apologise for abandoning you but in the circumstances, I can't think of anything else I can do.

I do like you, am halfway to falling in love with you, and I certainly find you physically attractive. But I can't get involved with a man I don't trust.

I thought we understood each other but that was obviously incorrect. It's not your physical injuries that are the problem, it's your mental ones. You've allowed your injury to sour your outlook on life and I just don't want to be involved with someone like that.

I apologise again for leaving you to find your own way home but when you've had time to think about it, you'll know I've made the right decision.

Could I ask you not to use The Sanctuary anymore and instead go somewhere else to eat? As it's my home, I have no choice but to remain.

I wish you all the best in your endeavours.
Best wishes,
Charlotte

After reading it through a couple of times she was satisfied she couldn't do any better. There was no easy way to break a man's heart. He had strong feelings for her and it was going to be difficult for him to accept the reasons she'd ended things so abruptly.

She stuffed the letter into an envelope and sealed it. She would hand it in with her key – she would also pay his bill, as that was only fair. There was no need for the letter to be given to Dan until after he'd had his breakfast tomorrow. He'd just assume she was sulking in her room when he came down to dine.

The ancient concierge listened carefully – thank goodness this old gentleman wasn't as deaf as the other one. Obviously, she couldn't tell him the truth, but then it was none of his business. She just stuck to the facts – she was leaving and her companion wasn't.

'I'll arrange for a car to take him to the station after breakfast tomorrow, ma'am. Shall I put that charge on your bill too?'

She paid what was a significant amount, but not exorbitant in the circumstances. She wouldn't be able to claim back the cost of Dan's accommodation and taxi and this would eat up most of her carefully hoarded savings.

She was relieved she hadn't actually told him the name of the base they were going to; it just hadn't come up in the conversation. She headed there and arrived as it was getting dark. There was no armed guard on the gate, no sign of anyone doing anything useful.

There was a grass strip, several blister hangars, a few wooden huts and a substantial brick-built building. The blackouts were drawn, which must mean that was where everybody was. The place certainly didn't require twenty general duties WAAFs – in fact she couldn't see that they needed any at all but they were certainly claiming the wages and the expenses for that many.

There was ample room in front of what she supposed was the mess hall and offices for her to park. This time she locked the car. If this base was so patently dishonest then it was possible someone might steal the car and she'd be stuck without transport in Norfolk.

There was only one way to do this – with confidence – and by drawing on all the officer training she'd so recently received.

Dan rolled out of bed, bracing himself against the substantial wooden frame. He had excellent night vision and within a few moments was able to see enough to find his cane and make his way to the large windows. He pulled the blackout curtains, checked not a chink of light could escape, and then found the switch on the wall.

His head was fuzzy, his mouth dry. These were the usual after-effects of taking those strong morphine-based tablets. He rarely took them but sometimes there was no option and today had been one of them.

He glanced at his watch – bloody hell – it was nine o'clock. Too late to eat and far too late to go in search of Charlotte and try and put things right between them.

She needed to understand how things were with him if they were to have any hope of a life together. Living in constant pain made him short-tempered but it didn't change the way he felt about her. She would have to make allowances, rise above his snarling and snapping, know that it wasn't him but the pain.

The surgeons had fought to save his leg and at the time he'd been grateful but more and more frequently he wished they'd amputated it. It would be easier to live without the leg than live with the agony it caused him.

He couldn't see losing half a leg would change how Charlotte viewed him but it would change his life. There'd be no need to take these bloody pills; he might be able to walk without his stick if he had a prosthetic leg. When he returned to the Smoke, he'd make an appointment to see the same surgeon and arrange to have the damn thing removed.

Of course, there was the little matter of arresting Jones and Smith to settle – but once that was done then he'd book sick leave. Afterwards he'd be in better shape physically and mentally. He undressed, glad he'd eaten such a substantial lunch, completed his ablutions and climbed between the sheets.

His relationship would have to be put on hold – he couldn't expect her to continue to see him in the circumstances. From what he remembered about others who'd had limbs amputated, if there was no infection after the operation, they recovered in a couple of weeks. The fitting of the false limb couldn't take place until the wound was completely healed, the scar hardened, but he'd be able to get around with crutches well enough until that happened.

The thought of being without the constant, dragging pain he'd endured since he'd been blown up in Dunkirk made him almost as happy as having Charlotte in his life. When he explained to her why he was doing this, what a difference it would make to both of them, she would be as pleased as he was that he'd finally made the right decision. No one wanted to be with a bad-tempered bastard – which was what he'd become.

Breakfast was served at eight o'clock and as he'd no intention of risking his life in the ancient lift he left his room fifteen minutes before the appointed time. He expected to see Charlotte waiting for him in the dining room but she wasn't there. Surely, she wasn't still angry with him? He was too hungry to worry about her absence and devoured everything that was put in front of him, expecting her to arrive at any moment.

After his second pot of tea he was seriously worried. He headed for the reception desk. The concierge handed him a letter. For a moment he didn't understand the significance. He dropped the key.

'Your account has been settled, Detective Inspector Chalmers, and the car will be here momentarily to take you to the station.'

He mumbled his thanks and took the letter to the door where he would be able to see when his taxi arrived. He slit open the envelope and read the contents. He didn't need to read it a second time. His initial reaction had been fury that she'd dumped him so unceremoniously, then a wave of misery almost unmanned him.

Angrily he blinked back unwanted tears, shoved the letter and envelope into his coat pocket, and went outside where he could blame the sea breeze for his wet cheeks. After a few minutes he recovered his composure and began to see this as the perfect opportunity for both of them.

Her decision was the right one as things stood – he didn't

blame her. When he was himself again, minus his leg, things would be different. He'd prove to her that he was no longer an unpleasant human being, but a man who loved her and would make her happy if she agreed to marry him.

He almost pitched head first down the steps. His subconscious had, without his permission, made assumptions about his feelings. Until that moment the fact that he was hopelessly in love with her hadn't been apparent to him.

He was smiling when he climbed into the car. He didn't care how long it took to persuade her to marry him. Even if it took years, one day they would be together and he'd make her happy, protect her, love her, provide her with everything she wanted and, hopefully, give them both children to love.

16

Charlotte was careful not to push the door open too vigorously. She wanted to arrive confidently but not dramatically. It didn't matter either way as she stepped into a large, deserted entrance area.

Ahead of her she could hear voices, the clatter of crockery and clink of glasses – that would be the mess. There must be officers, a base didn't run without at least a couple, but she doubted they'd have their own mess so everyone must use the one she could hear ahead of her.

She looked around with interest. The brown linoleum was polished to a high shine, as it should be. Through the open doors of the three offices she could see nothing to complain about. Desks were cleared, chairs neatly pushed in, no piles of paperwork waiting to be dealt with.

They might be dishonest here but they were certainly efficient and tidy. The wooden huts she'd seen must be the accommodation but there certainly wasn't room for twenty girls anywhere on this small base. It was a storage depot now – it had been used initially to train pilots on Tiger Moths but training had been moved to Canada, the wilds of Scotland and other remote places. Once the Germans had started bombing Britain the skies over Norfolk would have been far too dangerous for trainee pilots.

Her cumbersome haversack would be better off on a chair in one of the offices. She wanted to look her best when she strode into the mess. She didn't like being the centre of attention but had learned over the summer how to deal with it, how to take command, how to issue orders when inside she was as wobbly as jelly.

There was no point in procrastinating – she needed to introduce herself immediately. Hopefully, she'd then be offered a meal as her stomach was beginning to rumble and she didn't want anyone to hear it gurgling as that would be rather undignified. Her mouth curved at the thought. It would be hard to maintain discipline in those circumstances.

She headed for the mess and walked into a long room, which obviously served as a recreation hall, bar and dining area. In the few moments she had before anyone noticed her arrival she did a rapid headcount and there were approximately fifteen airmen, two WAAFs and no one above the rank of warrant officer.

Being the most senior person there gave her the confidence to march in, look around and wait for the room to fall silent. She stood until everyone was looking in her direction before speaking.

'Good evening, I'm Assistant Section Officer Fenimore. I've been sent from the War Office in search of twenty missing WAAFs.'

She was smiling as she spoke but watching the reactions of the personnel in front of her. No one looked particularly guilty; in fact, if anything, they looked pleased to see her.

A stout, middle-aged warrant officer was the first to get to his feet and walk towards her. He stopped and saluted. She reciprocated.

'Warrant Officer Riggs, ma'am, I can't say that we're thrilled to see you but in some ways it's a relief. Have you driven all the way from London on your own?'

'I have. Something smells delicious and I haven't eaten since lunchtime.'

He beamed. 'Then you've come to the right place. We might be small, but we have first-class catering here. It's steak and kidney pie tonight followed by apple cobbler and custard.' He pointed to the table from which he'd come. 'If you'd care to be seated, ma'am, I'll bring you your meal myself. Least I can do when you've come so far.'

'Thank you, but I'm perfectly capable of collecting my own food. However, I'd be delighted to join you.'

The general chatter had resumed almost immediately, which was reassuring. For some reason she didn't think the missing WAAF situation was exactly as it seemed. She'd expected to see shifty-looking individuals, hardened criminals possibly, but instead was in a room full of perfectly normal, friendly RAF personnel.

There were three WAAFs serving through the hatch in the kitchen wall and she immediately noticed a difference in the way they viewed her. None of them smiled. They weren't disrespectful but they weren't happy to see her.

She stored this information for later, collected her plates, relieved that she'd remembered to remove her irons from her haversack before she'd come in. All WAAF were expected to carry their own cutlery and tin mug – it would have looked unprofessional for her not to have had hers even though it wouldn't have mattered, as there were knives, forks and spoons readily available.

The table she joined was made up of two corporals and a sergeant. She was the only officer on the base. She didn't join in the conversation until she'd finished the delicious steak and kidney pie – even the cabbage and potatoes were perfectly cooked, which made a change as quite often the vegetables were all but inedible.

Apple cobbler and custard could be eaten hot or cold so could wait until she'd spoken to her table companions. 'You already know who I am. Would you care to introduce yourselves?'

They had one thing in common: apart from being RAF and not WAAF, they were all in their forties and obviously too old for active service. They were doing their bit for the war by running a storage depot but obviously in no danger from the Germans tucked away as they were in the wilds of Norfolk.

'I'm sure you already know why I'm here. Sergeant Blowers, would you care to explain why this small base apparently has twenty active WAAF working here and being paid every week for their services.'

She'd deliberately chosen the sergeant as he'd looked the most uncomfortable to have her at the table. The other three had carried on eating as if not bothered at all. One of the corporals had got out his Woodbines but she'd told him if he wanted to smoke then he could go outside and he nodded amiably and wandered off without protest.

Blowers shifted uncomfortably. He looked everywhere but at her; several minutes passed and she was still without an answer to her question.

'WO Whitely, put that man out of his misery. Tell me what's going on here. I've full authority to call in the RAF police and have you all arrested.'

'Well, it's like this, ma'am: a request was put in for five girls. We need them for catering, orderly duties and so on but someone at your office made a mistake and sent us a charabanc full.'

'I assumed something like that had taken place. However, that doesn't explain why you didn't send them back immediately but continued to pretend that they work here. Where exactly are the girls now, because we don't have any record of them being anywhere else?'

'It might seem a bit unusual, ma'am, but these girls didn't want to be sent back. They liked it up here away from the bombs and such. There are few small, inactive bases like this one dotted about and they were all crying out for a few girls to run the domestic side of things.'

She was beginning to see what had happened but kept her thoughts to herself and allowed him to continue his rambling explanation without interruption.

'All of them had made frequent requests for girls to be sent but these had been denied. It seems that unless you want dozens, you don't get anyone at all.'

'Let me get this clear. You parcelled the girls out to these other bases – they're all working as they should be doing general duties. The only irregularity being that they are registered on your books and are being paid here.'

He nodded. 'That's it in a nutshell, ma'am. I knew at once that you'd understand how things were.'

'Believe me, I do understand exactly. Unfortunately, what you've been doing is highly illegal. The only way out of a court martial is for me to attempt to sort this out whilst I'm here. I'll get the girls you have here legally assigned to you and then visit the other places and do the same for them.'

Sergeant Blowers was now confident enough to speak for himself. 'I've not been comfortable doing this all these months, ma'am, but although not strictly legal no one has benefited financially or in any other way from this peculiar arrangement. There's been a lot of toing and froing every pay parade to make sure the right girl gets the right amount of money every week.'

The other corporal spoke up. 'We get sacks full of letters sent here and then have to sort them out and make sure they go to the right person. It's been a blooming nightmare trying to keep it straight.'

'I'm sure it has, Corporal. I'll do my best to sort things out for you and the girls, but I can't promise someone more senior than I am won't decide to drop on the lot of you like a ton of bricks.'

Dan was slightly less relaxed about having been so summarily dismissed by Charlotte after being obliged to wait for two hours for a train to London at Great Yarmouth station. The journey, which under normal circumstances would take more no more than three hours, took four as the train stopped at every station, sometimes for as long as fifteen minutes.

This meant he didn't arrive at Liverpool Street until just before five o'clock – an entire day wasted as far as he was concerned. Simmons wasn't available until he was officially back on duty so either he had to hobble his way down to the underground or hope he might find a cab – although they were in very short supply nowadays.

Eventually, in a foul mood, he arrived at his apartment. He'd ordered a substantial dinner to be sent up as soon as it could be prepared. He drank whisky with his meal and began to feel a little mellower.

He wasn't expected at his desk until the day after tomorrow. He intended to spend the time searching out the surgeon and arranging for the amputation. As soon as he'd completed his investigation, had got enough evidence to arrest Jones and Smith, then he'd go into hospital. He thought he might have to resign his position as he doubted Bailey – who wasn't a fan of his – would allow him to have as much as six weeks' sick leave.

He'd become a policeman because he hadn't wanted to go into the army. As he'd told Charlotte, he didn't need to work but would be bored witless with nothing to do. He didn't see himself as a gentleman of leisure, drifting to his club for a snifter with his pals, riding to hounds, hunting, shooting and fishing and all that nonsense.

That said, he wasn't sure a one-legged detective inspector would be acceptable to his superiors. He knew they'd only taken him back because they were so desperately short of good men. When this bloody war was over they'd kick him out anyway and replace him with a healthy, fit, returning serviceman.

He was finishing his third glass of whisky when the phone rang loudly in the hall. Muttering profanities under his breath he snatched up his stick and, somewhat unsteadily, made his way to the telephone.

'Chalmers.'

'Thank God, sir, you're needed... please come in, please—' Wainwright was almost incoherent. Something appalling had occurred.

'Send someone to collect me and I'll be with you as soon as I can. What's happened?'

'Joan, she's been murdered.'

For a second Dan was too shocked to respond. 'We'll get the bastards. Where did this happen? Who's at the scene? Was she raped?'

'No, a couple of PCs were just doing a routine check as part of their beat and that's the first thing they checked. Her underclothes were undisturbed. Her body was found behind the Athenaeum Club in Waterloo Place. I'm the most senior officer on duty. Day staff clocked off an hour ago. The two PCs who discovered her are standing guard and waiting for me. I don't think I can do this on my own, sir. Me and Joan were stepping out.'

'Contact the photographer, notify the police surgeon. Pull yourself together. Ring first for the car, then make the other calls. I'll let the chief super know. No one kills one of ours and gets away with it. I'll organise as many boots on the ground as are available.'

He disconnected and informed his superior. 'My God. First someone tries to kill your young lady and then the WPC attached to your team is murdered. Take charge – you can have everything you want. Don't worry about the overtime – get in as many men as you need.'

'Yes, sir, I'll do that whilst I wait for Davidson and the car to arrive to collect me. I'd intended to spend a few days in the country – thank God I didn't. Davidson wasn't in uniform so I suppose there's a remote possibility this is unconnected.'

'Let's hope so, but I can begin to see a pattern.'

There was just time to change his shirt before he had to leave. He was waiting outside when the car drew up. He was surprised, but pleased, to see Simmons driving his usual car.

'Sergeant, my driver is supposed to be on leave. Wasn't there anyone else available?'

The girl answered his question. 'It was just as quick to get me out, sir, and I'm happy to be of service. Dreadful, dreadful business.'

Dan slammed the door and settled into the corner. How the hell did she know? This sort of thing shouldn't be common knowledge – Wainwright had been indiscreet, but now wasn't the time to give him a bollocking. That could wait.

He deliberately didn't open a discussion about the murder and his sergeant took the hint and remained silent. As they approached the scene of the crime he could see several other cars – most of these were official police vehicles and clearly marked as such. There were, however, two other plain sedans no doubt belonging to the police surgeon, or coroner depending who'd been on duty, and the official photographer.

The area was heaving with uniformed men but with no senior officer in charge they weren't doing anything useful. He was out of the car as soon as it stopped and within minutes had things organised. They needed light on the scene; if an ARP complained he'd get an earful.

Eventually the area had been combed for clues – none had been found – and the body of WPC Davidson was on the way to the morgue for a post-mortem. Not that he needed a report as the girl had quite clearly been shot. The body had been dumped behind the club but the murder hadn't taken place here as there wasn't enough blood.

He would inform her parents himself, but not tonight. The girl had digs somewhere close by so her parents wouldn't be sitting up waiting for their daughter to return. If he remembered correctly her home was somewhere outside Romford. He wouldn't leave this unpleasant duty to anyone else.

'Is it through and through, doc?'

'No, DI Chalmers, I'll be able to recover the bullet. She wasn't shot here – I'm sure you noticed that there's not enough blood.'

'Can you give me a rough estimate of the time of death?'

'She's cold, so several hours ago. I'll give you a more accurate time when I do the PM.'

This meant she'd been killed in broad daylight. To be shot was unusual. Unpremeditated murders were more commonly done by a blunt instrument, a brick or whatever came to hand, or sometimes a knife. For a gun to have been used pointed towards premeditation and he was certain the poor girl's death was linked to the investigation he'd involved her in.

The Athenaeum Club had been brought to a standstill. A dozen constables were methodically interviewing each club-goer, much to the annoyance of the management and the alarm of some of the guests. The fact that many of the men were with women who probably weren't their wives was none of his business.

He didn't expect to learn anything of value but it was possible someone had seen or heard something. The remaining uniformed men were canvassing the area. There were always dubious characters lurking in the club district and he was hopeful one of them might divulge something of interest in exchange for a ten-bob note.

It wasn't until two a.m. that he was able to speak privately to his sergeant. He'd sent Simmons home to get some sleep as he'd no intention of returning to his flat. He would make use of the camp bed if necessary.

It took Charlotte the whole of the following day to visit the other bases and get the WAAFs officially registered at these places. It was all highly irregular but nothing actually illegal had taken place really. The girls were all doing what they were trained to do, just not in the place they were supposed to be.

She departed at dusk, satisfied she'd done the best she could to sort out the muddle. Being so busy had been exactly what she'd needed as it hadn't given her a moment to dwell on Dan. Driving in the dark with pinprick headlights wasn't something she wished to do, especially on the narrow country lanes of Norfolk.

She was relieved to find a small hotel, more a public house with rooms, and booked in for the night. They didn't serve food apart from breakfast but the landlady kindly made her some sandwiches and a pot of tea, which Charlotte took up to her room.

Even if she'd wanted to sleep, she wouldn't have been able to as there was a noisy darts game going on in the public bar just below her. She completed her report, filed her papers in her briefcase, and then had nothing else to do. She wished she'd had the foresight to bring a book to occupy her time.

Had Dan got back to London safely? She wished they hadn't kissed and held hands – in fact if she was being honest, she wished they hadn't met at all. She'd never expected to fall in love, and certainly not with someone like him but inexplicably her heart had overruled her head and now she was bereft.

Why couldn't she have fallen in love with someone less complex? There'd been ample opportunity over the past two years but until she'd met him her senses hadn't been stirred in any way. Loving him wasn't enough to make her wish to continue the relationship – he would make the worst possible husband and father. She must be sensible and stick to her decision not to see him again.

Mind you, after she'd abandoned him, he'd never want to see her again. He wasn't the sort of man who would take kindly to being treated so disrespectfully. She sighed and rubbed her eyes. He had feelings for her too and it would be so much harder for him as the decision had been hers.

Angrily she pushed these thoughts aside. There was a war on and she was an officer in the WAAF. There was no time for such sentimental nonsense. She would do her duty as she'd been trained to do and he would do his. They would both have regrets, but they would get on with their lives and soon put this romantic interlude behind them.

17

'Close the door, Wainwright,' Dan said as he stumbled into his chair. 'I was going to tear you off a strip for revealing confidential information to my driver but it no longer seems to matter.'

His sergeant dropped into his place on the other side of the desk and yawned so widely his jaw cracked. 'I'm sorry, unprofessional of me.'

'Forget it, I have. Now, tell me again exactly what happened yesterday.'

'That's the thing, nothing out of the ordinary. After Joan had finished filing and so on, I gave her the rest of the day off. She said she was meeting a friend for lunch and then going to the pictures.'

'We still don't know the name of this friend. I need to speak to the other WPCs when they get in at seven thirty. Her landlady wasn't much use as she said she hadn't seen Davidson since the night before and didn't know any of her friends as they never came to the house.'

'We were out together last night, sir, and I walked her home at just after ten o'clock. As I was transferring to nights, I went home for some kip at the same time as she left to meet her friend yesterday.'

Dan flicked through his notebook, then did the same with his sergeant's but there was nothing written in either of them to give them the lead they wanted.

'Do you think she told anyone what you discovered in the evidence room?'

'Absolutely not. She wouldn't betray your trust like that.' He dropped his head in his hands for a moment then looked up. He seemed to have aged ten years overnight. 'I don't understand the motive behind the murder. If it's something to do with our case then all they've done is draw more attention to it. It just doesn't make sense.'

'I don't believe in coincidence. Dammit!' He slammed his hands on the desk, making the papers and his colleague jump. 'I can think of one possible explanation. She signed the ledger last week but was only murdered yesterday. I need to see the duty roster.'

'I'll get it, there won't be anybody in the office for hours.' His sergeant dashed off and returned a few minutes later.

Dan flicked through the pages. 'As I suspected. This Johnson has been on sick leave and yesterday was his first day in the basement. Jesus Christ – did you sign the book down there as well?'

'I didn't – I meant to, but I forgot. The old bloke was just clocking off when we turned up and would remember I was there if asked.'

'Then you need to watch your back, my friend, as do I.' He came to a decision. 'We need to remove those boxes before someone else does. I'm coming down with you. I know where the key's kept.'

Usually in the small hours the place was silent but tonight was different. Davidson might have been a WPC but she was still one of their own and the grim-faced constables he nodded to on his way through the building reflected how he felt.

He met Chief Divisional Inspector Michael Robins as he was heading downstairs. Dan liked this chap; he was ten years his senior – a good man who deserved his rank.

'Dan, I can't tell you how sorry I am about your WPC. I need to talk to you – need to know everything about the case the three of you were working on.'

'You were going to be my next port of call. Come with us – there's something we need to get from the evidence room.'

Wainwright went to the boxes in which the incriminating papers and evidence were hidden. And his sergeant's exclamation of triumph was a relief. He'd given Mike a quick summary of what had been going on.

'We need to take the boxes intact, not touch the interiors at all,' Dan said. 'Then find something identical from the stores, give them the same labels and a liberal coating of dust. With any luck, whoever comes to look won't realise we've removed what they're looking for.'

'We can't carry them through the building, Dan – there are quite possibly others in the employ of this bastard Bentley. I know where they can go for the moment.'

Less than fifteen minutes later the three of them were drinking tea in the canteen. Wainwright had had to go into the kitchen himself to make it, as the catering staff didn't arrive until seven. The boxes were hidden at the back of a broom cupboard and Dan was confident nobody would find them.

'My only concern is that we might have been seen going down to the basement,' he said.

'I'm sure we weren't. If anyone saw us in the corridor then they would just think we were coming here,' Wainwright said as he munched his way through his fifth digestive.

'Do you want me to go to Romford?' Mike asked.

'Her death's my responsibility. I got her involved in this.'

'That may be so, my friend, but she was a uniformed member of the police force and therefore it is I who must deliver the bad news.'

He could hardly argue as, even though they were friends, Mike outranked him. 'If you insist. There will be something in the morning papers about the murder but as Davidson wasn't in uniform, I'm hoping no one realises she was a policewoman. The article won't have her name unless someone at the scene spoke to a reporter.'

'You're right. Even so, I need to see her parents. The body will have to be formally identified by next of kin.' Mike shook his head. 'I'm still at a loss to know why, if your case and this murder are linked, that they needed to murder her. In fact, the whole thing makes no sense to me.'

'Nor to me. We need to track down this friend and discover Davidson's movements yesterday afternoon. I intend to send PCs to every cinema with a copy of her photograph. Unfortunately, we only have one of her in uniform, which will immediately reveal that she's a WPC.'

'The story will be plastered all over the rags as soon as you do that. This makes it imperative I go to Romford this morning. There's nothing else we can do at the moment. I'm going home for a couple of hours' kip. Why don't you two do the same?'

The three of them had carefully avoided discussing the boxes they'd removed and the significance of these items.

'I'll grab some shut-eye in my office and Wainwright's on duty anyway. Do I inform the chief super about earlier?'

Even asking this question was dangerous as it indicated he wasn't entirely sure of his superior's honesty.

'No need. Let's see what we find out today,' Mike replied.

Charlotte didn't stop for lunch the following day and therefore arrived at Victory House mid-afternoon. The WAAF from the motor pool gave the car a quick inspection and then drove it away. With her briefcase under her arm, she headed for her office, hoping her solution to the problem would be accepted.

There was the usual clatter of typewriters and jolly chatter in the main office. She nodded her way through but didn't stop. She could see the wing commander through the pebbled glass that made up half the door.

'Welcome back, Fenimore, tell me what you found and how you dealt with it.' He listened and smiled. 'Exactly what I would have done. Well done, my girl, I knew you were the right person for this job. Your in-tray is full – if it weren't, I would give you the rest of the day off.'

'Then I'll get on with it, sir.'

When she eventually left all the secretaries and clerks had departed. It was strange walking through the silence of a normally noisy, busy room. The nights were getting noticeably longer and soon she would be walking home in the blackout.

Her usual table was available and after dinner she retired, satisfied with a job well done. The bathroom was occupied and she hated using it immediately after someone else. Tonight she'd make do with a strip wash at the basin in her room.

Only as she settled down to sleep did unwanted thoughts of Dan drift into her mind. Just thinking about him and his kiss, the touch of his hand on her face, his lips pressed against her palm made her restless and uncomfortable.

Maybe having an affair with him wouldn't be so bad. There were prophylactics he could use to prevent an unwanted pregnancy – she didn't know much about these apart from that they were issued to servicemen.

Many of the women she'd served with had a relaxed attitude about sex. Their mantra was: "There's a war on – we could be dead tomorrow." It wasn't one she'd either agreed with or adopted as her strict upbringing had made her view extramarital relationships as beyond the pale. How she'd changed since she'd fallen for Dan. Falling for someone put a different perspective on this and she understood now that her views were outdated and somewhat prudish.

One thing was quite certain, she wasn't going to seek him out. However, if they met by chance and he looked at her in the same way maybe she'd throw her hat over the windmill and become a fallen woman. She smiled to herself in the darkness.

Would having an affair with him make her his mistress? She wasn't quite sure about that – maybe the term was only used when the man in question was married. If a married woman did the same would her lover be known as her master? She fell asleep smiling at her highly improper musings.

★

A few days after her jaunt to Norfolk she left rather later than usual. It was more dusk than dark but she hurried anyway. When she turned into Tothill Street she saw Dan's car parked outside. Either he'd eaten very early and Violet had returned to collect him – or he was there specifically to see her.

'The DI's waiting inside to speak to you.' Her friend didn't smile and Charlotte's stomach lurched.

She pushed her way past the blackouts and immediately saw him leaning against the wall. His expression was forbidding. He obviously hadn't come for a social visit.

'I need to speak to you in private, ma'am. Would you accompany me outside so we can talk in the car?'

His formality was chilling. 'Of course, sir. I'm sorry to have kept you waiting.'

He said nothing else, stood aside to let her negotiate the curtains and then followed her out. Violet had the rear door open and Charlotte got in and slid across the leather seat so her back was pressed against the far side of the car.

She needn't have bothered as Dan took the front passenger seat and slammed the door. Violet moved away so she couldn't overhear what was being said. He swung round so he was facing her across the back of the seat.

'I have to tell you that the WPC who was working with me has been murdered. My sergeant and I now have an armed plain-clothes constable keeping us safe.

Only then did she notice a man in a long coat, his hat pulled down so it obscured his face, was patrolling up and down the other side of the narrow street.

'I'm very sorry to hear this. But how is this of relevance to me?'

His façade of indifference fell. 'For God's sake, Charlotte, of course it has something to do with you. Remember, someone already tried to kill you and he was working for Bentley – the murdering bastard is behind this.'

It was as if a heavy weight had settled on her chest. 'That was then – we're not together now.'

His expression softened. 'Don't be dense, sweetheart, you know how I feel about you. They can get to me through you and I'm not going to let that happen. I'm pretty sure someone has been watching me and no doubt saw me leave town with you.'

She looked around nervously. 'Do you think they know that I live here?'

'I'm certain of it. You're safe enough inside but walking to and from work isn't going to happen again. My driver will collect me first and then take you to Victory House. Half an hour before you intend to leave, ring this number and we'll reverse the process.'

He handed over slip of paper. She pushed it into a pocket without looking at it. Her hands were trembling and she clasped them in her lap, not wanting him to see how scared she was.

'I'm sorry I left you at the hotel in Norfolk. I couldn't think of anything else to do in the circumstances.'

'It was a bloody nuisance getting back, but water under the bridge. I'm not certain how long this arrangement will have to continue – but until I've locked Bentley and his cronies up, I'm not taking any risks with your safety.'

As she was already pressed against the far side of the car she reached down and opened the door. There really wasn't anything else to say. She scrambled out, nodded to Violet, and all but ran into the safety of the hotel.

She paused, concealed behind the blackout curtains, giving herself a few moments to steady her nerves. Moments later the car roared away leaving her to process the dreadful news that an innocent girl had been killed by a villain just because she was working with Dan.

Obviously, he couldn't discuss the case with her but she wished she knew what he was involved in and how long it might be before everyone embroiled in the investigation was safe from this Bentley person.

Her appetite had deserted her and she couldn't face a full dinner. She paused at the concierge's desk and ordered soup, a sandwich and a jug of coffee – if there was any available – to be sent up to her room.

'Will tea be acceptable if there's no coffee, ma'am?'

'Yes, thank you.'

With her key in her hand, she fled up the two flights of stairs and almost fell into her room. Dan said she was safe here. But the concierge wasn't always at the front desk and it would be simple enough for someone to slip into the hotel and up the stairs without being seen. They could hide in the small pantry where the chambermaids made the early morning tea and then creep down the passageway in the dead of night.

Somehow the locked door no longer seemed sufficient protection. A determined murderer could kick the door in, kill her in her bed and escape before anyone could apprehend him.

★

Seeing Charlotte, and knowing that he'd put her in danger again, made Dan reassess his future plans. As the car sped the short distance back to the Yard he knew that this would be his last case. He loved being a police detective but he loved her more and, unless he became a civilian, he couldn't in all good conscience pursue his interest.

He'd made an appointment to see the surgeon at the end of October – this gave him two weeks to solve this murder and bring the perpetrators to justice. He wasn't a bloodthirsty man, wasn't even sure he agreed with the death penalty, but the man who'd pulled the trigger and the man who'd ordered it would hang if he had his way.

The atmosphere at work was no longer convivial. The plain-clothes and the uniformed policemen were eyeing each other with suspicion. Somehow, God knows who'd blabbed, the fact that corruption within the force was now being vigorously investigated, had leaked.

The chief super was taking it all very seriously. Dan and Mike had decided that this meant their superior wasn't part of the problem and had shared everything they knew. Consequently, they now had full authority to look through case files and interview anyone they wanted. This would make them extremely unpopular, but so be it.

So far Johnson hadn't been spoken to even though it was patently obvious he was in Bentley's pay. Everyone agreed they didn't want to alert the man until they had enough evidence to make it stick.

Dan had refused to have another WPC working for him so a grizzled, semi-retired constable was sitting at the desk outside his office. Dan had no intention of taking this bloke into his confidence so it remained for Wainwright, Mike and himself to look for the connections.

'Sir, we've got a clear timeline for Joan's movements. The photograph we circulated has proved invaluable.'

'It's also made the story front-page news. Bentley will be extra cautious not to attract any attention at the moment. Sergeant, tell me what you've got.'

'We already knew that Joan didn't turn up for her meeting so her friend went to the pictures on her own. We now know more or less what happened.' Wainwright was doing a good job but his feelings for the dead girl were making it harder than it should be.

'Show me what you've written.'

Dan scanned the notes. He was already aware that Davidson had received a phone call just before she left for home. What he hadn't known was that the telephone exchange had been able to place the call as having come from Bentley's office.

'I wish we knew what was said. Obviously, she was somehow tricked into meeting the bastard who abducted her.'

'I think your premise is correct, sir. Johnson must have looked in one of the boxes and found the items were missing. The fact that no one now works down there alone means he's had no opportunity to look in the others.'

'I see from this that we now know Johnson was always the one on duty when either Jones or Smith tampered with the evidence. We've a clear link between the three of them but need something more concrete if we're going to charge them.'

'What we need to do is catch the murdering bastard who killed my Joan.'

'We will. Two eyewitnesses saw Davidson get out of a black car. They both said she looked scared and the two men were holding her arms. That's enough to raid the place tonight. I've got the warrants but nobody else knows – I can't risk him being warned. The pathologist has the bullet and with any luck we'll find the gun it came from.'

'Then who's going to be with us this evening?' Wainwright asked, obviously keen to be on the list.

'The men are coming from another division. We have to assume that they aren't connected to Bentley.'

The armed DCs who now accompanied himself and his sergeant every time they left the premises were off duty and would return at seven thirty to accompany them on the raid. Both he and Wainwright would also be armed, but the uniformed policemen wouldn't be. He hoped having four revolvers would be enough.

He'd made arrangements for Wainwright to drive him in a different car, thus leaving Simmons free to collect Charlotte at whatever time she finished her duties at Victory House.

18

Charlotte staggered out of bed the next morning having had very little sleep. Every creak, every noise, she'd jolted awake. It was all very well for Dan to tell her she was safe in her room but he hadn't really considered this statement carefully enough.

She remembered when Jane was being followed by two men employed by her vile, abusive father, and how terrifying it had been for her friend. To be told so casually that this Bentley character would be aware that she and Dan had left town together, that someone might try and abduct her when she was walking to work, meant that there might be somebody watching her too.

Why would harming her be of any benefit to this criminal? She'd get Violet to drive her to Scotland Yard and she'd demand answers. Sanderson would be at meetings all day so he wouldn't even know she was late.

The remains of her mostly uneaten supper were still on the tray. Wasting food was against the law so she supposed she'd better eat it. Cold soup and stale sandwiches weren't very appetising but she forced them down. She dropped the soup spoon with relief, collected her haversack with her ever-present irons, and picked up the tray.

Halfway down the stairs she realised she'd be expected to eat breakfast – she was now on half-board, which was cheaper than buying dinner separately. She'd have to make up some excuse about being late and not having time to eat this morning. Even so small a white lie made her uncomfortable.

Violet had remained in the car, which was waiting outside the hotel. Charlotte opened the front passenger door and jumped in.

'I don't want to go to Victory House. Please take me wherever the inspector is at the moment. I need to speak to him urgently.'

'I can't do that. I've been told to drive you to work and if I do anything else then I'll be in trouble.'

'In which case, I'll walk to Scotland Yard. Do you think he'll be angrier if I do that than if you drive me? One way or another, that's where I'm going.'

'Well, if you put it like that, I don't have any choice, do I?' She smiled and pulled away smoothly from the kerb. 'You'll need to ask for him at the desk. You can't go up – it's not open to civilians.'

'As long as I see him immediately, I don't care where it is. He won't be particularly happy that he's got to walk down several flights of stairs.'

Violet glanced across at her. 'How do you know he's going to have to do that?'

'He told me his office is on the second floor. We've spent a bit of time together socially, you know.'

'Blimey, that's a turn-up for the books. He's not had a girlfriend all the time I've been driving him.' Violet nodded. 'Mind you, I've had my suspicions.'

'I'm not his girlfriend, just a friend.'

'If you say so.' She turned into the car park behind the big building and switched off the engine. 'I'll wait for you. You're going to work afterwards, aren't you?'

'I certainly am. I don't think this will take very long.'

She approached the uniformed sergeant behind the long, polished wooden counter. 'Excuse me, I'm ASO Fenimore and I need to speak to DI Chalmers.'

'To what does it pertain, Miss Fenimore?'

She stared at him, her expression hard. 'A, it's none of your business why I wish to speak to your inspector. B, you will address me correctly. Either call me Assistant Section Officer or ma'am.'

His mouth dropped open. He obviously wasn't used to being taken to task by a girl half his age even if she was an officer in the WAAF.

'I beg your pardon, ma'am, I'll make the call right away.'

'Thank you, Sergeant.'

He picked up the telephone receiver and spoke briefly into it and then turned to deal with the next enquiry. There were now two other people waiting so she stepped aside and went to lean on the wall. The middle-aged woman in a maroon felt hat that had seen better days had come in to report that someone had stolen her purse from her shopping bag whilst she was waiting in the queue outside a butcher's shop.

The other person was a shifty-looking individual with heavily Brylcreemed hair, a shiny suit and an unlit cigarette hanging from his lips. He spoke so quietly she couldn't hear what he'd said. The desk sergeant made another call and almost immediately a door to the left of her was unlocked.

She didn't see who was behind it, but shiny suit vanished through it and she could hear the lock being pushed across behind him.

She'd now been waiting over fifteen minutes and was beginning to think that Dan wasn't going to come down. Then the same door opened a second time and he stepped out. He didn't look particularly pleased to see her.

'Shall we talk outside?'

'Yes. Thank you for coming. I'm sorry to disturb your busy day but I really needed to talk to you.'

He held open the door and she stepped through into the autumn sunshine. He nodded towards a corner of the car park where there were no police cars parked.

'I was in the middle of a meeting, so I hope this is important.'

This less than encouraging comment made her wonder if she'd made a mistake by coming here. Then she remembered his words in the car – that he had feelings for her – and knew he'd understand and want to help.

'I didn't sleep last night after what you told me. Firstly, it would be easy for someone determined to do me harm to get into the hotel without being seen. Your assumption that I was safe inside is quite wrong.' She paused to see his reaction. He was obviously listening but didn't respond.

'The second thing I need to tell you is that I don't understand why, even if we were in a relationship, attacking me would be of any benefit to this Bentley character.'

He rubbed his eyes. He looked as if he hadn't slept for days. Without thinking she put out her hand and took his – it was an instinctive gesture and told her something she hadn't until that moment understood. She still reciprocated his feelings, which complicated things no end.

'I'm sorry, sweetheart, to have put you into this appalling situation. I didn't explain things properly. Bentley would abduct you in order to put pressure on me to drop my investigation into him and his minions. You're right to say there would be no point in coming into your room and shooting you.'

'Then why was that unfortunate WPC murdered?'

'She was abducted and taken to Bentley. They could hardly let her go after that.'

Charlotte couldn't prevent a gasp. 'So, if I was taken then I would be killed like her?'

He pulled her close, ignoring the two policemen who'd come out and were about to get in the adjacent car. His arms were strong; he gave her the comfort and strength she needed.

She was sorry when he released her. He still had hold of her hands. His expression was dark, his eyes glacial. 'No one will harm you. We're raiding that bastard's premises tonight. We've enough evidence to hang them.'

'There's more than enough killing at the moment but I won't shed a tear if they do get the death penalty. I bet that unfortunate WPC isn't the only person who's been murdered by that villainous Bentley.'

'I'm certain she isn't.' Now wasn't the time to remind her he already had two of Bentley's men in custody awaiting trial for the murder of the man who'd pushed her under a bus. He glanced sideways and saw they had an interested audience. The sensible thing to do would be to step away, pretend that the embrace had been to offer comfort and nothing more. He was on duty – but he didn't give a damn about that.

'Charlotte, I know I'm not good enough for you but I love you and I'm hoping that you return my feelings and will agree to be my wife sometime in the future.'

Her smile rocked him back on his heels. It took all his self-control not to snatch her back and kiss her breathless.

'I didn't want to fall in love with you. I meant everything I said when we were away, but I love you anyway and you'll have to work on your irascible temper.' Her smile was radiant as she continued. 'I will marry you. I couldn't envisage being anybody else's wife.'

He tightened his hold on her hands and she returned the pressure. 'I promise I'll make you happy. You'll not regret this. If we have to wait until the end of this bloody war then so be it. As long as I know that one day you'll be my wife, that's okay by me.'

'We can discuss it when we meet next time.'

'We can't stay out here any longer. You might not be aware of it but there are two PCs gawping at us. We'll be the main topic of conversation in the canteen today.'

He expected her to agree, to increase the distance between them and make the meeting seem an innocuous conversation and not in any way romantic. Instead, she stepped towards him, put her arms around his neck and what followed was inevitable.

For a few incredible, blissful moments he forgot he was a cripple, a detective inspector, and became just a man revelling in a kiss from his future wife. Then sanity returned and gently he removed her hands but retained them within his. They were small within his grasp. They weren't soft, but the hands of a working woman, which suited him perfectly.

'Dan, I'm sorry if I've embarrassed you in front of your men. I've got to get to work as I'm already late. I don't want to be put on a charge. Be careful tonight; don't take any risks. I don't think I could go on if anything happened to you.'

'I'm good at my job, darling – I won't come to any harm. I'm not sure when I'll get the opportunity to see you but I'll come to the hotel when I'm able. We've got so much more to talk about and we can't do it now as I've got a job to do as well.'

'Violet's waiting for me. Take care, my love. I'll be thinking of you tonight.'

Then she was gone. He watched her walk briskly across the car park and get into the front seat of his car. The world seemed brighter and despite everything, for the first time in a long time – perhaps ever – he was optimistic about his future.

He turned deliberately to face the two watchers. Instead of snarling at them, which was what he would have done yesterday, he limped across, smiling, which obviously unnerved them. They both jumped to attention.

'ASO Fenimore has just agreed to marry me. You might even see me looking happy occasionally from now on.'

The two exchanged a glance. 'Congratulations, sir, she's a lovely young lady,' one of them said and the other nodded his agreement.

His sergeant was waiting for him. 'I apologise for vanishing so suddenly. You can congratulate me; I'm now engaged to be married. Not something I ever thought I'd be lucky enough to say.'

Wainwright slapped him on the back and for a few minutes the atmosphere in the office was lightened. Then it was time to return to work.

'If a case has been dismissed then double jeopardy comes into play. Bentley can't be tried for the same crime twice. There must be something we're missing.'

'I was thinking the same things, sir. We can't retrieve the boxes now. We've got enough proof to arrest everybody we find tonight. The boxes are a bonus and we can look in them later.'

Dan spent the remainder of the day ensuring that everything was in place for the night raid – that there would be no legal loophole for Bentley to wriggle out of this time. He was hoping that either Jones or Smith would be scooped up too – it would make convicting them for corruption so much easier if they were found on the premises of a known criminal.

He was confident that a case could be made against the two corrupt men for tampering with evidence. Therefore, if they weren't picked up tonight then they'd be arrested at some point in the near future. Bailey had told Dan to wait until the investigation was complete.

Under normal circumstances Johnson, the bent sergeant in charge of the evidence room, would have been suspended until he was either charged or exonerated. This hadn't been done as they didn't want to alert Bentley that the police were closing in on him.

When this villain and his underlings were held in custody Dan was going to put pressure on the two already charged with murder. Offering them the opportunity to avoid the death penalty would hopefully be enough to get them to give evidence against their former employer.

He wasn't sure Wainwright was sufficiently in control of his emotions not to do something stupid when he confronted the man who'd ordered the murder of the woman he loved. He didn't blame him – if it had been Charlotte and not the WPC, Bentley and several others would already be dead at his hand. He'd decide later if Wainwright should be armed or not.

His sergeant was on the prowl in the corridors, offices and canteens asking casual questions and making mental notes. To actually write anything in his notebook would immediately alert this division that there was an inquiry being conducted into some of them. Mike had returned to his normal duties, which gave him much-appreciated time to himself. He shouted through the door and PC Reynolds stood up.

'Could you get me a pot of tea and whatever's going in the canteen? Get yourself something at the same time and put it on my tab.'

'Righto, sir. I'll not be a tick.'

Dan was enjoying his tea, sandwich and bun when the chief superintendent strode in.

Charlotte couldn't believe what had just happened. She'd gone to speak to Dan about the possibility of her being abducted and come away engaged to him. She was fizzing with excitement and couldn't wait to progress their relationship, as long as she was certain she wouldn't get pregnant.

Violet opened and shut her mouth like a goldfish, obviously desperate to say something about what she'd seen but not knowing if it would be inappropriate.

'Dan and I just got engaged. I didn't know until he proposed that I was in love with him.'

'Blimey, that's a surprise and no mistake. I reckon the two of you are a perfect match. Some girls mightn't want to marry a bloke with a mangled leg, but I think he's a real catch.'

'I think so too. We won't be getting married for a while as we've both got jobs to do. I'll have to make up the time I've missed this morning, so will you pick me up at eight o'clock?'

'I'll be waiting. The inspector doesn't want me tonight as he's arranged for someone else to drive him home. I should've realised he'd got feelings for you by the way he was being so protective.'

The day rushed past and she was able to solve several accounting anomalies without the need to visit the bases. However, this last one looked decidedly dubious. Whoever was running a hotel in Bournemouth, which was being used as a billet for trainee WAAFs, was claiming they had a hundred and twenty girls staying with them at any one time and were being paid accordingly.

She recognised the name of the hotel because she'd stayed there as a guest before the war. It only had twenty bedrooms and none of them were large enough to put more than three girls in. Unless they were using bunk beds – which was possible – there was deliberate malfeasance taking place.

It was too late to ring the hotel now but she'd get on to it first thing in the morning.

If they were actually putting six girls into one room that would also be unacceptable overcrowding. Also, there wouldn't be enough ablutions and she doubted the kitchen would be able to cater satisfactorily for such a large number. Whether the hotel was falsely claiming for sixty extra residents or actually squeezing them in, it was still something that had to be dealt with.

It was quite possible she'd have to visit and demand to see the accounts and inspect the bedrooms to prove they were claiming for double the number of women they had living there. Tomorrow she'd talk to her CO and see if he agreed with her assessment.

This particular hotel was used to house those doing their preliminary training, which lasted for three weeks. The WAAFs were then divided into groups and sent off for more specific training elsewhere. Therefore, it would be complicated to track anyone down and speak to them.

The offices on this floor were mainly deserted and her feet echoed in the corridor. There was the occasional light coming from under a door, which showed that she wasn't the only one who'd been working late.

On the ground floor it was quite different. Here there were always uniformed personnel dashing about, official cars coming and going, phalanxes of nervous civilian girls waiting to be inducted and WAAF officers and NCOs organising everything efficiently. Sometimes she rather wished she was one of those officers and not isolated from her peers as she was now.

Violet had driven into the large yard at the rear of the

building and was talking with two uniformed girls. The khaki of her uniform, although smart, wasn't nearly as attractive as Air Force blue.

'Good evening, Simmons, I'm sorry to have kept you waiting.'

Her friend saluted and rushed across to open the rear passenger door. Charlotte would have preferred to sit next to her but obediently ducked her head and got into the back. Once the car was on the main thoroughfare Violet apologised.

'I thought it would look a bit funny if you got in the front with me, Charlotte.'

'Doesn't Dan sit with you now?'

'That's different. Nobody would think he was there in order to have a chat with me but they would if it was you. I'm not very popular with the officer who runs the motor pool – she keeps telling me I've got a cushy number and if she had her way then I'd be back with her, covered in oil and rummaging about in the engines of cars and lorries that need repairing.'

'I must say I did wonder how you came to be Dan's driver – I didn't know that a member of the ATS ever worked for civilian organisations.'

'I don't think they do usually. DI Chalmers was one of ours before he was blown up at Dunkirk so I reckon an exception was made for him.'

The drive was so brief there wasn't time to do more than exchange a few pleasantries before the car arrived outside the hotel. 'I'll be here at seven thirty tomorrow to collect you.'

'Thank you, good night. Take care walking home in the blackout.'

*

If anyone had asked her what she'd eaten at dinner she wouldn't be able to tell them anything apart from it was hot and tasty. Her thoughts were constantly drifting to what might be happening to Dan and his men. She wasn't exactly sure when this raid was going to take place but knew it was going to be at a time Bentley wouldn't be expecting them to arrive.

The Agatha Christie crime story she'd been reading previously didn't seem appropriate tonight. She put the wireless on and fortunately it was Thursday and *ITMA*, and the silliness of the characters made her laugh and temporarily forget her worries.

When the news came on the home service she jumped up and turned it off. Maybe it was her patriotic duty to hear which submarine had sunk which frigate, how many bombs the RAF had dropped on Germany and what was happening in Africa with Montgomery. No one would know she deliberately wasn't listening.

She'd just returned from the bathroom when the siren went off. It was unlikely to be a full raid as the Blitz had stopped in the summer but the Luftwaffe still sent fighter-bombers across at regular intervals just to keep the citizens of London on their toes.

As she was grabbing her necessities she paused and went to her bedroom door and opened it. The occupants of the other four rooms were definitely there – there were lights under two of the doors – but none of them appeared to be taking it seriously.

There were voices on the stairs so some residents were

going down to the cellar, which had a perfectly adequate bomb shelter. She decided not to go with them. Somehow it seemed right that she was in a modicum of danger as the man she loved was at this very moment risking his life to bring a murderer and his henchmen to justice. Once the lights in her room were off, she drew back the heavy blackout curtains. The sky was crisscrossed with searchlights, the ack-ack guns were firing, but she couldn't hear the terrifying drone of a squadron of bombers approaching.

If there were no German planes over London then why were they wasting their ammunition firing into an empty sky? Would this non-existent air raid ruin Dan's plans or would it actually help him? She yanked the curtains closed and switched on the wireless, relieved there was now an orchestra playing what she thought might be Mozart.

19

The police vehicles were parked in side streets. Dan had decided they would approach on foot, thus making the element of surprise more likely. He could still manage his revolver and his cane without making a complete arse of himself, even if it was bloody dark.

The uniformed men from the other division, under Mike's command, seemed a decent bunch and were following orders as they should. The moon was hidden behind clouds, which was good as they were less likely to be seen creeping along towards the large building where Bentley had his offices.

The man had a large, modern house in Romford where he kept his family cloistered and well away from his nefarious and criminal activities. The poor woman was about to get a nasty shock in the morning when she discovered the man she thought was a legitimate businessman was in fact a murdering bastard.

One of the undercover detectives from another division had been keeping watch on the building. 'DC Davies, sir. Bentley's not left the premises. There's four other men in there as well. Unfortunately, four tarts went in half an hour ago.'

'That's the best possible news. It means they'll be too busy with them to hear us coming.'

He checked the luminous dial on his watch. Five minutes to ten – five minutes before they moved in. Wainwright was armed and had given his word not to shoot anyone unless forced to. Then the night air was split by the howl of the siren. The sky was lit by search lights and the thump thump thump of the guns almost drowned out the wailing.

'Wainwright, make sure everyone sticks to the plan. There's no need to head for a shelter. It'll be a hit-and-run fighter-bomber or two and it'll be the East End, not here, that gets their attention.'

His sergeant conveyed the message and they continued to creep towards their destination. They were walking single file, almost crablike, backs and shoulders pressed firmly against the wall, making them almost invisible. At least he hoped so. It would be a bloody disaster if the occupants of Bentley's premises decided to head for the communal shelter at the end of the road.

Then his mouth curved in the darkness. Not a single door had opened, not a single person had rushed out carrying their blankets, flasks and torches in order to spend the rest of the night in the shelter. Londoners had survived the Blitz; half a dozen German planes overhead wasn't enough to scare them.

Dan intended to bang on the front door flanked by half a dozen uniformed constables. Wainwright, Mike and half a dozen more PCs would go around to the rear of the building and burst in from there. He was glad that his friend had arranged for the CID from his division to help out as they would also be armed. He had a nasty suspicion this was going to be crucial.

He made his way to the main entrance. The building was brick-built, of Victorian construction, three storeys high and had only been used as offices for the past few years. Prior to that it had been a factory of some sort. On the left was a solid wooden gate, locked of course; on the right an entrance wide enough for a car to drive down – this must have been for a horse and cart originally.

A plain-clothes detective, revolver in his hand, was standing with another couple of constables out of sight, on the gate side. He waited whilst the almost invisible wave of blue uniformed men flowed down the right passageway.

He nodded and one of the constables hammered on the door with the end of the crowbar he was carrying. 'Open in the name of the law. We have a search warrant for these premises.'

As expected, nobody opened the door. 'Do it, Constable.'

This young man was an expert at prising open doors and within a couple of minutes they were inside. He held up his hand and moved forward to listen. There was no sound of running feet, shouting or scuffling – the only sounds drifting down to him were of loud band music, male voices and the shrill laughter of the prostitutes.

'They didn't hear us. The siren has drowned out our approach.'

The ground floor and basement were used as storerooms, for ill-gotten gains no doubt, but they could be investigated later. They would find the kitchen, bedrooms and offices on the upper two floors.

He was about to ascend when Mike, Wainwright, and the others appeared having also broken their way in successfully.

'We collared two buggers in the yard and they've been dealt with,' Wainwright told him quietly. His sergeant's teeth flashed white in the darkness. 'This should be easy, sir, sounds as if we'll catch them literally with their pants down.'

Negotiating the stairs would slow Dan so he moved aside and let Mike and Wainwright take the lead. 'Don't be complacent. It's been easy so far but these are hardened criminals. They won't hesitate to shoot to kill.' His whispered words were acknowledged quietly.

The racket was coming from a closed door directly ahead. For obvious reasons they hadn't switched on the lights and he swung his torch beam from one end of the corridor to the other. There were windows all along the passage overlooking the street but these were painted black. All the rooms were at the back.

'Mike, Wainwright, with me. Those of you who are armed, watch the other doors in case anyone comes out.' There were two closed doors on the left and one on the right – there was the sound of grunting coming from the nearest so that was obviously occupied.

He had overwhelming numbers and this should be sufficient to arrest everybody without bloodshed and without any of the occupants being able to barge past the ring of constables and escape into the night.

This time the bobby with the crowbar kicked the door open and the passageway was flooded with light. Now there was noise. Shouts of rage, screams from the girls, and the sound of chairs crashing to the boards.

With Mike on his left, his sergeant on his right, he stepped into the room. One glance was enough to tell him Bentley wasn't there. The bastard must be in one of the other rooms with a girl. Smith and Jones were also missing, which was a damned nuisance. However, the others were familiar faces and these would do for a start.

Their sudden appearance had been enough to gain the advantage. None of the four rough men attempted to reach for their weapons. It would have been suicide and they knew it.

'Wainwright, cuff this lot. Get them outside and into the vans. Then get back here.'

Mike was already approaching the nearest door. Whoever was in there must have heard the racket and would have had time to snatch up his gun.

'Wait, we need to be careful now. Bentley is in one of these rooms and he'll shoot to kill. He's got nothing to lose.'

The doors opened inwards, which meant there would be no protection going in. He glanced back into the main room and pointed at an upended table. 'Constable, grab hold of that. It'll give us a bit of cover.'

One of the detectives, he didn't know his name, pointed towards the door he was standing in front of – the one furthest away. 'Definitely someone in here, sir.'

'Don't go in. Wait where you are but be ready to thump whoever comes out. Try not to shoot anyone you don't have to.' Dan had a gut feeling Bentley and the tart were in the room he was about to enter.

Once the makeshift shield was held up in front of himself and Mike, Dan gestured for the constable with the crowbar to force open the door. He did this from a crouch, having been warned that whoever was inside would shoot at chest height.

As the door crashed open, there was a fusillade of gunshots and if he and Mike hadn't been behind the solid oak table, they would have both been dead. The air stank of cordite; his ears rang from the noise. Then a second shot was fired but this time from behind him.

'Got the bastard, sir, he won't be murdering anyone else,' Wainwright yelled triumphantly.

The two constables who were holding the legs of the table promptly dropped it, allowing Dan to see into the carnage. Bentley was indeed dead – a chest shot that would have killed him instantly. He was still holding a gun.

His night-time companion was whimpering in a corner, the sheets pulled around her naked body. 'Get dressed, be quick about it,' he ordered and immediately the girl snatched up her discarded clothes and began to pull them on.

The man he'd been trying to bring to justice for years had just had time to pull on his trousers but his chest – what was left of it – was bare, as were his feet.

There were raised voices coming from the room next door as the occupants were arrested. Dan turned, interested to see who the sixth man was.

Charlotte slept fitfully – not because she was fearful of being assassinated in her bed but because she was desperate to know that Dan and his colleagues were safe. She awoke the next morning gritty-eyed and yawning.

Her alarm clock was still haranguing her with its strident bell; she reached over and switched it off. Then she noticed there was a note pushed under her door. She fell out of bed and snatched it up.

My darling Charlotte,

Everything went perfectly last night. Bentley is dead, we've made several important arrests and none of my men were harmed.

I reserved a table for tonight at seven thirty. Don't smile – the night concierge was very accommodating.

I'm going to grab a few hours' shut-eye.

I love you,

Dan

Her eyes brimmed and she read it again. Things were going to be different now – the danger was over – this dreadful man had met his just deserts. She almost skipped to the bathroom and ran considerably more than the statutory five inches and added the last of her precious bath salts to the water.

It wasn't just the heat that made her hot all over, it was the thought of what might be going to happen between them. Not tonight – but quite possibly in a week or two she would agree to spend the night at his apartment. He could hardly do so here as she would be instantly evicted.

She was surprised that the hotel manager, or the waiter who served, didn't comment on her happiness as she was quite sure she positively glowed. After she'd talked to Dan about their future she would write to her best friends and give them the good news.

Violet was unable to give her the details of last night's endeavours but was equally excited about the result. 'It'll be quite different at the Yard today. They've been after that blighter for years. Mind you – I reckon there'll be some quaking in their boots as to what might come out about their involvement with that villain.'

'I don't care about any of it as long as Dan's safe and that monster's no longer a threat. I'll ring you when I'm ready to leave tonight. I'm hoping I'll be able to get away by six thirty as we've got a table booked for seven thirty at the hotel.'

'Righty ho. I'm to pick him up in Kensington after I've taken you to work.'

Charlotte was surprised and somewhat alarmed to find her CO waiting impatiently for her to arrive. She was half an hour before her allotted time and he rarely turned up until half an hour after her. There must be something important going on.

Immediately she was focused on her duty and pushed aside all thoughts of her personal life. She saluted – not something she usually did and he returned the gesture.

'Excellent, I'm glad you're early.' He stopped pacing and indicated she be seated. 'I see you've earmarked Seaview Hotel in Bournemouth for investigation.'

'I have, sir. I stayed there a few years ago and know the hotel can't possibly accommodate one hundred and twenty girls.'

'That's unfortunate because the wretched place is owned by the family of a bigwig at the War Office.'

'Are you suggesting that we have to overlook this dishonesty because the people who own it are important?'

'Not quite as bad as that, my dear. Your investigation could be unofficial, your report not filed. I'll take it to the appropriate person and I can assure you the correct figures will be submitted in future.'

'That's appalling, if you don't mind me saying so, sir. I could be arrested for feeding a crust to a pigeon and yet whoever these people are can defraud the government of thousands of pounds and get away with it.'

He drummed his fingers on the table. 'You're right. There's a war on. It's tantamount to looting and you can be executed for that. No, ASO, do your duty. Forget that I said anything.'

'So, I should continue as I intended? Drive there tomorrow, visit the hotel and present you with my official report as I did last time?'

He refused to look directly at her, shifted uneasily in his seat. 'I'd be eternally grateful, my dear girl, if you would leave me out of this one? I'll be out of the office Monday and Tuesday of next week, so send your report directly to the War Office.'

It had taken her a while to grasp what he was hinting at. Someone close to him, possibly a member of his own family, was involved in this fraud. Her estimation of Sanderson plummeted. Weren't those in command supposed to be setting an example to everyone else? How many more of these scandals were waiting to be uncovered?

In the short time she'd worked in this office it had occurred to her more than once that in order to eradicate dishonesty, discover the fraudulent claims being made, it really needed more than one WAAF and one wing commander. There were thousands, literally, of requisitions being made for personnel every year and she couldn't possibly be expected to sift out all those that were actually bogus from those that were genuine mistakes.

Good heavens – of course it wasn't just her and Sanderson

involved – there were dozens of girls in the main office reviewing and fulfilling the numerous requests. The vast majority of those would be perfectly ordinary, legitimate demands for extra staff to do work of national importance on an RAF base somewhere in the country. The WAAF were vital as they released the men for active duty.

'I don't think I'm suited to this position, sir. I'd like to apply to be a wireless operator – I'm proficient with the Morse code and I believe that's a requirement. Could I ask you to support my transfer?'

He understood immediately. Quid pro quo. She would do as he asked if he returned the favour. With a sigh he pushed himself to his feet. 'I'll get the letter written and sent to the appropriate person before I leave tonight. I've enjoyed having you here these past few weeks, ASO Fenimore, and wish you well in your next post.'

She stood to attention and saluted him for a second time – this time he just nodded and walked out, leaving her feeling deflated and disappointed that someone she'd come to admire wasn't the man she'd thought he was.

The car had to be booked, petrol applied for and arrangements made for the drive. It was little over a hundred miles from London to Bournemouth and shouldn't take her more than three hours. She didn't like driving in the dark with only the pinprick of light allowed from her headlamps, so she'd have to find somewhere to stay.

She was in the canteen munching a spam sandwich when the stupidity of what she'd done finally registered. Her tea slopped into the saucer ruining the digestive biscuits resting there.

It was too late to withdraw her request for a transfer and

heaven knows where she might be sent. It certainly wouldn't be in London and she'd have to leave her comfortable billet and probably live in a Nissen hut. Not too bad during the summer months, but absolutely horrid in the winter.

At least this time as an officer she'd have an orderly to take care of her needs and not have to share a room with anyone else. Leaving this post so soon after taking it up would make the chances of further promotion remote. But, far worse, she wouldn't be able to see Dan, possibly for months.

Dan was back at his desk by nine o'clock the next morning. This was good going as he hadn't left until just after four. It had taken that long to interview those who had been arrested and he'd only managed to write up half his reports. His sergeant had been given three days' compassionate leave and had taken it gratefully. The young man needed time to grieve for the girl he'd loved.

Smith, the corrupt DC who'd been suspended along with Sergeant Jones, had been the man in the other room. Once the head of the snake, Bentley, had been removed his underlings were only too ready to cough up what they knew. This is what had taken so long last night.

There was now an arrest warrant out for Jones and he was hopeful the man would be picked up sometime today. It made him uneasy thinking of that slippery blighter being at large. Johnson and two other uniformed constables had been arrested as well as three DCs. A sad day for Scotland Yard.

There was an unpleasant atmosphere in the corridors

– nobody liked a nark, someone who betrayed the trust of their comrades – but even more unpopular were those who acted on this information.

The chief superintendent was scowling when he strode in. 'This is a bloody nightmare, Chalmers. How many more crooked cops are you going to arrest before you're done?'

'As many as I find, sir. However, I'm confident your house is now squeaky-clean. Smith has been singing like a canary and if there was anyone else he could have put a finger on then he would have done so in order to reduce his own sentence.'

'Thank the good Lord for that. What about your ex-sergeant? Have you any idea where he's hiding?'

'I've got every man available searching for him. If he's still in London we'll have him in custody soon enough.'

'Nasty business – be glad when it's sorted. Good work, Chalmers, it won't go unnoticed. There will be a promotion in this for you, I shouldn't be surprised. You're the best man I've got here.'

Dan was tempted to hand in his resignation as he'd already written the letter and it was in his desk drawer, but decided to leave it until he'd spoken to Charlotte that evening. This needed to be done before he was officially offered a promotion as he might be tempted to take it.

He wanted to go home and change before his dinner date with his future wife. A fiancée – he had a fiancée of his own and he could scarcely believe his luck. He now had in his possession the engagement ring that he'd sent Simmons to collect. It had been stored in a bank vault in the city along with all the other family valuables and had belonged to his grandmother.

The door swung open and Mike burst in. 'I know why Bentley was so desperate to get his hands on those boxes that he was prepared to murder a policewoman.'

'Tell me. It's the one thing that didn't fit.'

'We both got it wrong about when missing evidence causes a case to be dismissed. As this evidence was tampered with by corrupt policemen, all three cases could have been reopened. Also, the items had been logged in and never left the evidence room. This makes everything admissible.'

'Of course, bloody stupid of me not to have known that. A case can be reopened if the evidence has been tampered with by the police officers involved with the case, as happened here.'

20

Charlotte wished she had civvies to change into – something other than her uniform. Dan had never seen her in anything but grey-blue and she thought she looked rather spiffing in a silk evening gown. He'd fallen in love with her when she was wearing her hideous, beige lisle stockings, frumpy shoes and a less than well-fitted skirt and jacket. This was a miracle in itself.

Unlike her two friends she wasn't particularly attractive – at least she didn't think so. Her figure was reasonably curved, her hair an unexciting brown and she was a little above average height. She wasn't exactly plain, had been complimented on her hazel eyes a couple of times, but was certainly nothing special. Tonight was important, so at least she could put on a clean collar.

The collars on her shirts were detachable and she knew that some WAAF took them to a Chinese laundry to be washed and starched, but she just scrubbed them in her sink and then put them under her mattress so they would dry flat.

Having her laundry done by the hotel was expensive but there was no alternative as she could hardly wash her knickers and bra and hang them over the back of the chair to dry. Summer knee-length knickers, pink silky affairs known as twilights, weren't so bad the but the winter ones she was now in, her blackouts, were too hideous to be seen even by a chambermaid.

Being able to put on a clean collar while wearing the same shirt meant she only had to send laundry down once a week. The daily amount she was given for her expenses didn't cover the extra costs involved by living in a hotel. She had to use her wages for the things that would be included if she was living on base.

Her hair was freshly swept up and neatly pinned. She added a smudge of red lipstick, feeling rather daring as she did so, and hurried downstairs for what she knew was going to be the most exciting and important dinner of her life.

Dan was watching the stairs. His smile rocked her back on her heels. He really was the most handsome man and she was so lucky that he'd chosen her when he could have had anybody. He held out his hand and she rushed over to take it.

'I'm sorry, have you been waiting long?'

'No, I arrived a moment ago.' He leaned down and whispered, his breath warm against her ear and it made her feel rather odd. 'Do you think anyone would object if I kissed you?'

She looked up at him, laughing. 'I certainly wouldn't.'

He matched words to deeds and her head was spinning and her knees decidedly weak when he eventually released her.

'Might I be the first to offer my congratulations, Detective Inspector?' The head waiter was smiling so he hadn't been offended by their inappropriate behaviour.

'Thank you, much appreciated. ASO Fenimore is now my fiancée. This is a very special evening for both of us.'

Dan had his arm firmly around her waist, holding her hard against his side. He'd spoken loudly enough that other diners turned and nodded their congratulations.

'If you would care to follow me, ma'am, sir, your table is ready.'

This time they weren't tucked away in her usual place but in the main dining room. She stopped, her eyes wide. 'Are we sitting there? How did they know to get this ready for us?'

The table had the best napery, crystal glasses, silver candlesticks and what looked like a bottle of champagne waiting in an ice bucket. Not only were there champagne glasses, but also some for water.

'I asked them to do something a bit special for us when I booked the table earlier. I'm glad you like it, darling, I wasn't sure.'

Not one, but two waiters were there to pull out their chairs, place the white napkins across their laps and light the candles. They weren't offered a menu so she supposed that despite the extravagant table setting they would still be eating the same as everyone else. She just hoped it wasn't liver and bacon as she really didn't like that.

As soon as they were alone Dan reached into his waistcoat pocket and removed a small, leather ring box. 'This was my grandmother's and I never thought I'd be lucky enough to be able to give it to anyone. If it doesn't fit then it can be altered.' He flicked open the box and held it out.

'Is that a sapphire in the middle? Diamonds around the edge? It's beautiful, but I can't wear something so valuable when I'm working.'

He took her hand and pushed the ring onto her finger. It fitted perfectly, which had to be a good omen. 'I love it, and I'll wear it when I'm off duty.'

'I'm glad it fits and that you like it. Couldn't you wear it on a chain around your neck when you can't have it on your finger?'

'I was thinking that myself. I've got a gold chain that would be perfect. Thank you so much, my love. I can't tell you how happy I am.'

He grinned, making him look years younger and even more attractive. 'You certainly can tell me; in fact, I insist that you do so at every possible opportunity.'

'Do you know what's on the menu tonight?'

He smiled and shook his head. 'The chef is cooking something especially for us. God knows what it'll be, but it won't be offal, then spotted dick for dessert.'

He pointed to the champagne and she shook her head. 'I'd much prefer the water. They've even found some slices of lemon to put in it – such luxury! I wonder where they got those from as I've not seen a lemon, orange or banana since the war started.'

She hadn't realised one of the waiters was standing behind her. 'Chef has access to a hothouse in Surrey and had it sent up especially for tonight, ma'am. The flowers came from there too.' The elderly man moved round, picked up the jug and filled both their glasses without spilling a drop despite the fact that his hand was shaking.

'Thank you, that will be all for the moment,' Dan said firmly.

She leaned forward so she could speak without danger of being overheard. 'If we've got lemon in our water, goodness knows what we'll get to eat. Do you think the other guests will make a fuss if they see we've got something they can't have?'

'I'm afraid that if you've got the money to pay for it you can have whatever you want. No, sweetheart, don't frown. I'm usually frugal even though I've got so much of it, but tonight is different.'

They were so close their hair was touching. He smelled wonderful – something lemony. 'You smell like my water.' She hadn't meant to say this and he chuckled.

'Then my work here is done. I wouldn't like to tell you what I sometimes reek of.'

'No, please don't. I can imagine and don't need a detailed description.' She sat back hurriedly. Being in such close proximity to him was making her silly, and she hated not being in control.

She needed to tell him her bad news but didn't want to spoil the evening so decided to keep it to herself until they were saying goodbye.

'I've got to go to Bournemouth tomorrow so I won't be able to see you in the evening. I'll be back the day after and we can meet for dinner then, if you're free.'

'I wish I could come with you but there's too much going on at the moment. I don't like you travelling so far on your own especially with Jones still on the loose. Take Simmons and my car – nobody will object as I'm the blue-eyed boy at the moment.'

'I think it'll be too late to rearrange things.'

'Leave it to me, darling, I'll get it organised later this evening. What time were you intending to set out?'

'Eight o'clock – I want to be there before lunch.' She

changed the subject. 'I expect this Bentley business will be leaked to the press, however careful you are. Will you be mentioned by name? I don't suppose you'll be popular with everyone at work. Am I allowed to ask exactly how many CID and uniformed men have been arrested?'

'Too many – I was horrified to find how deep the corruption in the force is. It's going to create a stink when the public read about it. The prime minister has been informed and he wasn't happy. What does he expect? There's a bloody war on and it's so much easier for criminals to get away with it at the moment.'

She wished she hadn't mentioned it as he sat back in his chair. His expression was severe, and he no longer looked like the happy, relaxed man he had a few moments ago.

Dan was lost in his unpleasant thoughts and when he glanced up to his horror he saw tears in her eyes. He said something extremely impolite under his breath. He reached over and grabbed her hand before she could hide it under the table.

'I'm sorry, darling. You know what a bad-tempered sod I am, but you love me anyway, don't you?' His tone was light but he scanned her face anxiously. She blinked and then her lovely smile was back.

'You know I do. I wasn't upset because you looked so forbidding, I was cross with myself for ruining our evening by talking about it. I've got to learn to...'

'No, stop right there. I don't want you to change for me. You don't have to learn anything – it's I who needs to change. Which leads me...'

They were interrupted by the two waiters arriving with their appetisers. She couldn't see what it was as the contents were obscured by domed silver lids. The plates were put down and the covers removed with a flourish.

'Thank you, that looks quite delicious.'

'Would madam like extra bread to be served?'

Dan snorted into his napkin and she kicked him under the table. 'No, thank you, we have sufficient here.'

The waiter retreated allowing her to speak freely. 'Where did they get smoked salmon from? Surely they didn't send to Scotland for it?' Her stomach gurgled loudly in anticipation of the treat.

'Does it matter?' His eyes were dancing as he pointed to the champagne. 'Would madam like a glass of champagne?'

'No she wouldn't. If you call me that again you're likely to be wearing your meal and not eating it.'

Neither of them spoke as they ate this delicacy. As far as she was concerned it was the most delicious thing she'd tasted for years – possibly ever. Her father had gambled away the family fortune so there was rarely anything luxurious to eat when she was home apart from what could be shot, or picked from the kitchen garden. Her boarding school fees were paid from a trust fund set up for that purpose – if he'd been able to get his hands on it, she was sure he would have done.

A squeeze of lemon and a pinch of black pepper was all it needed. The triangles of real bread – not the nasty British loaf – were spread with actual butter, which made them even more delicious.

'I wonder what we're getting for the second course. I can't remember when I had three courses – I think it might have been the last Christmas I spent at home. I'm surprised it's not against the law.'

'I'm going to have a glass of bubbly. I want to toast my future wife with something other than water.'

He didn't need to snap his fingers to call a waiter to open the bottle. The wine waiter appeared as if summoned by a genie. 'I'm a little unnerved by all this attention. It's like eating in a goldfish bowl. Also, we've had a lot of black looks from the other diners.'

She was rather hoping the cork would fly across the room in a dramatic fashion but the waiter knew what he was doing and turned the napkin-wrapped bottle, rather than the cork itself. There was a disappointing pop, no gush of champagne – she supposed it was better to do it properly and not waste a drop.

Dan waved the obsequious waiter away, refusing to let him pour the golden fizzy liquid into the glasses. She wasn't overfond of alcohol of any sort, but as this was a special occasion she was determined to enjoy the champagne. She doubted she'd get a chance to drink it again before the end of the war.

She picked up the half-full glass and held it in front of her. He did the same.

'To you, my future bride. I just hope that you're as happy as I am right now.' His eyes blazed into hers. If anybody doubted this was a love match then they only had to look at him to know they were wrong. They both took a mouthful and it wasn't as unpleasant as she'd expected – in fact it was rather palatable. Not sweet at all and the bubbles were very celebratory.

'To you, my future husband. I love you and am so happy I could burst just like these bubbles.'

They drank a second mouthful and before she could prevent him he pushed himself upright, put one finger under her chin to tilt her face, and then kissed her in full view of everyone.

This time she'd kept her eyes open and was staring into his from a few inches away. It made her quite dizzy with excitement. Fortunately, he resumed his place before they did anything else to shock the dining room.

The main course was fetched – it was chicken à la something or other – with duchess potatoes and a medley of vegetables. When he refilled her glass, she didn't object. She couldn't remember having had such a wonderful night before.

There was some sort of elaborate meringue dessert served with oodles of whipped cream which she was certain had brandy in it. She'd had a further glass of champagne and thought she was now just a little bit tiddly. There was something really important she was supposed to tell him but she couldn't for the life of her remember what it was.

'Come along, darling, I've ordered coffee – the real stuff – to be served in the small lounge. Can you walk unaided or do you need my stick to hold you upright?'

'Maybe I should go outside for some fresh air and clear my head. I really shouldn't have had that third glass. I don't have a head for alcohol.'

'I can see that. Are you coming or shall I ask the waiter to assist madam?'

She didn't make the mistake of trying to stand up too quickly but her head still swam unpleasantly. She prayed she wouldn't be sick as that would be such a waste of a delicious meal and certainly wouldn't be popular with either Dan or the hotel staff.

'Actually, my love, I'm going straight to bed. Thank you for a wonderful evening.'

He didn't argue or attempt to stop her. 'Probably wise. I'm glad you enjoyed it – I certainly did. What time do you think you'll be back the day after tomorrow?'

Tomorrow? Where was she going? She hadn't the foggiest what he was talking about. 'I don't know. Good night.'

Her ability to march, ramrod straight, proved useful and she reached the stairs without faltering. Her key was in a pocket so she didn't need to stop at the desk. She rested her hand as lightly as she dared on the banister and made her way briskly to the first floor.

She really wanted to have a lie-down on the soft carpet in the hallway, which looked very inviting. No – she would persevere and not stop until she was safely inside her own little haven.

She woke the next morning with a horrible headache, a nasty taste in her mouth, but nothing a couple of aspirin and a glass of water couldn't cure. She had very little recollection of the previous night but did know that she'd had a lovely time.

She threaded the beautiful ring onto the chain and then fastened it around her neck. It was probably safer there than leaving it in the room. The smell of breakfast made her stomach churn so she dropped her key on the counter and walked into the street.

Violet wasn't there, which was unusual, but just this once it wouldn't matter if she walked to work; after all it was only half a mile and there were plenty of pedestrians about.

For some reason the car wasn't where she expected it to be but she could see it parked neatly on the other side of the large yard. She collected the key, checked the tank was full, that there was a spare can in the boot, and then tossed her overnight bag and haversack on the front passenger seat.

There was no sign of a WAAF from the motor pool to check everything was tickety-boo. Presumably she was now considered an experienced driver and was therefore allowed to set out without all the rigmarole of last time.

As she was driving through the suburbs heading for Slough the headache that had been hindering her ability to think coherently finally responded to the aspirin. With a horrified shriek she swerved to the side of the road and skidded to a halt.

The car hadn't been waiting for her because she shouldn't be taking this one. Violet was supposed to be driving her in Dan's car. She dropped her head on the steering wheel and her stomach lurched. For a horrible moment she thought she was going to be sick, which would make things even worse.

She remembered to look over her shoulder before she opened the door. It was pure chance that she had actually pulled into the kerb and wasn't obstructing traffic. She got out and almost staggered around the car to lean against the passenger side.

There was another thing she hadn't done and that was tell Dan she was going to be posted out of London when she returned – probably on Monday or Tuesday.

There would be pandemonium, not only at Victory House when they discovered the car was missing, but also when Violet saw that she wasn't waiting outside as had been arranged. Her head cleared a little. What she needed to do was find a telephone box.

When she tipped the coins from her purse into her hand she realised she only had enough to make one phone call – the second would have to be a reverse charge. She wasn't even sure how that worked.

There was no point in panicking – she had to keep a cool head and continue to drive towards Bournemouth whilst keeping a lookout for a red box so she could make the necessary calls.

21

Dan had been waiting for half an hour outside his Kensington home. Simmons had never been late before and he was becoming slightly anxious about the delay. He was about to go inside to use the telephone when the car screeched to a halt beside him.

His driver threw open the car door and jumped out. 'Sir, she wasn't there. I'm late because I've been looking for her. She left the hotel at half past seven but isn't at work.' She looked so worried that he immediately reassured her even though he was unsettled by this news.

'I'm certain that there's a simple explanation.' He clambered into the front of the car knowing his fear for Charlotte's safety wasn't apparent to her. 'Where have you looked?'

'Just along the route from the hotel to Victory House. It took ages to get anyone to go up to her office and check if she was there – that's why I'm so late. They said her office is closed and they've no idea where she is. That Wing Commander Sanderson is on sick leave.'

'The Yard, as quick as you can.'

She took him at his word and they covered the short distance in record time. 'Stay with the car. I might need you again at short notice.'

He slammed into his office pleased that Wainwright was already there. 'Charlotte's missing. She wasn't there when Simmons went to collect her – definitely left the hotel – but failed to arrive at her workplace.'

'Sod me! Do you think Jones has taken her?'

'Christ, I hope not. Get boots on the ground asking questions. I'm going to speak to the chief super. He needs to know this is my priority at the moment.'

He was given *carte blanche* to do whatever was necessary to find her. Could Jones have gone back to the premises that had been raided the other night? It's what he would have done as the place had been searched and every item of stolen property removed. What possible reason would there be for the police to look there again?

This search proved fruitless. He rounded up half a dozen villains who had a vague connection with Jones. He was at his worst during the interviews. These men were hardened criminals but today they couldn't withstand his snarling interrogation. They knew nothing about Jones or Charlotte.

'Let them go, Sergeant, a total waste of bloody time.'

The uniformed custody sergeant smiled. 'I don't think so, sir. You put the fear of God into them – I doubt we'll have any trouble from them for a while.'

It was now three hours since the search began and so far they'd found no one who'd seen her. The reports he'd had from the constables who'd interviewed the WAAFs at Victory House had provided no useful information.

Then his eye was caught by a sentence at the end of one of them. The man had written that they had a problem of their own as a car had been stolen that morning. He stared at the words. For a second the import of them didn't register.

Then he understood and, after an initial rush of relief, he was consumed by fury. She hadn't been abducted but had forgotten she was supposed to travel with Simmons.

The telephone on his desk jangled and he snatched it up. 'Excuse me, sir, but the operator says there's a caller asking if you'll accept the charges of the call.'

'Yes, put it through.'

There was the usual whirring and then the operator cheerfully told him he was now connected. 'Dan, I'm so sorry…'

He cut her short. 'Have you any idea the trouble you've caused? How could you be so irresponsible? So stupid? I had half the force out looking for you. What the f….' He just managed to stop himself. Swearing at her wouldn't help. 'They think the car's been stolen.'

He paused trying to rein in his anger. There was no response to his tirade. All he could hear was a faint crackle on the line. Had she hung up on him?

'Charlotte, for God's sake say something. I've been going out of my mind here thinking you'd been abducted.'

Then the operator answered. 'I'm sorry, the caller has disconnected. Do you wish me to try and reconnect the line for you, sir?'

'No, thank you.' What a bloody shambles he'd made of it. He didn't blame her for hanging up – he'd behaved like an absolute brute. Not given her a chance to explain what had happened – had just made an assumption.

Cold sweat trickled between his shoulder blades. She could have had an accident and have been ringing for his help. He'd no idea where she was and now it was too late. One thing he could do was straighten things out at Victory

House. He'd go round there in person and not telephone it was the least he could do in the circumstances.

It took him several minutes to contact the necessary people and have the search called off. God knows how much time and resources had been wasted on this unnecessary hunt. He would make the appropriate apologies when he returned.

He grabbed his outdoor garments, shrugged into his coat, rammed his hat on his head and picked up his cane. He paused at the desk outside on the way out. 'Going to be out for an hour.'

He was back in less than that and his temper was even more frayed than it had been when he'd left. It had been a pointless journey. Charlotte had rung them some time ago. Fortunately, it had been in time to prevent a major incident and had been put down to inefficient paperwork. This meant Charlotte was unlikely to be put on a charge.

As he didn't know the name of the hotel she was investigating he couldn't contact her and apologise for his boorish behaviour. His reaction had been uncalled for. He was a police inspector, for God's sake, and had years of experience in controlling his emotions in difficult circumstances.

The report came in that Jones had been seen in Stepney – it seemed reliable as the informant was well known to him.

'Wainwright, I want to arrest him myself. I'll take a couple of uniformed blokes with me.'

'I'm up to my neck in paperwork here. Are you sure you don't need me to accompany you? I could do with a break.'

His sergeant now had a desk on the far side of the large

office. 'If you go then I'll have to remain here and complete that lot.'

'That's true, sir, but your fiancée could call back and you want to be here to take the call, don't you?'

'Manipulative bugger. All right – before you go bring that lot over to me. I'm damned if I'm going to sit at your miserable desk when I've got such a magnificent one of my own.'

The young man grinned. 'Would you like me to fetch lunch before I go?' His remark had been facetious but Dan decided Wainwright had the better of the deal so fetching his food was only fair.

'Yes, sandwiches and a pot of tea – see what our constable outside would like. Put it on my tab.'

'I think Dawkins would like an hour off to buy his own lunch, sir.'

'Right, tell him he can go for an hour but that means you've got to come back with my meal.'

There was no further call from Charlotte and not hearing from her made him uneasy. Not because he really believed she'd met with an accident or been abducted by Jones, but because he guessed she was so appalled by his ranting at her she didn't want to speak to him.

Jones had been apprehended, charged, and would go before the magistrate in the morning. Then he would be sent to Wormwood Scrubs to await trial. He would join the five other corrupt policemen arraigned there along with the remaining seven members of Bentley's band.

★

It hadn't occurred to Charlotte that Dan would instigate a full-scale manhunt for her. With hindsight it would have been better to have used her pennies to ring him and then asked him to contact Victory House. Even so, he had been absolutely vile to her and she'd hung up before he'd finished snarling at her.

There was nothing she could do about it at the moment and she regretted her impulsive decision to disconnect the call and rush out of the telephone box. He might well be worried that she'd met with an accident and this was the reason she hadn't contacted him earlier. If that was the case then it would be no more than he deserved for being so beastly.

She arrived at Seaview and as she'd suspected they had been falsely claiming for WAAF trainees. She interviewed the catering staff, the orderlies and the sergeant who was in charge of the premises.

'No, ma'am, there's never been more than fifty here and even that's a bit of a squeeze. I always check before I sign the paperwork so they must be falsifying it afterwards. Shocking behaviour – there's a war on and every penny counts.'

'I agree with you, Sergeant. I have everything I need to make my report and none of it reflects badly on you or those you have under your control. Is everything satisfactory here? Do you have any complaints?'

'No, ma'am, all tickety-boo. The girls love it and are always sad to move on once they're trained.'

Satisfied the hotel could continue to accommodate the

trainees, and that it was the owners, not the people running the place, who were culpable, Charlotte went in search of them. She was unsurprised to find Mr and Mrs Culley had been called away unexpectedly from their grand house half a mile away from the hotel. The housekeeper was happy to speak to her.

'I didn't know they were going until yesterday evening. They got a phone call from London – I think it was madam's brother who's a bigwig in the RAF.'

'I see. Did they say where they were going or how long they might be away?'

'No, they said to put covers on the furniture. That means they don't expect to be back for a good while. Mr Culley has family in America – I think they might be going there. Mind you, I wouldn't want to cross the Atlantic with all those U-boats out there, would you?'

'No, I certainly wouldn't. Thank you for your help. I've got all the information I need.' She stood up and brushed the crumbs from her skirt. 'That was a delicious tea. I won't need much dinner tonight after eating all that. I don't suppose you could recommend a decent bed and breakfast or guesthouse?'

'Stay here, ma'am, there's only me and Joe – my hubby – living here. Madam will never know and it will save you the money.'

'If you're quite sure, then that's very kind of you and I accept. I'll just fetch my overnight bag from the car and then join you.'

Further conversation with the garrulous housekeeper

confirmed her view that the wing commander had warned his sister and that the Culleys had fled before they could be arrested. He'd asked her not to mention his name, but he was as culpable as them even if he wasn't getting any financial benefit from the arrangement.

That evening when she retired she had ample time to consider her options. She could hand in a report that didn't mention the connection or give a true version of events. Doing this would mean she wouldn't get the transfer she'd asked for but, on the bright side, it was quite possible the man she worked with would be the one transferred and she could continue in the posting that she enjoyed.

Whatever the outcome she knew she'd do the right thing. The report was finished and in her briefcase waiting to be handed in on her return. She was looking forward to seeing Dan that evening and, having had some time to think it over, had forgiven him for his bad temper. Just because they were engaged didn't mean his character had changed overnight – he was short-tempered and prone to unpleasant outbursts. She'd fallen in love with him the way he was and would just have to grow a thicker skin and not get upset when he spoke to her like that.

She parked the car on her return, hung the keys on the appropriate hook, and headed inside. Instead of going to her office she took the report directly to the office of the air commodore, as some instinct made her wonder if she handed it to anyone working in Sanderson's department it might never reach the appropriate authorities.

He would be away until Monday or Tuesday. There was no such thing as a weekend in the services and the building was as busy as it was on a weekday. There was the usual pile of files on the desk and she settled down to deal with them.

Every time she heard footsteps in the corridor she expected someone from the office of the air commodore to be coming to speak to her. The same when the telephone rang – but she completed her duties without interruption.

Then, as she was thinking about ringing Violet and asking her to come and collect her, a WAAF knocked on the door and handed her an official-looking envelope. Charlotte tore it open and her legs gave way beneath her.

She was being transferred, but not to be trained as a wireless operator. She was being sent to Scotland to work in an administrative role. The posting was immediate. With shaking fingers she examined the travel warrant. Her train left Euston in two hours' time.

She snatched up the receiver and asked the switchboard operator to connect her to Scotland Yard. Dan wasn't there and she could hardly leave a personal message like this with the desk sergeant.

Hastily she scribbled a letter telling him what had happened and saying she would contact him as soon as she was able. If she handed it in to the concierge at the hotel then she could be sure Dan would get it.

She ran all the way home and burst in almost colliding with two elderly matrons who were crossing the foyer. 'I beg your pardon, I'm in a frightful rush. I've been transferred and my train leaves in an hour and a half.'

'That's quite all right, my dear, you have to do whatever you're told,' one of them said with a somewhat startled smile.

The concierge had overheard and shook his head

sympathetically. 'I'll have your account ready when you come down, ma'am. What you want us to do with your pictures, ornaments and wireless?'

She handed him the letter addressed to Dan. 'I've asked DI Chalmers to collect them. He doesn't know I'm leaving and it's going to be a shock to him.'

'I'll make sure he gets the letter and I'll see to it personally that those items are packed away and kept safe until he can collect them. We'll be sorry to see you go, ma'am.'

'Not as sorry as I am to leave. Could you see if you can find me a taxi? I daren't miss my train as I'm already in a lot of trouble.'

As she was pounding up the stairs she realised she shouldn't have revealed that information. Having had to pack at speed several times before, it didn't take long to have her belongings neatly stowed in her kitbag. The tin hat and gas mask had been handed in some time ago so she didn't have to worry about those.

She stopped at the door and looked around the room for the last time. She'd been happy here and was desperately sad at having to leave under such circumstances. The only consolation was that she hadn't been demoted. Someone in the war office hadn't liked the fact that she'd incriminated Sanderson and this was her punishment – expulsion to the wilds of Scotland. She was pretty sure Wick was about as far away from London she could be sent as it was on the westernmost tip of the Highlands. Wick airbase faced the Moray Firth, which then led into the icy depths of the North Sea.

★

Dan headed for the chief superintendent's office with his letter of resignation in his hand. He wanted to have reorganised his future before he saw Charlotte tonight. He'd already booked two months' sick leave as he was due to go into hospital next week. He was hoping that this letter would be welcome in the circumstances.

There were two civilian secretaries hammering away on their typewriters in the outer office. One of them immediately rang through to announce his arrival.

'Good morning, Chalmers, just the man I wanted to see. Sit down, I've got good news for you. I told you we appreciate the work you've done for us in bringing that villain and his men to justice.'

'Thank you, sir, just doing my job. I couldn't have achieved such an excellent result without those who worked with me.'

'True, true, but you set things in motion and your investigative skills were the main reason for the successful outcome as far as we're concerned. Therefore, you are now Detective Chief Inspector Chalmers. When you return to work you will have the pick of the CID to add to your team.'

This was unexpected. 'Thank you, I appreciate your confidence in me. I feel that I must point out I don't know whether I'll be returning...'

'Nonsense, of course you will. You've managed perfectly well as you are and will do even better on a tin leg than you do with a stick.' Dan's hesitation was noted and his boss continued. 'This is just the start, DCI Chalmers – we need a man we can trust and I can guarantee that your promotion to superintendent will follow rapidly.'

To refuse now was impossible. 'I'll do my best, but...'

'No buts, young man – you have a bright future ahead of you here and won't let us down. If you are thinking of retiring then put that idea firmly aside. You would be bored in a month if you were at home doing nothing.'

'That's probably true, sir. However, at the end of this blasted war those who volunteered will return and you'll have a surplus of excellent men to choose from.'

'By then it will be you in my position doing the choosing. I can't see this conflict ending soon.'

'If the Americans join us then I think we've got a chance of winning, but without them we're fighting alone.'

'Then let's hope they stop procrastinating. By the way, word reached me that you're to be congratulated on your engagement. Is that correct?'

'It is. We've no plans to get married at the moment.'

'Shame, I think having a little woman at home would be of benefit to you. Give you something to look forward to.'

Dan hid his smile by standing up. Charlotte had no intention of being anybody's "little woman". She was an independent WAAF officer and he wouldn't want her any different.

The increase in salary wasn't mentioned as they both knew he'd no need of the money. It was fortunate he hadn't told her he intended to resign.

'It's because of my relationship with her that I intended to stand down. My work has put her in danger and my future wife is more important than this job.'

'Nonsense – as a senior officer you won't be so personally involved in your investigations. Nobody has ever made any attempt to harm my family.'

It would hardly be polite to point out that the chief superintendent had never conducted an investigation into such dangerous criminals as he had.

'I'm not going to resign at the moment, sir, but I just want to warn you that if any further threats are made against Charlotte then I'll walk away.'

'Very well, I can't quibble about that. You already did your bit for your country at Dunkirk and since then have cleaned house, removed the corrupt officers and have made dozens of significant arrests.'

Dan had only been gone half an hour but already someone had replaced the name on his door and it now read, in large gilt letters, Detective Chief Inspector Chalmers. He couldn't wait to see Charlotte tonight and give her the good news.

22

Charlotte arrived with minutes to spare and a guard with a soft Highland accent grabbed her kitbag from her and all but shoved her onto the train, then slammed the door behind them. She scarcely had time to catch her breath before another guard blew his whistle and the train slowly steamed out of the station, belching and coughing smoke, making her eyes sting.

'I'll be seeing your ticket then, lassie.'

She showed him her travel warrant, which entitled her to absolutely nothing on this overnight train.

'You're the lucky one. I'm having an empty sleeper. It was reserved but the passenger hasn't come in time.'

She walked behind him down the rocking train – he still refused to give her back the kitbag although she was perfectly capable of carrying it for herself. She was disappointed that he wasn't wearing a kilt or at least a tartan tam-o'-shanter.

The sleeping compartments were towards the front of the long train and they had to make their way down the narrow corridors and through the dining car. This was already full of those who could afford the exorbitant prices. She wondered what they could serve now there was such strict rationing.

Her escort stopped at an empty table laid up for two. 'Now you sit here, lassie. The least I can do is see that you're fed. There'll be no charge as the missing passenger has paid.'

'If you're quite sure you won't get into trouble, then that's absolutely splendid. I haven't eaten since breakfast.'

'I'll take this along to your sleeper. I'll be back to show you where it is in an hour or so.' He nodded and smiled. 'Where exactly are you being posted to?'

'Caithness somewhere. I've never been to Scotland but wish I'd been able to come in the summer and not as winter's approaching.'

'It does get a mite chilly in the Highlands but you WAAF lasses have your thick coats like the cattle. You'll do fine.'

Charlotte was so hungry she didn't care what she was served but in fact the meal was excellent. A thick vegetable soup followed by a beef stew and apple dumplings with cream. What made it even better was the real coffee.

Her guard returned and led her through the sleepers, all with closed doors and most of them obviously occupied. He stopped and unlocked the door in front of him. 'You'll be more comfortable in here than in a seat. There's everything you need provided. What time will you be wanting breakfast? It's served from six o'clock until seven thirty.'

'What time does the train arrive in Wick?'

'Bless you, lassie, this train doesn't go that far. This carriage terminates at Inverness at nine.'

'I see. My travel warrant is to Wick but I'm not sure how I'm supposed to use it if there's no train.'

'There's a train, just not this one. There are local trains but they don't run frequently. You'd have been better off getting a seat in an RAF aircraft. I'm surprised they wanted you to find your way overland.'

'There's no urgency for me to arrive quickly. I'd like to have breakfast as late as possible so can I reserve my table for eight?' He nodded and jotted it down in his notebook. She wondered if she should tip him now. 'Thank you for your assistance. Will you still be on duty tomorrow morning?'

'I'll be here to carry your bag, lassie, don't you fret.'

She'd expected there to be two sets of bunks and that she would be sharing with three strangers but as this was first class, she had it to herself. There were real sheets, starched and crisply ironed and already turned down for her. The walls were panelled with what she thought was walnut, there were numerous interesting cupboards with shiny brass knobs. There was even a bedside light.

She lifted the lid of the corner unit and discovered a small sink. Underneath was a pristine china chamber pot hidden away in a discreet cupboard.

There was no sign of her kitbag but she guessed it had been put somewhere out of sight. All she had to do was keep searching and she'd find it. Sure enough the two doors under the bed opened to reveal a long storage space ideal for luggage.

Should she undress? She wasn't entirely comfortable about removing her clothes on a train even in a private compartment with the door locked. She compromised and decided to sleep in her blackouts and vest. These knee-length knickers were hardly flattering but warm, and made sure no WAAF revealed more than she should beneath her skirt.

Breakfast the following morning was obviously kippers

as she could smell them as she approached the dining car. Hopefully they would have an alternative as she wasn't fond of these bony, salty fish. The alternative, naturally, was porridge and she disliked that even more.

'Could I just have coffee and toast, please?'

The waiter nodded pleasantly and returned with a full rack, butter and marmalade. This was more like it and she ate all four slices and drained the coffee pot. She left half a crown under the saucer and wobbled her way back to her compartment.

With the blinds up she was able to view the Scottish landscape. She'd never been this far north and wished with all her heart that she wasn't there now. Dan would be devastated she'd gone but would hopefully understand it had nothing to do with him.

She would probably have been transferred anyway after handing in that damning report, so at least she couldn't blame herself for the separation. He would be expecting her to telephone this morning but it was highly unlikely she'd be able to do so until she arrived at Wick and, from what the helpful guard had said, that might not be until tomorrow.

She had one of her precious ten-shilling notes ready for when he arrived. His happy smile told her she'd given him more than he expected and she was pleased. This time she was able to get out just along the corridor and didn't have to walk the length of the train.

'Thank you so much. You've made a difficult situation so much easier. I got engaged two days ago and didn't have time to say goodbye to my fiancé.'

His reply was drowned by the racket the engine was

making. She jumped onto the platform and held out her hand for the bag. It was decidedly colder here and she was glad she was wearing her heavy greatcoat.

She turned, expecting to see the long snake of carriages but instead there were only four and a much smaller engine. Now she understood his cryptic comment, "this carriage terminates at Inverness." The rest of the train had terminated back down the line – possibly Glasgow.

Dan intended to go with Simmons when she went to collect Charlotte and wandered downstairs at seven o'clock knowing this was about the time his driver usually left.

'I've not heard anything from ASO Fenimore, sir. I expect she's working late.'

'We won't wait for the call. Please drop me off at the hotel and then go and find her.'

He needed a beer and a chance to unwind before she arrived. He had a lot of grovelling to do and wasn't familiar with apologising as he rarely felt the need to do so. Being in love with Charlotte was changing him, and for the better.

The hotel manager himself was behind the desk. He reached into the recesses of a pigeonhole and walked towards him.

'I'm very sorry to tell you, sir, but ASO Fenimore was unexpectedly posted to Scotland. She left this letter for you last night.'

My darling Dan,
I can't tell you in a letter exactly what happened but because of something I did I'm being sent to Wick for

the foreseeable future. There isn't time for me to contact you.

I'm sorry about the mix-up with the car and I'm sure you're sorry about snarling at me.

I'll be in touch as soon as I can. I love you and I'm so sorry this has happened when everything was so wonderful between us.

I'll be thinking of you every night and hope you understand this wasn't my fault.

All my love,
Charlotte

It took him a moment to assimilate what he'd read. Where the bloody hell was Wick? 'Do you know exactly where Wick is?'

'It's in Scotland, on the coast, as far away from here as you could possibly get.' The manager looked as shocked as he was. 'Is that where they've sent her?'

He nodded, too numb to answer. She must have done something far worse than take a car without permission to have been posted that far away at such short notice. Then something about the letter caught his attention. He read it again. She didn't mention that she'd been demoted – surely this should have been the first thing to happen? There was something odd about this posting.

It was too late to make enquiries at Victory House but he'd start an investigation tomorrow. He had a couple of days before he reported to the hospital for the amputation and intended to use them to uncover what was behind her being sent to the Highlands so suddenly.

'I'd still like to dine here, if that's possible?'

'Of course – you can have the table that you reserved for both of you. ASO Fenimore asked us to pack up and keep safe several personal items and then hand them on to you.'

'Thank you. If you could have them behind the desk my driver can bring them out to the car.'

'They'll be waiting for you, Inspector Chalmers.'

'It's chief inspector now.'

'Congratulations, sir, well deserved.'

He'd expected Simmons to be upset that her new friend and vanished so suddenly without a word but the reverse was true.

'It's a blooming cheek, that's what it is. I always thought that Wing Commander Sanderson was a rum one. I reckon it's something to do with him – he's had her transferred because she found out something she shouldn't about him.' She shoved the large cardboard box onto the rear passenger seat with such force it shot to the other side.

'I think the same as you. Pick me up at seven tomorrow and we'll start our enquiries before Victory House is busy.'

'I'll have a chat with the WAAF from the motor pool – I might be in khaki but we've got the same job.'

'Yes, that's an excellent idea. In fact, it would be far better for you to go and for me to keep a low profile. I've got a few friends at the war office and will start my enquiries there.'

Simmons volunteered to carry the box to his apartment and he agreed. After all, she'd spent a couple of nights in his spare room so the place was hardly off limits to her.

One of the men he wanted to speak to was more likely to be available late at night than he was during the day. Air Commodore Frank Fulton was his godfather, a contemporary of his defunct father, and had always been a good friend to him.

A bottle of whisky had mysteriously appeared on his desk earlier that day and he thought it was probably from the stolen goods and black-market items found in Bentley's storerooms. This commodity was in such short supply that, despite its dubious provenance, he was delighted to have it.

He poured himself a generous measure and settled on the chair by the telephone. He hoped Charlotte had arrived safely but had a nasty suspicion she might still be travelling. There would be a telephone call as soon as she had the opportunity, of that he had no doubt.

The operator connected him. 'Uncle Frank, it's Dan. Can you spare me a few minutes? I've got a problem I think you might be able to help me with.'

'Dan, my boy, good to hear from you. We must get together for a drink at my club sometime soon. How are you? Let's start with your news before we get to the problem – it's been far too long since we spoke.'

Dan told him about his promotion, about his decision to have his leg removed, and that he was engaged to be married.

'You made the right decision about your leg. The promotion is well deserved and I hope you'll bring your future wife to meet me and Betty when you can. Now, tell me why you rang.'

'Can you tell me anything about Wing Commander Sanderson?'

There was silence for a moment and he knew he was onto something.

'Why do you ask?'

'Before I answer that I want to tell you that I've just been instrumental in removing six corrupt policemen from Scotland Yard.'

'Are you suggesting that Sanderson is corrupt?'

Briefly he explained his interest in the man and that he didn't know exactly why Charlotte had been transferred so suddenly but it was something to do with Sanderson and her investigation in Bournemouth.

'You've put me in a bit of a spot, my boy. I do know something about that and of Sanderson's involvement. I can't divulge anything further but I can assure you that your young lady won't be in Scotland indefinitely. Is that good enough for you?'

'It's absolutely splendid, Uncle Frank. Would you prefer it if I didn't investigate this myself?'

'To do so would be stepping over several lines, my boy, so better leave it to those better placed to put matters right. Your young lady will no doubt carry out her duties as she should wherever she's posted.'

'I know she will. Thank you for your advice and for your help. She doesn't know about my hospital appointment and now I'm glad I didn't tell her. Hopefully, when she returns I'll be a new man, albeit minus half a leg.'

He was tempted to ring Simmons and tell her not to chat to the WAAFs in the morning but decided it wouldn't hurt to pick up a bit of gossip. The fact that his godfather was already aware of Sanderson being involved meant whatever Charlotte had uncovered was pretty serious as the information had gone straight to the top.

The transfer had been made by Sanderson and wasn't

official. This meant Charlotte wasn't in serious trouble and would be back in a few weeks. There was a war on – as everybody said all the time – and bringing a single WAAF back from Scotland wouldn't feature very high on anybody's list of priorities.

Charlotte asked a porter and was told there were no trains running to Wick until the following morning. She couldn't afford to pay to stay in a hotel as having to settle her bill yesterday had taken all her spare cash. She had only a few shillings left until the next payday.

She hefted her kitbag over her shoulder and made her way into the forecourt. There were a lot of RAF personnel about so there must be a base nearby. Remembering what she'd been told about it being easier to fly to Wick than to travel overland she thought it might be worth hitching a lift to the base and seeing if she could organise that. After all, she was part of their services, wasn't she?

Several airmen saluted her and fortunately she'd had the foresight to put her kitbag on her left shoulder, which left her right hand free to respond. She needed to find an officer – they would be able to help. She was surprised there were so many Air Force personnel around as it was still early.

Outside on the street she immediately spotted a young flight lieutenant strolling in her direction. She was of equivalent rank so thought he'd be the best person to speak to.

'Excuse me, Flight Lieutenant, I need to get to Wick. Do you think there's any chance I might be able to snag a lift from your base today?'

He smiled and held out his hand. 'Here, let me carry your bag. I'm a foot taller than you and probably weigh twice as much so no arguments please.'

'I wouldn't dream of arguing with a fellow officer. However, you haven't answered my question.'

'I'm Peter Sullivan.'

'Charlotte Fenimore.'

'Well, Charlotte, it's a couple of miles to the base and there's a regular bus run especially for us chaps. There's an ancient Tiger Moth used for delivering people and parcels to Wick. I'll take you there myself as I'm on four days' leave.'

'That would be absolutely spiffing, Peter, thank you so much. Are you quite sure you won't get put on a charge for borrowing the Moth?'

'As I said, its sole purpose is delivering people and parcels and I think you qualify as one of the former. Believe me, there'll be a queue of bods eager for the chance so I've just got in first.'

He was striding down the pavement and she was almost running to keep up with him. She'd forgotten what it was like to be with a man who could walk faster than her. She swallowed a lump in her throat as she thought about Dan and how abruptly she'd left him.

'I'm engaged to a police inspector,' she announced suddenly.

He looked down at her and grinned. 'Good for you, didn't expect an absolute corker like you to be available. Can't say I approve of you tying yourself to a policeman but at least he's in uniform.'

They arrived at the bus stop, which gave her time to catch her breath. 'Actually, he's a CID inspector, so plain clothes.

He was a lieutenant in the army at Dunkirk where he was horribly injured so got invalided out.' Why on earth was she revealing so much personal information to a complete stranger?

'Poor sod – and good for you taking pity on a wounded hero.'

The bus trundled up so she didn't have time to take issue with his casual comment. The bus was full of air force personnel and there were several WAAF amongst them. The journey was only a few minutes and the ancient vehicle wheezed to a halt and they all disembarked.

The guard at the gate didn't look up from his newspaper, which she thought was rather lax. Just because everyone was in blue, it didn't mean they shouldn't be asked to identify themselves.

'Have you ever flown in a Moth?'

'I've never flown in anything. I know it's a two-seater biplane, open to the elements. My greatcoat is thick and I've got a balaclava somewhere.'

'If you hang on here a minute, Charlotte, I'll speak to my Win Co and get the okay. Then I'll grab my gear and see if I can find transport. The kite's on the far side of the base – take too long to walk there.'

He dumped her bag against the wall and vanished into the building. She'd never worked on a base and found everything fascinating. She'd expected to see aircraft coming in and taking off constantly but while she waited there was nothing happening in the sky or on the ground.

As far as she could see there was only one runway so perhaps this wasn't an active base at the moment. There were a couple of hangars and a few aircraft parked around the perimeter. She could see the River Ness behind the buildings and smiled at the thought that maybe the mythical monster from the loch might occasionally swim down this far.

Peter had been gone some time and she was beginning to wonder if he'd forgotten about her. She'd nodded and smiled to a few airmen and a couple of WAAF but nobody had stopped to talk to her. Was she uninteresting or were they just too busy?

There was a roar of an engine and a dilapidated van rocked to a halt beside her. Peter was inside. He leaned across and shoved open the door. 'This is the best I can do, but better than walking.'

He now had his flight suit and flying boots on and looked much better prepared for an open-air flight than she was. 'Thank you so much for doing this. I don't actually have to be there at a particular time – in fact, I don't even know if they're aware that I'm coming.'

'The trains are haphazard at the moment so you'd probably have to wait hours to get one. Better that I take you.'

The gears crunched and they sped off, heading for the far side of the base. It was too noisy to continue the conversation, which was fortunate, as the closer she got to the point where she was going to be airborne, the more nervous she was.

23

Dan spent the day clearing his in-tray, making sure all his ongoing investigations could be continued by Wainwright – who was taking over until a new CID inspector was appointed – and so that when he left he wouldn't be worrying about work.

The atmosphere in the corridors had improved now the culprits were incarcerated and he was no longer poking about in other people's business. The men arrested at Bentley's premises were falling over themselves to provide information in the hope they might get a lighter sentence.

They now knew exactly what had happened to WPC Davidson. Mike had joined him in his office, bringing a welcome tray of tea and biscuits.

'That poor girl didn't stand a chance,' Mike said sadly. 'When one of them telephoned impersonating her cousin and asking for help, of course she was going to go. We know the name of the copper who gave Bentley the information they used to entice her into their neighbourhood.'

'We also know which of the bastards pulled the trigger and then dumped the body. I wish Bentley hadn't died. In my opinion it would have been better if he'd stood trial and then been hanged as an example to the others who might want to step into his shoes.'

'Let's hope the newspapers find something else to write about. It's unpleasant having the fact that the Yard was rife with corruption plastered over the front pages.'

'I've yet to meet your future wife,' Mike said, deliberately changing the subject. 'My wife wants to know if you'll come for dinner Thursday night.'

'I'm sorry, that's impossible. Charlotte was posted to Wick the day before yesterday; it's somewhere in the Highlands north of Inverness.'

'Good God! I thought she was happy where she was and doing a good job.'

'She was. I can't discuss the details but the transfer was an error and she'll be back, possibly not to the same place, in a few weeks. Hopefully she'll at least be in England next time.'

'Does she know about your promotion?'

'No, I was going to tell her last night but she'd already gone. She doesn't even know I'm going into hospital tomorrow night. To tell you the truth, Mike, I've not heard from her apart from the brief note she left.'

'It doesn't take two days to get to Wick. Can't you contact the base and at least find out if she arrived safely?'

'I'm going to do so when I get home tonight. She promised to ring me as soon as she arrived and I expected to hear from her yesterday.'

'Do it immediately. You're a chief inspector and can do what you damn well please. As long as you pay for the call, or at least offer to do so, nobody will complain if they do find out.'

Dan had already got the number to hand and after several minutes of clicking, whirring and tinny voices he was finally connected to the base at Wick.

'Good afternoon. I'm Detective Chief Inspector Chalmers from Scotland Yard. I'm making enquiries about a WAAF officer – Assistant Section Officer Fenimore. She was posted from London two days ago and is a possible witness in an ongoing inquiry. I need to speak to her.'

'If you would hold on for a moment, sir, I'll find out where she is and see if I can put you through.'

The line went dead and he thought he'd been cut off. He looked at Mike and raised an eyebrow and his friend smiled and poured them both another cup of tea. Tea was the panacea for all ills – the Women's Voluntary Service had provided gallons of it to those bombed out in the Blitz.

The woman he'd spoken to before eventually returned. 'I'm sorry, Chief Inspector, but no one of that name is stationed here and we have no record of her having been posted to this base.'

There was no point in arguing. If Charlotte wasn't there, wasn't even expected, then that was the end of the matter as far as they were concerned. Somehow he managed to answer. 'Thank you. I must've been misinformed. Good afternoon.'

He dropped the phone on the desk. Mike reached out and returned it to the base set.

'She's not there; they know nothing about her.' Dan pulled out the letter he'd been carrying in his waistcoat pocket and showed it to Mike, who read it quickly.

'No doubt about it, she was definitely being transferred to Wick. So where the devil is she?'

'I'm going round to Horse Guards. My godfather's an air commodore and he knew all about her transfer. He won't want to talk to me, but he has no choice.'

'Wainwright's quite capable of dealing with anything that might arise this afternoon. There has to be some simple explanation – good luck, my friend.'

Dan was gritting his teeth by the time he was eventually escorted to the upper floor where his godfather had his office. They'd tried to dissuade him, but he was determined to see him. Uncle Frank had definitely known all about the transfer – meaning it had been official after all – so why the hell didn't the people he'd spoken to at Wick?'

'I'm sorry to interrupt your day, sir, but this won't wait.' Addressing his godfather formally had been the right thing to do as it immediately set the tone for an official meeting.

'Right. Sit down, Detective Chief Inspector, and tell me why you've come.'

Dan kept his explanation simple and to the point. When he'd finished he certainly had Uncle Frank's full attention.

'This is very strange. She was definitely transferred; I've seen the paperwork and a copy of the travel warrant she was issued.'

'Then why didn't Wick know that she was being sent there?' He pulled out a chair and flopped onto it. His bloody leg was killing him today. 'It's possible she missed the train and is still en route but that doesn't explain why they don't have knowledge of her imminent arrival.'

'Exactly. Would you like coffee? I need to speak to a few

people and get some telephone calls made. I might be some time.'

'Coffee, as long as it's the genuine article and not the ersatz rubbish that's being called by the same name.' This was hardly polite but too late to do anything but shrug apologetically.

'It's the real thing. I've friends at the American Embassy; they have a constant stream of the luxury items we don't have arriving daily.'

'Good to know, sir. If the Yanks eventually decide to join us, maybe some of their largesse will filter down to those who need it most and not remain with the rich who can afford to buy on the black market.'

'I assume you're not suggesting you would prefer people like us to break the law if that meant more for the underprivileged?'

'Obviously, that's not what I mean.' Dan rubbed his eyes and shrugged. 'I think that I'm becoming a bit of a Bolshevik, Uncle Frank. There's so much deprivation, genuine hardship, and the government puts out propaganda films pretending everything is tickety-boo.

'The powers that be seem to think a cup of tea and a wad will keep people happy when they've lost everything, have nowhere to live, and no prospect of finding a home or anything to put in it, in the foreseeable future.'

'Don't just complain about how things are, my boy, do something about it.'

Dan was about to protest that there wasn't much one person could do to alleviate the suffering of thousands of people but his godfather had already rushed off. A short while later a young woman, not in uniform, appeared with a tray.

'Air Commodore Fulton asked me to bring this up to you, sir.'

The coffee was everything it should be and he savoured every mouthful. The rich and powerful might well have difficulty getting coffee soon, even on the black market. That is, of course, unless they had American friends.

He had drained the pot before he heard footsteps approaching the office.

The Tiger Moth, Charlotte decided, looked sturdy enough even if it had no cockpit and the pilot sat behind the passenger. She noticed Peter had a parachute but there didn't appear to be one for her. Did this mean he would bail out and leave her to die? That didn't seem very heroic for a RAF pilot. She was tempted to ask but decided as he was being kind enough to fly her to Wick then it wouldn't be very gracious to do so.

'I've got some spare goggles. Do you have anything in your kitbag you can put on under your greatcoat? It's a short flight, but it'll be bloody cold.'

'I've got the balaclava I mentioned earlier, gloves and a scarf.' These items were neatly packed at the top of the bag as being the most likely to be needed. Whilst she was sorting herself out, he pulled on his helmet, gloves and goggles before picking up her bag and ramming it under the seat she was about to sit on.

'In you go. I need to check for myself that you're safely strapped in.'

When she was settled he leaned in and clipped the metal fasteners shut. She wasn't entirely comfortable about his proximity and instinctively held her breath and breathed in to make herself smaller.

'Right – don't be sick over the side as I'll get it in the face. There's a bag if you need it.'

He strode to the front of the plane and heaved on the propeller a couple of times. The engine roared into life and she wasn't entirely confident about being in it when it was alive, so to speak, without the pilot in his place behind her.

The lights on the runway were green, which meant they could take off without having to hang about. The little biplane accelerated furiously. She held her breath and closed her eyes. Then the rattling and groaning stopped and they were airborne.

She risked a quick glance and was horrified that they were heading out to sea. The wind whipped past her and within seconds she couldn't feel her cheeks despite the scarf wrapped around them. After a few minutes Peter straightened the little aircraft and they were now flying close to the coast.

This made sense as it would lead them directly to Wick but she would much prefer to be looking down at dry land. Not that it would make any difference if they ditched – she didn't have a parachute and would die anyway.

She hunched as low as she could and pulled her greatcoat tighter. Thank God it was a short flight as she'd known as soon as they were up that she really didn't enjoy the experience. This would be her first and, hopefully, last trip in a plane.

They'd only been flying for a few freezing minutes when quite suddenly a bank of fog rolled in. One moment they were in sunshine; the next in thick, grey, impenetrable cloud. She felt the Tiger Moth change course and although somewhat disorientated she was pretty sure Peter was flying towards the coast.

Her bladder almost emptied when she got a sharp poke in the back. She looked over her shoulder and he pointed to the ground. She nodded. He was going to find somewhere to land and the sooner the better as far as she was concerned.

He was obviously trying to get in front of the incoming sea fog. Landing completely blind in such a hilly and desolate place could only end in disaster. Then, miraculously, they were in sunlight again. She looked down and there seemed to be an area of what looked like reasonably smooth heather. Not ideal but better than the rocks and cliffs, which she knew were somewhere close behind them.

The engine note had changed. They circled slowly and then began to descend. Only as they got closer to the ground did she realise that what she'd thought was relatively smooth, was in fact the reverse. There were rocks everywhere and the surface undulated alarmingly.

There wasn't time to pray. She barely had time to brace herself as the heather rushed up towards them. The wheels hit, the plane bounced several times and didn't seem to be slowing down at all. Then one of the flimsy wheels must have hit a rock.

With a hideous tearing sound her world upended and everything went black. The racket continued, deafening, terrifying, then abruptly there was silence. Why was it so dark? Why was she upside down? Then she realised the plane had turned turtle and she was suspended from her harness.

Everything hurt, but she was alive, which was a miracle

in itself. Slowly she flexed each limb bracing herself for searing pain, but nothing was broken. How did the wretched harness undo? Surely they should be quick release? She pressed and prodded, her stomach churning, feeling dizzier by the minute, until more by luck than anything else she did what was required.

The straps, which were cutting into her, opened and she was face first in the dirt. She blinked a few times wondering why everything was blurred and wet when just before they'd landed the sun had been out. The fog had caught up and completely enveloped them.

She wriggled forwards and was relieved to be out from under the plane. Then her stomach plummeted. Peter was ominously silent. Please God, don't let him be dead or badly injured.

'Peter, Peter, are you hurt?'

Nothing – not even a groan. Now her eyes had adjusted to the murk she could see a yard in front of her. This was more than enough to crawl to the rear of the plane and peer under the crushed fuselage.

He was hanging from his harness as she'd been a few moments ago. She took a steadying breath and reached out and put her forefingers where his jawbone met his ear. Her breath hissed through her teeth. He was alive – a regular, reasonably strong pulse. He was unconscious, possibly concussed, which was a lot better than being dead.

She reached in and this time hit the harness in the correct place and it snapped open. She did her best to hold him steady but he was too heavy for her. When he was crumpled in the small space under the pilot's seat she reached in and grabbed the collar of his flight suit and slowly backed away.

It took her several attempts but eventually she'd pulled him clear. She quickly checked he had no obvious breaks in his legs or arms and then rolled him into the recovery position. Thank God she'd attended a basic first-aid course. She put her cheek up against his mouth and was reassured that he was breathing strongly.

She sniffed and was satisfied there was no petrol leaking from the engine. Until the fog lifted, they had to stay where they were. It had taken all her strength to move him a couple of yards. It would be impossible for her to drag him any further.

As nobody at Wick was aware she was arriving by air they wouldn't mount a search party when she failed to arrive. Presumably he'd filled in a flight plan so, when he failed to return to his base, they would be alerted. He'd told her he wasn't due back on roster for four days, so it was quite possible nobody would realise he was in trouble until then.

Anyway, nothing would be airborne in this fog. It might be hours, possibly days, before rescue arrived. She didn't know much about this part of the Highlands but from what little she'd seen before they'd come down, the coast was mostly inaccessible cliffs and the land consisted of acres of impenetrable moors.

The first thing she needed to do was rig up some sort of shelter. They were in the lee of the wreckage, which gave them some protection from the icy wind coming in from the sea. However, Peter couldn't remain on the ground without getting horribly cold – although, as his flight suit was padded and waterproof he was probably better placed than she was.

It took her several attempts to drag her kitbag from under the seat but at least she was warmer by the time she'd achieved her goal. Then she extracted his overnight bag and rummaged around for the first-aid kit and emergency rations. Once these were out, she checked the batteries were working in both their torches. She didn't smoke so didn't have matches or a lighter, and didn't like to search through his pockets and see if he had either.

A fire was essential, as not only would it keep them warm it would also act as a beacon to any aircraft that came in search of them. She'd seen no roads or villages just before they crash-landed so had no idea how anyone would reach them even if they did know where they were.

'Your young lady definitely caught the night train to Inverness, Dan,' Uncle Frank announced as he burst in. 'I managed to speak to the adjutant at Wick and her paperwork has now arrived and they are expecting her. However, she's yet to appear and should have been there by now.'

'Did she get off the train?'

'Definitely. A porter remembered her as she tipped him ten bob. She was seen at the station yesterday morning but was too late to catch the train to Wick. She was last seen catching the bus to the base at Inverness in the company of a pilot.'

'That makes sense. It would be far easier to get a flight to Wick than to hang about waiting for the next train.' Then the enormity of what he just said made something clutch at his heart. He leaned against the doorjamb to stay upright. 'If she'd caught a train this morning then she would be there later today. But if she got someone to fly her up then she would have been there yesterday lunchtime. Something's happened.'

'Nonsense, you know what these huge bases are like – well maybe you don't. Wick is coastal command and there's constant toing and froing of kites and personnel. She might well be there several days before she can access the telephone. Don't look so worried, my boy.'

Dan's breathing slowly returned to normal. 'I expect you're right. However, I won't be comfortable until I've heard from her directly. I wish she hadn't been posted quite so far away.'

'I can have her transferred back to her old position. Sanderson has been dishonourably discharged for his actions. He posted your young lady out of spite for being caught with his hand in the honey pot. It's fortunate that his sister and her husband have vanished. We don't really want to find them as it will kick up a frightful stink if people know the government has been defrauded by thousands of pounds over the past two years.'

'It's not up to me to decide what Charlotte wants to do. Perhaps she could be given the option to stay where she is for a few weeks before deciding if she wants to be transferred? I'd rather like to be back on my feet when I see her again. I don't want her to worry about what I'm going to do.'

'When do you expect to be fully functioning again, my boy?'

'December. I'm due back to work after Christmas. I was going to resign, but to tell you the truth I don't know what I'd do with myself if I wasn't working.'

'Good God, men like you are needed at Scotland Yard, especially with what's been going on there recently.'

'I came to that conclusion myself. Thank you for your assistance. I'd better get back to the office.'

'I take it you're not intending to look after yourself when you come out of hospital?'

'No, of course not. I've made arrangements to go to an excellent convalescent home. My prosthetic leg will be fitted whilst I'm there. I'll let you get on and I apologise for disturbing your day.'

He couldn't ignore the gut feeling he had that Charlotte was in trouble and decided to cancel his hospital visit and go to Scotland and find her himself. When he told his godfather, he nodded.

'Your leg can wait but this can't. Maybe you're right to be concerned. Your instincts have never let you down so far. Get your driver to take you to Hornchurch – I'll arrange for someone from the ATA to take you to Inverness. There'll be a taxi Anson you can cadge a lift in. It'll mean changing kites a couple of times as none of the ATA pilots are asked to fly the length and breadth of Britain.'

'That means I'll be there today with any luck. Shall I ring you at home this evening with any news?'

'Do that, my dear boy. I'd hate to think that anything untoward has happened to your young lady.'

24

Charlotte pulled out the rubberised square that had been the only protection against the elements, and was officially a gas cape, which WAAFs had until greatcoats were issued. This was also intended to be used as a groundsheet so would be ideal in the circumstances.

She also had a tin of emergency rations – these weren't supposed to be issued to the WAAF but when Nancy had been working in the stores, before moving into catering, her friend had found a box with a dozen or more of these tins left in it and had been told she could have them.

After spreading out the waterproof sheet she carefully positioned Peter's canvas holdall as a makeshift pillow and was then ready to either roll him onto it or wriggle it under him. He was still breathing evenly; she could see even in the gloom that his colour was good – if she didn't know better she would just think he was deeply asleep.

'Peter, Flight Lieutenant, you can't lie there on the wet grass any longer.' Shaking and shouting was fruitless as he didn't stir. She put her knee into the small of his back, put one hand on his shoulder and the other on his hip and pushed.

It worked and he rolled smoothly onto the surface she'd

prepared. There was no point in being prudish – she had to look in his pockets and see if there was a lighter or a box of matches. They really needed a fire if they weren't to suffer from hypothermia when it got dark.

The wind whistling off the sea was bringing in more fog, but hopefully this would be gone in a few hours and then if anyone came to look for them at least they would see the wreckage of the Tiger Moth.

There was nothing of use in the pockets of his flight suit. She seemed to recall that pilots carried an inflatable dinghy and a flare attached to their suits. Presumably, they only did this if they were in a fighter and likely to be shot down.

She undid the front and slid her hand inside and in the top pocket of his jacket she found a lighter. She was becoming more concerned about his continuing stillness – having a young lady put her hands all over his body should definitely have got a reaction. There was no sign of a lump, no bruising anywhere on his head, but the only explanation must be that he'd suffered a head injury – a serious one – or he would be coming round by now.

Visibility was still minimal and even with the torch she couldn't see very far in front of her. It would be far too risky to move away from the wreckage to look for something combustible. Therefore, it would have to be the plane itself that was burnt. It certainly couldn't fly again so she couldn't see anyone could object.

The Moth was basically made out of wood, which would make an excellent fire. All she had to do was clamber over the wings and pull off as much as she could. Obviously, the fire had to be several yards from the wreckage in case the wind changed and blew sparks into the engine.

There was probably a tankful of fuel just waiting to explode.

She scrambled, wrenched and swore and eventually had satisfactory pile of timber. Her dilemma was that if she started the blaze near enough to be any benefit to either of them then it would be far too close to the Tiger Moth.

Her greatcoat was tucked around the comatose pilot. She could keep warm by moving about so his need was greater than hers. The wind was no longer howling past them and it had been making her eyes water despite wearing a balaclava and goggles.

She could build the fire but first she needed to find fresh water. The rations didn't include anything to drink and water was more essential than food. He would be warm enough for the moment and didn't need a torch as he was unconscious. She'd already peeled off the tape that covered most of the glass around the bulb and stopped too much light shining in the blackout.

With one positioned so the beam shone skywards and the other in her hand, she set out to look for a stream and also anything flammable. She walked backwards initially, keeping her eye on the narrow pillar of light to make sure she could see it. This was her beacon and would ensure she didn't get lost on the moor.

Satisfied she was safe to move further afield she faced front and shone her torch in an arc in the hope she might see a stream or small pond. There were none. There was heather, other low-growing shrubs, rocks and slopes but nothing else at all.

Until now she hadn't realised that they'd landed in a hollow, enclosed on three sides by small hills, the third open to the sea. It had occurred to her that a competent pilot should have been able to fly above the fog, or use the instruments to guide him. Why had he chosen to crash-land and risk both their lives by doing so?

This was something she'd ask him as soon as he was conscious. This made it even more imperative she built a fire because it was just possible there was a village, or even a small hill farm, near enough to see the smoke and come and investigate.

Pulling up dead heather was easier than she'd anticipated and soon she had a double armful, exactly what she needed to use as kindling. She straightened and turned to walk back towards the light of the torch. It was no longer visible. Had the battery run out so soon?

The grey, wet fog swirled around her and her panic rose. She breathed in and out slowly through her nose, trying to calm her thundering heart. Yes – she could hear the sea but instead of being on her left it was behind her.

How stupid! She was facing in the wrong direction. She made a quarter turn to the left and immediately saw the flickering torch beam. Twice she almost tripped and fell in her eagerness to get back.

She tore up a manual of some sort that she'd found under the pilot's seat and hoped it wasn't something crucial. After a couple of failures, the paper ignited the twigs and in a few minutes there was the welcome heat of a substantial blaze.

Peter was still several yards away. She grabbed the end of the rubber sheet and after a few abortive efforts managed to drag him away from the danger of an exploding fuel tank and close enough to the fire to feel the benefit.

Her face was damp from the fog. Was there enough

moisture in the air for her to collect it for drinking water? With the two torches and the fire she could see the area well enough to be able to walk around freely without fear of tripping over anything or becoming lost.

There was a piece of canvas dangling from a broken wing. Would this do? What she needed was a receptacle into which the water could drip. Then she remembered her trusty irons and tin mug. After twenty minutes of fiddling she stepped away, satisfied she'd done the best she could with what she had. Any condensation, moisture, rain even, should hopefully trickle down the canvas and into the waiting mug.

Dan was able to speak to his surgeon and postpone his operation. Then he got Simmons to drive him home where he packed what he'd need for a few days. He had a shower and changed from his underwear to his suit. He didn't want to travel smelling of criminals.

This was the longest journey Simmons had undertaken with him but she was up to the task and threaded her way through the traffic with aplomb. As they were approaching the armed guards at the gate of the fighter base, he told her to pull over.

'I'll walk from here. Too complicated to get us both through the gate. Hopefully, I'll be back in a few days but I doubt I'll be fortunate enough to return the way I'm going. I'll need picking up at Euston station.'

He showed his warrant card and the guard nodded. 'If you would care to wait a moment, sir, there's transport on its way. The Anson's waiting for you.'

Fifteen minutes after arriving at Hornchurch he was in an ATA aircraft being expertly piloted by a young woman. There were half a dozen other passengers – all in the distinctive navy blue of the Air Transport Auxiliary. He was glad there were still a couple of empty seats. He wouldn't have wanted to have displaced a pilot needed to ferry new aircraft from factory to base.

He had to disembark and then travel in two further Ansons before finally landing at Inverness just as the light began to fade. The pilot, another young woman, had told him she wasn't allowed to fly in the dark so he was lucky to have got there tonight.

This time there was no waiting transport and it looked a daunting distance from where the aircraft had landed to the huddle of buildings on the far side of the base. He slung his overnight bag over his shoulder, took a firm grip on the handle of his cane and set off as briskly as he could.

He'd not gone more than a hundred yards when a dilapidated van pulled up. A friendly WAAF wound down the window. 'Hop in, sir, it's not often we get civilians here.'

He'd expected her to have a Scottish accent but she spoke the same English he did. 'Thank you, much appreciated. Got this lot at Dunkirk.'

The main building, which housed the offices, and from the racket and clinking of glasses was also the Officers' Mess, was busy. The doors to the rooms were open and he approached the first. There were two WAAFs clattering away on typewriters, but the first one saw him and immediately came over.

'Can I help you, sir?' She asked the question but her

expression told him that she didn't expect she'd be able to be of any assistance at all.

'Yes, I need to speak to the CO. I'm DCI Chalmers from Scotland Yard here on a matter of the utmost urgency.'

She jumped to attention and immediately became interested in his request. 'If you would care to come with me, sir, I'll take you to Wing Commander Anderson. You're lucky, he's just had a telephone call, so I know he's in his office.'

She knocked on a door and when told to enter opened it, stood in the doorway and saluted smartly. 'I have Detective Chief Inspector Chalmers from Scotland Yard here to see you, sir.'

There was the sound of a chair being pushed back and as the girl stepped aside Dan came face-to-face with a man about his own age, but with only one arm.

'Come in, old boy, take a pew. You look as if you could do with a chair.' He waggled the stump of his right arm. 'I won't offer to shake hands for obvious reasons.'

He mimed drinking from a cup at the WAAF and returned to his place behind the paper-strewn desk. 'I suppose being deskbound is better than nothing – but I hate paperwork, would much rather be flying. I lost my arm at the Battle of Britain last year. Where did you get your injury?'

'Dunkirk,' Dan said tersely not wanting to make small talk. 'Assistant Section Officer Fenimore, my fiancée, arrived here two days ago with an unnamed pilot officer. She was supposed to report to Wick but has failed to arrive. Do you have any officers or aircraft missing?'

'Flight Lieutenant Sullivan requested permission to fly a WAAF to Wick. He's on leave until tomorrow so obviously hasn't been reported missing. Have you spoken to Wick?'

'Charlotte hasn't reported for duty.'

'Give me a moment. I'll ring the adjutant there – he'll have a record of Peter's arrival.'

Dan ignored the tray of sandwiches and tea that arrived as he was more interested in the end of the conversation he could hear. None of it was reassuring.

'Bloody hell. He must have gone down in the fog that blanketed the area two days ago. I'll send someone up to look for them.' He paused, his expression grim. 'He would fly along the coast. If they ditched in the sea then....'

'I understand. Was the aircraft in good repair? Regularly maintained?'

'Of course it bloody was. This is the RAF – everything's properly maintained.'

'Is this Sullivan a competent pilot?'

'Yes, one of the best. He's only here for R&R, totally knackered after flying dozens of ops, and will be back with an active squadron at the end of the month.'

'In which case, would you say that it's likely that if he had engine trouble then he would be able to land safely and not in the sea?'

'I get your drift, now, Chief Inspector. Yes, it's possible they *are* still alive. However, it's damn cold at night and they've been stranded for forty-eight hours. Even if neither of them are hurt they could well be suffering from hypothermia by now – let alone the problems caused by lack of water.'

'Wing Commander, you're not helping the situation with your pessimistic attitude. Whoever you send to search must believe he's looking for survivors and not corpses. I can assure you he's more likely to find them if he thinks they might be alive.'

'Point taken, Chief Inspector. There's still about an hour of flying time – let's hope they see something before it gets dark.'

The fog, which had rolled in so suddenly, disappeared almost as quickly. They must have been on the ground for several hours by now and it was probably only a couple of hours before it began to get dark and much colder. Charlotte could now see in all directions – not that it helped. There was a teaspoon of water in the bottom of the mug, which wasn't much use to either of them, but maybe overnight more would drip into the receptacle.

After adding wood from the wreckage to the flames Charlotte walked to the top of the nearest hill in the vain hope that she might see smoke from a chimney somewhere in the distance. There wasn't even a sheep grazing on the heather – in fact the landscape was empty of any sign of human existence. The Highlands might be beautiful but they were a desolate place and she knew with absolute certainty they weren't going to be rescued today and possibly not tomorrow either.

Peter had said he'd got four days' leave, which meant no one would be looking for him for another three. She shivered and pushed her gloved hands into the sleeves of her uniform jacket. If it was this cold with the sun out God knows what it would be like in the dark so close to the coast.

Without urgent medical attention it was quite possible the young pilot, who'd so kindly offered to fly her to Wick, might die and that would be her fault too. She wasn't given to praying, wasn't even sure there was anybody listening, but it couldn't hurt to ask for divine intervention at this point.

Her prayers were interrupted by a shout. She spun round so fast she lost her balance and slid down the hill on her backside. Peter was sitting up and laughing at her.

'Sorry, old girl, I didn't mean to startle you.'

She was at his side in seconds and dropped to her knees. 'You look absolutely fine. You've been unconscious for hours and I thought you had a serious head injury.'

He grinned and unravelled himself from her coat. 'You look as though you need this more than me. Excuse me, I need a pee.' He scrambled to his feet, tossed her coat to her, and then, as if there was nothing wrong with him at all, vanished behind the wreckage.

Prayers were obviously miraculous things and from now on she'd be speaking to the Almighty more often. Until he'd mentioned needing to empty his bladder she'd been perfectly fine but now she was as desperate as he. As soon as he was back she'd nip around the back of the Tiger Moth herself. Everything looked much brighter and the return of her greatcoat meant she was warm again.

When she returned he was warming his hands by the fire. 'Well done for getting this going, Charlotte. We've got a couple of hours before dark so I think we need to get as much fuel as we can from the old girl.'

An hour later they had enough plywood to keep the fire burning for a couple of days. Together they managed to construct a rudimentary shelter using some of the struts and the fabric from the wings and fuselage.

They sat on her groundsheet out of the wind and ate half

the rations from her tin. 'What we don't have, Peter, is any water and that's more important than food.'

'There's still enough daylight to look for a burn.' He pointed to a particularly colourful patch of moor a few hundred yards away. 'See there, I think it's quite likely there's water under that patch of heather. Shall we go for a recce?'

'I'll go. I don't think you should be gallivanting about when you were unconscious for so long.'

'I wasn't knocked out, just exhausted. Sorry if I scared you.'

'Another thing, why didn't you just fly above the fog, use your instruments? You must have known that there was nowhere safe to land around here.'

'Good question. You wouldn't have noticed it, but the engine was playing up and I couldn't risk climbing. I think I made a bloody good fist of it, considering everything.'

'You completely wrecked the plane, nobody knows where we are, and we both could have been killed, so sorry if I disagree.' His friendly smile vanished and for a second she wondered if she'd made a catastrophic error criticising him. She knew nothing about him – he could be a violent young man.

Then he nodded. 'Fair enough. It's entirely my fault as I didn't bother with the preflight checks. If I had done then I'd have noticed there was something wrong with the engine. Rookie error – unforgivable.'

'Let's not worry about it now. Shall we investigate your theory about the water?'

He was right. They had to dig down a couple of feet but eventually water pooled in the bottom of the pit. They managed to fill the mug.

'It's not clean enough to drink but I think if we leave it overnight most of the mud will settle to the bottom and it won't be too bad.'

'Even if it doesn't, we'll have to drink it. I doubt that a bit of dirt will do us any harm.'

'Why haven't they sent out a search party already? They know you set out for Wick this morning and they know you didn't arrive.'

'It's a huge base, a major part of coastal command and there are half a dozen Spitfire squadrons as well as Mosquitoes, Hampdens and Beauforts stationed there. It might be days before they notice that I didn't arrive.'

'How will they rescue us when they do find us? They can't land an aircraft – from what I can see the coast around here is too dangerous for a boat, and there are no roads or even paths.' Was she going to see her beloved Dan again? Things looked bleak but she'd never give up hope – she had too much to live for.

25

Dan was invited to remain with Anderson. He was about to decline then changed his mind. He would learn more about the progress of the search if he was in the office of the CO. He turned his attention to the tea and food provided earlier.

'When you find them, how are you going to rescue them? From what I can gather there are no roads to speak of. Do you have land vehicles that can cope with that terrain?'

'We've got bloody great lorries with four-wheel drive. It doesn't matter if it's dark – they can still cover the terrain safely. I've got medics standing by.'

'I'll be going with them.' This was a statement of fact and unless he was locked into a room somewhere, nothing would stop him clambering into the lorry. He didn't contemplate for a minute that his beloved girl wasn't safe somewhere – the alternative wasn't acceptable.

'I won't point out the obvious, old boy, that with your duff leg you'll be more of a hindrance than a help.'

'I don't intend to get in anyone's way. I'll remain with the vehicle. I just want to be there when they bring her in.'

'It'll be rough terrain, but I don't suppose that will bother you.'

The roar of an aircraft taking off drowned out Dan's reply. He moved to the window and saw a Spitfire vanish into the sky. These nimble fighters could fly safely at ground level and would be perfect for the search.

He returned to his abandoned sandwich. 'How long will it take him to fly from here to Wick?'

'At cruising speed, around half an hour.'

'I take it he was told to fly inland first?' Dan asked. If they'd crashed in the sea there was no urgency as they would both be dead and the pilot would just be looking for floating wreckage.

'Absolutely. I've checked with the Met chappie and the fog came in a few minutes after the Tiger Moth took off. Therefore, they might very well be nearer to Inverness than to Wick.'

He only just had time to swallow the last mouthful when the distinctive sound of the Spitfire returning had him back on his feet and peering out of the window. He laughed out loud as the pilot circled overhead waggling his wings.

The Spit didn't land but soared back into the sky. The pilot obviously intended to lead the rescue party directly to the wreckage.

The band around his chest relaxed and, for the first time since Charlotte had gone missing he was able to breathe freely.

'He's found them and they're both alive. Thank God for that.'

'Inspector, the lorry's already on the move. You'd better get outside pronto if you want to go with them.'

★

On the third day Peter looked like a pirate, but with a ginger beard instead of a black one. The rations were gone but they'd managed to keep just about hydrated with the vile, muddy water. She was cold, smelly and ravenously hungry but at least she was alive.

'Bloody hell, I can hear a Spit,' he said as he jumped to his feet. 'Chuck everything we've got onto the fire. He needs to be able to see it.'

She hadn't heard anything, but now there was the distinctive roar of a Merlin engine. They stepped back from the flames and watched the sky.

'Look, I can see it. He's seen us. He's circling round.' She grabbed Peter's arm in her excitement.

They both waved frantically and the Spitfire flew so low they could see the grinning pilot in the cockpit. He gave them a thumbs up and then roared back into the sky.

'How long will it take them to reach us by land?'

'An hour or so as long as the smoke from the fire's visible. It's a damned nuisance that we're in a dip. We'll need to stand on that hill as they're more likely to see us if we do that.'

Charlotte was frantically stuffing her belongings into her kitbag. Most of them were mud-stained, wet and practically unwearable. She hoped she wasn't put on a charge for being inappropriately dressed and minus several items that should be in there. Her mouth curved. How silly to be worrying about something so trivial right now. They were going to be rescued and she would be able to telephone Dan and tell him what had happened. Did he even know she'd almost died?

She'd barely finished when the fighter was back overhead.

It circled slowly, a lot higher than it had been before, and she realised he was guiding the land party to them.

'Are we going to put the fire out or just let it burn?'

'Good point. Although there have been no Luftwaffe recently, we can't really leave it for them to see. We need to cover it with mud. There's plenty of that about, but we'll have to use our hands.'

'We're both so filthy I can't see it makes any difference,' she said cheerfully.

It took them more than an hour to completely douse the fire, collect their kit and make their way to the top of the hollow where they could watch for the arrival of the rescue party. The Spitfire had gone and then returned and Peter had said it had gone back to base in order to refuel.

They stood like a couple of dilapidated scarecrows watching the horizon. 'I can hear the lorry but I can't see it. It must be in that dip over there,' she yelled as she hopped from foot to foot.

Then, first the cab and then the rest of a massive lorry lumbered into sight. The plane overhead performed a loop-the-loop and then roared off into the sky. There was no need to attract the driver's attention as they could quite clearly hear the horn honking triumphantly.

'Let's walk to meet them,' he suggested.

'I'm happy with that. The sooner I'm in the warm and have a hot drink and something to eat the happier I'll be.'

He slung her kitbag over his shoulder and this time she didn't argue. The lack of food, water and sleep, as well as being cold and wet, had sapped her strength and she wasn't even sure she could walk that far when carrying nothing at all.

Chin up, best foot forward and all that – she thought to herself as she stumbled after him. He was obviously a lot fitter than her, as being deprived of everything for three days hadn't really affected him at all.

He stopped and put his arm around her waist. 'Come along, Assistant Section Officer Fenimore, don't give up now. We'll get a bloody medal for this I shouldn't be surprised.'

He knew why she'd been sent to the wilds of Scotland and was convinced that she'd be back in London in no time. 'Good grief, why ever would they do that? Nothing heroic about surviving a plane crash – what else could we have done but what we actually did?'

The distance between themselves and the approaching lorry seemed to be growing rather than shrinking and she wasn't sure she was going to make it. The vehicle also kept vanishing as it drove through repeated dips. 'I'm going to sit here and wait for them. Feel free to carry on, Flight Lieutenant.'

He dropped her kitbag immediately. 'Absolutely not. We'll sit on this, Cinderella, and wait for our carriage to arrive.'

'I certainly look like a Cinderella and not when she was going to the ball. I don't think you pass muster as the handsome prince either.'

She collapsed gratefully onto the bag and he joined her. 'It's strange that my hair's a fairly innocuous reddish blonde, but my beard is carrot-coloured.'

'Good thing you don't wear a handlebar moustache then, as a lot of your fellow pirates do.' She managed a weak laugh. 'I meant fellow pilots, of course.'

'You've been an absolute brick, Charlotte. You'd already

got things well organised before I came round. You deserve a bloody medal even if I should be taken out and shot for landing us in this mess.'

'I wish I didn't smell so awful. I'm going to be horribly embarrassed when our rescuers rush forward and then reel back gagging.'

He'd remained in his flight suit, which was now filthy and beyond repair. He peered inside and nodded happily. 'My uniform's tickety-boo. Just need a clean shirt and underwear and I'll be ready to go.'

'Kindly don't mention your intimate apparel, sir, highly inappropriate.' She was staring down at her ruined lisle stockings and what had once been shiny shoes. 'Forget medals. We'll probably both be put on a charge. Don't forget I used your Tiger Moth for our fire.'

'It wasn't going anywhere and someone would probably have put a match to it anyway. Look, rescue's approaching.'

She tried to stand but her legs refused to obey her command. 'I'm sorry, Peter, but I'm going to have to wait here. I really can't stand up on my own. My legs have turned to jelly.'

'Then stay where you are. There will be several strong medics eager to carry you to the lorry.'

'At least I don't have limbs hanging off. I'm just filthy, malodorous and exhausted.'

Dan was sitting in the front of the vehicle and his eyes had been fixed on Charlotte ever since the two of them had appeared on the brow of a small hill. The driver looked across at him.

'I can't go any faster, sir; would break the back axle. Your young lady looks just fine. I reckon she'll be surprised to see you.'

'I'm sure she will.'

The pilot had set off carrying her kitbag but after a hundred yards he'd stopped and put his arm around her waist. She wasn't as well as he'd thought. They trudged a bit further and then it was obviously too much for her and her companion dropped the bag and they both flopped onto it.

He pulled back the flap that separated the front of the lorry from the rear. The two medics immediately looked up. 'The pilot's fine but my fiancée looks completely knackered. I'd carry her myself but because of my bloody leg I'm incapable of doing so.'

'Don't worry, sir, we'll bring her in safely. Once we've got her wrapped in blankets and she's had a hot drink and something to eat she'll be in better shape.'

'When we stop, I'll transfer to the back.'

The driver continued for another fifteen minutes and then gently applied the brakes and the large lorry rocked to a halt. 'I can't get any closer, too many rocks. I've got room to turn round here as well once they're both on board.'

Getting out of a high vehicle was trickier than getting in but he was damned if he was going to ask for help. He twisted on the seat and dropped out feet first, making sure he landed on his good leg. He didn't know if things would be any easier when he had a tin leg. Douglas Bader was flying a Spitfire with two tin legs so getting in and out of the car or lorry with one should be a doddle.

The two medics were already running towards Charlotte and the pilot by the time he'd made his way to the rear of the lorry. He didn't want to distract her or them by his presence so, using his arms, heaved himself into the back.

Whilst he was waiting, heart pounding, he got out the two large thermos flasks, greaseproof-paper-wrapped sandwiches and slices of cake and was ready to pour the tea and hand out the food as soon as both of them were inside.

The canvas flaps had been tied back so he could see out but the lorry was parked with the side facing the direction they were coming. He rubbed his hand across his eyes when he finally heard her approaching. No time for sentiment – he didn't want her to know how terrified he'd been of losing her. He couldn't hear exactly what was being said, but obviously she wasn't on a stretcher.

Then he definitely heard her squeal and pounding footsteps followed. He scarcely had time to compose himself before she was throwing herself into his arms.

'Dan, I don't know how you're here, but I can't tell you how glad I am to see you.'

He crushed her to him, unable to respond for a moment. 'Not as glad as I am to see you, my darling.'

She looked up, her face mud-streaked, her hair tangled, but she'd never looked more beautiful to him. He kissed her and she responded passionately.

'All right, you two, that's quite enough of that. I've got no one here to kiss me better.'

Reluctantly he raised his head and grinned at the equally filthy young pilot. 'Too bad, old boy. I'm sure there's a queue of young ladies at the base waiting to offer you comfort.'

The medics handed out the tea and food. The pair of them wolfed it down. Whilst Charlotte ate he had time to look at her more closely and was concerned to see how much weight she'd lost, how pale her skin was, how dark the shadows under her eyes were.

Nobody else touched the tea or rations until Charlotte and the pilot had finished eating. The doctor who'd examined both of them said neither of them needed to be hospitalised. 'Nothing a long soak in a hot bath and several square meals a day won't put right. You'll be ready to return to duty in a week.'

With Charlotte safely wrapped in two blankets and snuggled on his lap everything was right in his world. The lorry slowly turned and begun its stately journey back to Inverness. He breathed in deeply and almost choked.

'My God, I hate to say it, sweetheart, but you smell absolutely appalling.'

She settled more firmly into his embrace before answering. 'So would you, my love, if you'd worn the same knickers for as long as I have.'

He laughed and wished they were alone. Just the mention of her knickers – in need of changing or not – made him want to make love to her there and then. There was so much he had to say to her, so many things to decide, but they could wait until she was fully recovered.

His shoulder had gone to sleep and his arms were cramped by the time the lorry eventually lumbered into the base. She'd slept the entire journey as had her companion. It was now totally dark.

'Right, sir, let me take her. We've got a small sickbay here. You can rejoin your fiancée later. She's totally knackered and needs a hot bath and a long sleep and you being there for either isn't a good idea.' The doctor grinned apologetically.

'Okay – I've got some telephone calls to make but will come to the sickbay as soon as that's done.'

First, he rang his godfather at his London home. 'Is she well? What the devil happened?'

Dan explained. 'The doc says he's going to keep her under observation for a couple of days and then she'll need at least a week to fully recover. I've not had an opportunity to talk to her so can't tell you what she wants to do.'

'Actually, I already have a position lined up for her as soon as she's declared fit. The officer in charge of the WAAF detail at her previous posting was involved in a traffic accident and will be *hors de combat* until the end of December. She is needed to run the place until the Queen Bee returns. She has been promoted to section officer from today.

'That sounds perfect. Whilst she's in Suffolk somewhere I'll get my leg done. I haven't discussed it with her yet, but I intend to marry her at Christmas. I hope you and Aunt Betty will be able to come?'

'We'll be there. Just let us know the time, place and date.'

Charlotte's bath was as full as it could be without slopping over onto the lino when she got in. A young WAAF nursing assistant insisted on accompanying her, saying it was the doctor's orders. The girl washed her hair efficiently and scrubbed the bits that Charlotte couldn't reach. The water was disgusting by the time she'd finished.

'Give me your arm, ma'am, and I'll help you up. I expect you're a bit wobbly on the old pins.'

Being seen naked by another woman was something

she'd got used to and she was glad to have the assistance. 'I can't believe how feeble I am. I need to sleep but I'm not going to until I see my fiancé again.' A warm flannelette nightdress was slipped over her head as she spoke.

'He'll be allowed in soon. Let's get you to bed and dry your hair. The doctor wants you to eat and drink something before you go to sleep.'

'I'm not hungry, but I could certainly do with another mug of tea.'

'We've been saying how romantic it was that your chap was flown up here especially to be at your side. He's gorgeous – and a CID chief inspector!'

The girl stopped rubbing her hair for a moment then resumed.

'I know. From the moment I saw him across the street a few months ago I was hooked. I'm sure he wouldn't have even looked at me if he hadn't been so horribly injured.'

Dan answered, 'That's bollocks, and you know it.'

She twisted and looked at him smiling down at her with the wet towel in his hands. 'I'm sure you shouldn't be in here but I'm glad you are. My hair's fine. Sit next to me so I can see you.'

He leaned down and kissed her, his lips hard, demanding and a wave of something she recognised as desire flooded through her. It was a good thing he broke the kiss as she'd wanted it to go on for ever.

'I volunteered to bring in your final meal of the day – or I should say night as it's after twelve.'

'If it's after midnight then it's tomorrow and actually the morning.'

He placed a tray across her knees and although she'd

thought herself unable to eat anything the appetising aroma of vegetable soup wafted up to her, making her stomach rumble and her mouth water.

He removed the tray when she'd eaten and drunk everything on it. 'You need to sleep, darling. I'll stay here. I've slept in far more uncomfortable places before now.'

She listened and there wasn't a sound. 'I think everybody's gone to bed, Dan. There's ample room for you on here.' She saw a flash of desire in his eyes and shook her head. 'No, not in my bed but on top of it. I don't want to sleep with you until we're married.' She smiled at him, making it clear it wasn't because she didn't want to. 'I love you but would really like to wait I wasn't sure how I felt about this but now I'm sure.'

'In which case, will you marry me at the earliest possible opportunity? What about Christmas?'

'Remember we've been invited to spend it with Nancy and David in Chelmsford and Jane and Oscar will be there too.'

'Perfect. We'll get married in Chelmsford. Now, stop talking and go to sleep.'

'Yes, sir, I'm yours to command.'

His snort of laughter made her giggle. 'And I'm the Queen of Sheba.'

He kicked off his shoes without bothering to undo the laces. His jacket, tie and waistcoat were dumped on the chair and his smart Bracers were now dangling down the back of his trousers. He looked positively rakish and she loved him so much it hurt.

He'd obviously come prepared as he'd brought a pillow and a couple of blankets with him. She shuffled across giving him as much room as she could. He dropped down beside her, slid his arm under the blankets and around her waist and drew her close so her bottom fitted into his lap.

'Good night, darling. If you wake and want anything just ask.'

26

Dan was up early and slid off the bed without waking Charlotte. He didn't want to raise any eyebrows when the nurses came in first thing. He tucked his borrowed bedding under her bed and then went in search of a bathroom.

On his return he bumped into the doctor who smiled. 'I looked in on my patients and didn't have the heart to disturb you two. I'm clocking off now but if you need me for anything I'll toddle over.'

'Her colour's better this morning. Are you anticipating any problems?'

'Not at all. You might as well spend the nights in her room. A lot more comfortable than the alternative.'

As he approached her door it flew open and she dashed out looking frantically up and down the passageway. He pointed to the bathroom door. 'In there, darling.'

'Thank you, my need is desperate.'

He straightened her bed whilst he waited and then tipped out the contents of her kitbag. There was nothing clean in there she could wear – God knows what she'd been doing with it. He heard her coming back and said without turning round. 'If you didn't change your knickers then how did everything get so muddy?'

'My undergarments are none of your business, DCI Chalmers,' a pleasant female voice replied, much to his embarrassment.

He turned, grinning apologetically and somewhat red-faced. 'I'm sorry, obviously I thought you were my fiancée. I don't believe we've met?'

The speaker was a lovely, fair-haired WAAF officer about his own age and, if he wasn't already in love with Charlotte, he would definitely have taken an interest.

'I'm SO Fullerton. I have details of SO Fenimore's new posting.' She looked at the ruined contents of the kitbag and laughed. 'I'll see if we've got replacements for all that – it doesn't look as if any of it is usable.'

Charlotte came in, ignored the other girl, and walked straight into his arms, which was exactly where he wanted her. A satisfactory few minutes later she winked at him and hopped back into bed.

'I apologise for being improperly dressed. As you can see I've nothing to wear. I also lost several items from that bag as well as my irons, which were abandoned at the crash site.'

'I'm SO Fullerton and I'm here to tell you that you've been promoted from assistant section officer to SO like me. Congratulations.'

'How absolutely spiffing. I expected to be put on a charge so to be promoted in the circumstances is quite extraordinary.'

Dan walked to the far side of the bed and then stretched out beside her. The other WAAF looked somewhat taken aback that he hadn't left them to talk in private. He closed his eyes and pretended to be asleep, which was the best he could do.

He heard the girl sit beside the bed and then his pretence became reality and the voices became distant and he drifted off to sleep. He didn't wake until something hard and sharp was poked into his midriff.

'Stop that, SO Fenimore; let a fellow sleep, why don't you?'

'I'm the one who should be asleep after my experiences. Someone from London wants to speak to you.'

He sat up so suddenly they almost cracked heads. 'You should have led with that, sweetheart. I'd better get a move on but I doubt it's anyone important.'

'I'll understand if you have to go today. I've got to be back at my old posting in four days so I've got to leave here soon as well.'

He called back as he reached the door. 'We can travel back together. I'll explain why when I return.'

A WAAF was gesticulating to him at the end of the passageway and he increased his pace. 'Whoever it is, sir, isn't very happy at being kept waiting so long.'

He picked up the receiver, which was practically vibrating from the racket the caller was making. He didn't recognise the voice. 'Good morning, DCI Chalmers here; how can I help you?'

'Good God, what took you so long?' The question was probably rhetorical but Dan decided to answer anyway as he'd taken an instant dislike to the speaker.

'I was asleep. To whom am I speaking?' He held the receiver away from his ear as the man on the other end shouted his reply.

'I'm Sir Henry Winstanley. I want to know what the devil you think you're doing in Scotland when you should be at your desk.'

The name Winstanley vaguely rang a bell but he couldn't quite place him and certainly didn't think the man had any right to harangue him for something that was patently none of his business.

'I've never heard of you, Sir Henry. I'm on unofficial sick leave until the New Year although it's nothing to do with you....' He was interrupted.

'If you're on sick leave you should be at home in your bed and not halfway across the country doing God knows what.'

Dan was tempted to hang up but managed to contain his anger and reply relatively calmly. 'If you wish to continue this conversation then I suggest you moderate your tone. The Chief Superintendent of Scotland Yard is aware of my reasons for absence and is satisfied they are justified. Might I enquire, sir, what this has to do with you?'

Sir Henry was about to answer but this time Dan interrupted him.

'I'm having my leg amputated and although on sick leave it will be unpaid.'

His comment was met by a disturbing silence. He could hear the man breathing heavily and hoped he wasn't having a heart attack.

'I seem to have got off on the wrong foot here, DCI Chalmers. I'm at the Home Office and your absence was brought to my attention by someone at the Yard. I was told it was unexplained and that you'd gone off on a jaunt with your young lady.'

If he hadn't been so angry Dan would have laughed at the absurdity. 'Sir Henry, might I suggest next time that you check your facts before making totally unsubstantiated accusations. Good morning.' He dropped the receiver back on the cradle and turned to see the two girls who worked in this room watching him with open-eyed admiration.

'Can you get me an outside line, please? I need to speak to Scotland Yard.'

Five minutes after the deeply worrying call from this mysterious Sir Henry he was talking to Mike. After quickly bringing him up to date with Charlotte's situation he moved on to the extraordinary telephone conversation he'd just had.

'I know exactly why someone is stirring up the shit, Dan. Not everybody was as pleased as we were to boot out the dirty cops. Several other divisions have also started investigations of corruption and I can tell you that your name is not popular in several places.'

'Will you speak to Bailey for me and warn him he's likely to get a call from this Winstanley chap complaining about my insubordination. If I get any more of this flak then I'll hand in my resignation – you can tell him that as well.'

'I'll do that. Give my best wishes to your fiancée.'

Dan disconnected and then returned to Charlotte's room. 'What was all that about? You're rather tight-lipped and grim so someone has obviously upset you.'

They were both laughing by the time he'd finished describing his conversation. Everything seemed better when he shared it with her. 'I told him something that I should have told you first. I'm going into hospital as soon as I get back to London and I'm having my leg amputated. I'll do far better with a prosthetic and won't have the pain.'

Her eyes widened and she shook her head. 'Isn't that a

really risky thing to do? Please don't do anything dangerous. I couldn't...'

'Sweetheart, don't cry.' He gathered her into his arms and tried to explain and reassure her. 'No riskier than any other surgery and I trust my surgeon implicitly. I'd intended to tell you the night you left so suddenly. I should have gone into hospital yesterday. It will make things easier for you as I'll not be such a bad-tempered bastard because of the pain.'

'I can't believe you'd do something so drastic for me. Please, darling, only go ahead if it's what you want.'

'It's for both of us.' He kissed her and for a few blissful moments he forgot about what he was about to face. When they were both able to speak again she nodded.

'Then I suppose delaying it by a few days won't make a lot of difference in the long run. I'd better write to Nancy and Jane and give them our good news. We could be married just before Christmas, preferably Christmas Eve, that way you'd never forget our anniversary.'

An orderly appeared with a trolley and there was a magnificent cooked breakfast for both of them. Food was a priority always and particularly now as Charlotte needed to replace the weight she'd lost.

'I absolutely hate porridge; I was dreading breakfast as it's the staple food up here.'

'Not only eggs, real and not reconstituted, bacon, fried bread and tinned tomatoes. There's also toast, marmalade and butter. An absolute feast.'

He put the tray with her food over her lap and then moved the trolley so it was in front of him whilst he was sitting on the chair. It made a reasonable table. Conversation could wait until they'd both eaten.

'That was delicious. I really don't need to be in bed but until SO Fullerton returns with my new kit, I've got nothing to put on.'

'The doctor said you were to rest, so I'm glad you can't get up. He won't be happy when he knows you've got to be in Suffolk in four days' time.'

'I intend to leave as soon as I've got my full kit and the bag to put it all in. You said we can travel back together.'

'We were talking about our forthcoming wedding, sweetheart. I'm quite happy to marry you in Chelmsford so your friends can be there and to have our wedding breakfast at Nancy's house, but I'd prefer to travel back and spend our honeymoon in our apartment.'

She was about to disagree but then realised that his suggestion made sense. She felt the colour travelling from her toes to the crown of her head and he watched her, his eyes glinting with amusement.

'I see you understand why I made that suggestion.' He picked up her hand and kissed the knuckles and just the light touch of his lips on her skin was like electricity travelling through her.

'I don't know anything about that side of things, my love, but I can't wait for you to show me. I assume you've got the experience I lack?' She widened her eyes and hoped her innocent expression would fool him.

'I've had a couple of affairs, if that's what you're hinting at. However, it will be completely new for me as well as I've never been to bed with a woman that I'm in love with.'

'We better talk about something else before we do

something we shouldn't. Move your chair a yard from my bed at once, DCI Chalmers. I don't trust you to behave if you're sitting as close as you are right now.'

With a smile he stood up and moved the chair. 'I was going to suggest that we shared a sleeper when we return but I think in the circumstances that would be unwise.'

'You keep telling me how rich you are – why don't you book two singles for tomorrow night? You get a wonderful dinner and breakfast included and I've never slept so well as I did on that train.'

'I do hope you're not marrying me for my money, SO Fenimore?'

'Well, I'm hardly marrying you for your intelligence, charm, good humour and looks, now am I?'

They were still laughing when two WAAF arrived with her uniform freshly sponged and pressed and this, and the other items placed on the bed, looked almost as good as they had before.

'Here you are, ma'am. I've taken the liberty of sewing on your new stripes.'

'Thank you. Is that the rest of my kit? I can't believe you managed to resurrect it. I thought everything was only fit for the ragbag.'

'Everything present and correct, ma'am. Your greatcoat isn't quite dry and you'll need a new waterproof.' The second girl had dumped a pile of clothing on the bed and conspicuous amongst them were her very unflattering knickers and bras. Dan was doing his best not to laugh as he eyed the pile.

'The things that are missing will arrive along with a new kitbag later today.' The girl didn't salute and Charlotte was glad; returning the gesture would have been silly whilst wearing a nightie.

As soon as the two girls had gone he picked up her blackouts and held them up a look of incredulity on his face. 'I can't believe this is what you've been wearing under that skirt. I've never seen anything so unflattering in my life.'

She tried to snatch the item from his hand but he moved it out of her reach. 'My underwear is my own business.'

With a wicked smile he dropped them onto the bed. 'Your underpinnings might be none of my business now but after we're married then I'll be taking a very personal interest.'

'I don't care how interested you are, I still have to wear those things and the hideous bras as well. Everything is issued and no exceptions allowed if we don't want to be put on a charge.'

'I'm going to buy you some more flattering lingerie, which you can wear when you're off duty. You do realise that if you get pregnant then you can leave and we can be together all the time.'

'Just because my friends are having babies it doesn't mean I want to do the same.'

His expression became wary. 'Never, or just at the moment?'

'Of course I want children with you one day, but we've both got important jobs to do and I don't think now is the time to be bringing babies into the world.'

'Fair enough. Avoiding the middle of your menstrual cycle is one way, but it's not guaranteed.'

This should have been a difficult and embarrassing conversation but talking to him about such intimate matters just seemed like any other topic. 'There's something a man can use that's more successful, isn't there?'

He nodded. 'I'll take care of that side of things but nothing's absolutely guaranteed apart from sleeping in separate beds.'

'If we were going to do that then there'd be little point in getting married. If we take every precaution and I still get pregnant then there's nothing we can do about it.'

'If you do, then I'll resign and we'll move into the country where it's relatively safe. I told you about the ancestral pile that's now in the hands of the RAF as a convalescent home – I didn't mention that I also own a small manor house in Surrey in a village a few miles from Guildford.'

'Saying small and manor in the same sentence is rather a contradiction, isn't it? The house I grew up in had seven bedrooms, as well as half a dozen more in the attics and nursery floor. Are you talking about something the same size?'

'Yes, more or less. There's a park – now ploughed up for potatoes – stables and the usual outbuildings as well as a walled kitchen garden. It's empty at the moment as the last tenant died a few months ago and I've not got around to leasing it again.'

'It sounds far too big for just two of us. I suppose we'll just have to fill it up with a dozen children, a nanny and nursemaids as well as several inside servants and another dozen outside.' She said this with a straight face and for a second he believed her.

'What about a butler, housekeeper and cook? No family should be without those, don't you think?'

She sighed and thought she was being ungrateful not to

want to live in the lap of luxury. 'Go and talk to somebody for half an hour as I'm going to get up. I don't care what the doctor said – I'm perfectly well and refuse to malinger here a moment longer.'

Getting dressed wasn't as straightforward as she'd anticipated. Attaching the collar to her shirt proved almost beyond her shaking fingers. She obviously wasn't as recovered as she'd thought but she wasn't going back to bed, however feeble she was.

He pushed open the door as she was struggling to do the laces on her shoes. Tears of frustration trickled down her cheeks and she hated for him to see her like this.

'Idiot girl, why didn't you call me? Now perhaps you can see why the medic said you needed to rest for a few days?'

'I won't put these on. I'll just lie on top of the bed for a bit until I feel better. Why are my hands trembling? I wasn't in any real danger once we were on the ground. I was deprived of food, water and sleep and was really cold, but I wasn't injured and I'm not ill, so why am I so useless?'

He joined her on the bed, then lifted her onto his lap so he could put his arms around her and she was able to rest her wet cheek against his shoulder. 'You've heard of shellshock? People from the trenches in the first lot suffered from it.'

'That's different – they were in very real danger and saw the most horrendous things.'

'The soldiers who returned from the beaches in Dunkirk suffered from the same sort of reaction – I know that dozens of pilots have become incapable of flying after thirty or so ops.'

She was beginning to see where he was going with this. 'So this is just my body's reaction to a stressful situation?'

'It is. Give yourself time and you'll soon be back to normal.'

'I'd better be, as I have to report for duty in four days.'

'If the medic doesn't sign you off then you can't go. Let's talk about our wedding plans. This should take your mind off things. There are about a dozen people I'd like to ask – do you think Nancy and David would be all right with that?'

'I'm sure they would. I was thinking, if we could borrow your staff car and tankful of petrol, couldn't we go to your house for a honeymoon?'

'It would be a flagrant and unacceptable use of my powers. We could travel by train easily enough and there's a bus from Guildford twice a day to the village.'

'Then let's do that. If we're going to be living there when the war's over, or possibly before, I'd really love to see it.'

He kissed the top of her head and slowly the tension drained from her body and she drifted off to sleep, safe and comfortable in his arms.

27

Two days after her rescue Dan was satisfied that Charlotte was now fit enough to resume her duties. The young pilot who'd crashed the Tiger Moth had introduced himself and apologised profusely. His apologies had been accepted but Dan was glad the young man didn't hang about.

He'd done as she suggested and booked adjacent first-class sleepers and a car was waiting outside to drive them to the station. They didn't have to catch the bus as she had when she'd arrived a week ago. He was expected at the hospital tomorrow evening and the operation would take place the following morning.

On the short drive to the station they were both quiet. He loved that about her – she was happy to just be with him and didn't feel the need to fill the silence with empty chatter as most girls would. She'd insisted on carrying her own kitbag, which made him feel emasculated. He hoped that once he'd got a tin leg, he'd be able to do everything a man should do.

'Look, Dan, it's the same guard who let me use an empty sleeper when I came up here last week.'

'Then I'll be sure to give him a suitably extravagant tip when we get off tomorrow morning.'

She was so excited about showing him the interior of the sleeping compartment he hadn't the heart to tell her that he'd travelled this way several times before.

'I have to go straight to Liverpool Street in order to catch the train to Felixstowe. I wish I could be at the hospital with you.'

'I'm damned glad you won't be. I'm going to be a horrible patient and you'd change your mind about marrying me. I'm going to concentrate on getting fit and am determined to walk beside you without my stick when we get married.'

'I won't be able to telephone you very often – it's emergency use only at this place. Also, all my letters will have to be redirected as I can't tell you exactly where I'll be for the next couple of months.'

'I'm not going to feel up to writing every day so neither should you. A weekly letter will be fine.'

'As I can't tell you what I'm doing and you've just told me that you'll be too grumpy to say anything pleasant, shall we just ignore each other until our wedding day?'

He knew her well enough to tell when she was teasing him. 'What about a telegram? I think I could manage to be pleasant with just a few words and you could probably manage not to reveal any state secrets.'

Her smile made him feel ten foot tall. 'Right, telegrams it is. Did you say goodbye to everyone you should?' He was wondering if she'd spoken to the handsome pilot.

'Nobody I needed to speak to personally. Come on, let's go to the dining car. I'm permanently hungry nowadays.'

The meal was certainly better than he'd expected and they were the last to leave, having had two pots of coffee and a brandy. She'd had one and he'd had several but she was as inebriated as he.

They tottered back to their respective compartments. He kissed her briefly knowing that with the slightest encouragement he'd follow her in and make love to her, which they'd both regret in the morning.

'I'm perfectly capable of finding my way to Liverpool Street, my love, and I'm sure you've got things to do before you go into hospital later.'

'I wasn't offering to come with you because I thought you unable to get there without my assistance, darling. I'm just reluctant to say goodbye as it's going to be weeks before we see each other again.'

They were standing under the clock at Euston station. His arms were around her and she was looking up at him with such love in her eyes he was almost unmanned.

'Dan, don't you think it quite astonishing that we feel the way we do when we've only known each other a few weeks? I just realised we're going to spend longer apart before our wedding than we have together. Do you think we're quite mad to be getting married so soon?'

'Absolutely not. I'm sure some people require months to make up their minds but we knew almost immediately. If there wasn't a war on, then no doubt we'd take things at a more decorous pace.'

'I don't think we would have. We're both decisive people and have no family to disapprove of us being so precipitate. I've changed my mind...' She laughed at his look of horror. 'No, you idiot, not about marrying you, but about writing.

I'm going to write every day whether you want me to or not because doing so will make me feel closer to you.'

'And I'll reply when I have the energy. You have the telephone number of the hospital and the convalescent home as well as their addresses. Let me know that you arrive safely and even if you can't tell me what you're doing, you can tell me who you're working with.'

He kissed her and then stepped aside to give her room to her toss her kitbag over her left shoulder. Her eyes were glittering with unshed tears, as were his. They both nodded as if to a stranger and she marched off without a backward glance, leaving him to watch her vanish into the bowels of the earth where the underground would take her to Liverpool Street.

An ancient taxi with an equally ancient driver rattled to a halt as he stepped out onto the pavement and he was fortunate to be the first to hail it. He'd got several telephone calls to make before he left for the hospital tonight and also wanted to make sure he had sufficient reading material, stationery and stamps to take with him.

Charlotte had already posted the letters to her two close friends with their news. His job was to contact the town hall at Chelmsford and book the registry office for 22nd December. He would also book the tickets for the various trains they would have to catch in order to get to Guildford.

Finding sufficient food for the wedding breakfast would be difficult for Nancy – everything was in short supply, particularly sugar, butter and everything else one might need to make something celebratory.

He intended to speak to the chef who ran the kitchen at his apartment. He was hoping, if enough money was on offer, that he would be able to buy what was needed and have it sent directly to Chelmsford. There would be around twenty guests and as there was no father of the bride it was down to him to pay for everything.

Presumably Charlotte would marry in her uniform. He had, as all plain-clothes officers did, his best blues but had no intention of digging them out. He'd got half a dozen excellent suits and any one of them would do for his special day.

By the time the car that he'd ordered arrived to take him to hospital, he was satisfied everything was in place and he was as ready as he'd ever be to lose the lower half of his leg.

Charlotte had travelled back and forth on this route several times and was familiar with the stations. There was always an ancient blue bus waiting outside Felixstowe station for any RAF or WAAF personnel heading for the radar station across the Debden. This bus was driven by a man, almost as ancient as his vehicle, who talked continuously but was quite incomprehensible because of his Suffolk accent.

It was strange to be returning to her first official posting but this time in command of the WAAF who were stationed there. She'd been saluted several times and her right arm was tired from responding. She'd left here as a warrant officer, the highest non-commissioned rank, and was returning as an SO. Not something she'd ever expected to do as when she'd left in May she'd thought her days of being involved with the top-secret radar installation were definitely over.

It seemed far longer than a few months since she'd last been here. So much had changed for her but everything would be the same here. The food would still be dreadful and illicit toast would be made on the makeshift cookers in each billet. There would still be the weekly dances in the magnificent building where all the female staff lived. This was the only occasion the men and women were allowed to fraternise.

It was now going to be her job to deal with those who broke the rules and she wasn't looking forward to that side of her new role. She would also be in charge of the rotas, issuing passes for those who wished to go to Felixstowe and no doubt a dozen other things she was as yet unaware of.

The busier she was the happier she'd be as it was going to be difficult not seeing or speaking to Dan from now until their wedding day. She'd told him they couldn't use the telephone as this wasn't allowed where she was stationed, but that wasn't quite correct as she could use the public call box in Felixstowe when she had her free days.

She signed in at the small guard hut situated at the bottom of the path that led up to Bawdsey Manor. The actual village of Bawdsey was a couple of miles inland to the north. The estate of over 168 acres could be reached via Woodbridge overland, but it was far easier to cross the Debden by boat from Felixstowe. This little ferry ran every half an hour and she was an expert at boarding it without getting her feet wet – something that happened frequently to those new to the experience.

She walked briskly up the path again, smiling to herself as she remembered the first time she'd arrived and had barely been able to carry her bag. Several of the girls who'd arrived at the same time had just dragged them along the grass, finding them too heavy to manage.

Several WAAF and airmen snapped to attention as she walked past and she saluted them equally efficiently. The officers' quarters were somewhere on the ground floor but naturally she'd never ventured that far herself.

On entering the office that was to be hers for the next few weeks she saw a desk piled high with unopened letters, stacks of forms and document wallets. There should have been a clerk sitting at the desk outside – so where was she?

Her kitbag could be hidden behind one of the filing cabinets. She didn't want to add to the clutter of the room with her belongings.

The telephone on her desk rang noisily and she picked it up. 'SO Fenimore.'

'Are you the new officer in charge?' the plummy male voice enquired abruptly.

'I am. Who are you?'

'I'm Wing Commander Richards – your opposite number so to speak. Been absolute chaos since Sybil had her accident. Can you find your way to my office?'

He outranked her by several levels but this was her command and she wasn't going to be bullied by an RAF officer. 'I'm sorry, sir, but I can't possibly spare the time to see you today. I need to get myself orientated and clear my desk. I'll come and see you soon as I can.' She replaced the receiver and waited for it to ring again and be given a direct command.

She had two options – start on the paperwork herself or go in search of the clerks who should be dealing with the routine matters. It might be lunchtime but someone should always be on duty. Things had got very lax since she was here a few months ago. It must be down to the new officer in charge who had now broken her leg.

All the letters had been opened and stacked so the ones that were urgent could be dealt with first when she heard laughing and chattering approaching. She was tempted to hide behind the door and then step out and terrify the two clerks who should have been here an hour ago.

Instead, she remained at the desk with her arms folded, staring at the door, waiting for the two outside to realise they weren't alone. After a few minutes the chattering stopped and a very young WAAF stepped into view.

The girl's horrified expression almost made Charlotte smile. Slowly she stood up, still without saying a word, and walked around the desk and stood in the centre of the office.

The second clerk joined the first looking equally terrified but neither of them stood to attention or saluted. This lack of respect was unacceptable under any circumstances.

'Attention!' she snapped and for a second nothing happened and then the girls exchanged glances before bringing their heels together and standing more or less straight.

'I am your commanding officer. You are both on a charge for disrespect, dereliction of duty and being absent from your positions without permission.'

The reaction she got was completely unexpected. Both girls burst into tears and ran out sobbing. There was no point in shouting at them as the outer office was already empty. There must be at least two sergeants, a corporal or two, several leading aircraftwomen and hopefully another officer, or at least a warrant officer somewhere who she could send after them.

There was no option but to go in search of someone who could find those two girls and bring them back. The NAAFI would be the best place to look first. She had only reached the door when the missing clerks were bundled back through the door at the end of the corridor by an irate sergeant and a corporal.

'These two are a disgrace, ma'am – they've been allowed to get away with things for far too long.' The sergeant saluted smartly but kept a firm hold on the arm of her charge. The corporal said nothing but did the same.

'Put them in the lock-up. I'll deal with them later. There must be more than two administrative clerks – have two of them report here immediately.'

It took Charlotte several days to stamp her authority and get things running smoothly. The two inefficient and insubordinate clerks were on fatigues and confined to barracks until they improved their attitude. They'd been allowed to do as they pleased because one of them was the niece of the injured CO.

Cordial relationships had been re-established with the RAF. She wasn't able to take any time off so hadn't been able to contact the hospital and see how Dan was after his operation. She assumed if anything had gone wrong then she would have been contacted immediately.

She wrote her first letter four days after arriving and knew it would make him laugh. She didn't expect him to reply immediately but was concerned when she'd sent three letters and still had no response from him.

Dan couldn't understand why he still had pain in the leg that no longer existed. The surgeon said this was quite usual and in time his brain would adjust to the new reality. The letters he received from Charlotte were exactly what he wanted to take his mind off what he was enduring. He'd refused to continue with the morphine for more than a day after his operation and a couple of aspirins every four hours hardly made a dent in the pain.

Two weeks after the amputation his leg had healed and he moved on to the convalescent home. Finally, he had the energy and inclination to write to Charlotte – not that he had anything particularly interesting to tell her – she seemed to be having a far better time ruling with a rod of iron at her new posting.

He had no visitors because he'd told no one where he was going to be. He learned to get around the place at high speed on his crutches, determined to be fit, so when his false leg was fitted he'd be able to walk on it immediately.

He'd brought the wireless he'd given to her with him and had it in his bedroom where he spent most of his time. He only emerged for meals, physiotherapy and appointments with medics. On 7th December he was listening to the news when he heard the newscaster announce that Japan had bombed the American naval fleet in Pearl Harbor.

Thousands of sailors had lost their lives in this lightning attack and more than half the fleet had been destroyed. The following day Britain declared war on Japan and everything changed. The Yanks were coming and, for the first time in a long bleak year, Dan began to think that maybe Hitler would eventually be defeated.

28

Charlotte viewed the beautiful frock that Nancy had made her and shook her head. 'It is absolutely lovely, but I must wear my uniform. I'm proud to be a WAAF and in years to come, when my children look at my wedding photographs, I want them to see me as I am now.'

Jane picked the dress up and held it in front of Charlotte. 'It seems such a shame not to wear it when Nancy's gone to so much trouble to make it for you.'

'I'm sorry, Nancy, I won't wear it for the ceremony but I'll change into it as soon as we get back here.'

'Don't be daft. Then you've got to change again when you leave this evening. It's my wedding gift to you anyway so you can wear it on your honeymoon. This house of Dan's sounds ever so posh. When this blooming war's over we can all come and stay with you. You'll have a house full of screaming kiddies of your own by then.'

'Dan and I have decided we want to postpone our family for a bit. Mind you, now the Americans are on their way, and Hitler has been held up in Russia, I'm beginning to believe that we can win this and it won't be more than a year or two before we've done so.'

She hadn't seen her future husband since he'd got his tin leg – in fact she hadn't seen him since she went to Bawdsey Manor. They'd spoken on the telephone a few times but he'd refused to talk about anything but their wedding and the arrangements he'd made.

'You must be desperate to see him after so long apart,' Jane said as she carefully folded the new dress and put it into the open suitcase on the bed.

'I'm not sure if I'm more nervous about getting married or excited about seeing him. By the way, Jane, are you sure that your baby isn't due until March?'

Her friend smoothed her voluminous maternity smock over her massive bump. 'I didn't want to tell you as it's your special day, not mine. David said he's certain I'm having twins – he could hear two distinct heartbeats.'

'Two babies at the same time? I'm not sure that sounds like fun but I'm sure you'll cope marvellously. At least you'll be living with your mother-in-law so you've got plenty of help. What does Oscar think about double trouble?'

'He's a bit anxious as carrying two isn't quite as straightforward as carrying one. David said I need to take things easy, rest as much as I can and put my feet up. I can also expect them to be born before the due date, but the closer I can get to it the better it will be for them.'

'Then sit down and put your feet up, Jane – my hubby knows what he's talking about.'

Although she wasn't going to wear the new dress Charlotte allowed Nancy and Jane to fuss around with her hair and make-up. Every button on her jacket was shining; she wasn't going to wear her greatcoat despite the fact it was December. This garment was warm and practical but not smart enough for a wedding.

Downstairs the children were playing quietly, the baby asleep in the pram, and wonderful appetising smells wafted from the kitchen. Nancy had been overwhelmed by the luxury items Dan had managed to find for their wedding celebration. The house looked festive as the tree and decorations had been put up. The two men were making themselves scarce but she could hear them talking quietly in the sitting room.

'I've just got to put on my hat,' Nancy said, 'and then I'm ready too.'

Her friend had made herself a stunning suit in a royal blue. Since her husband had managed to find her a treadle sewing machine there'd been no stopping her. She did alterations and dressmaking for the neighbourhood and in return they supplied her with material and oddments.

Jane waddled across to the coat stand and was about to pick up the dark blue cloak that Nancy had made her as nothing else fitted, when Oscar arrived at her side. He looked startlingly handsome; his ash blond curls and bright blue eyes were a perfect complement to his RAF uniform.

'Allow me, darling.' He swirled the vast garment around her shoulders and then handed her the matching cloche.

David was wearing a new suit and looked equally smart. Jenny, the live-in helper, was coming too so she could take care of Billy and Betty.

Two local women were in charge of the catering, which

meant Nancy would be able to relax and enjoy the day. They would also keep an eye on the sleeping baby until everyone returned.

'Where have you shut Polly and the puppy for the day?' Charlotte asked as they headed out into the garden.

'One of the gardeners has taken them home and will return them tonight. Thank God there were only two in the litter – a neighbour took the other one,' David said as he adjusted his spectacles.

It seemed strange walking along with her two best friends and their husbands, and only she and Oscar were in uniform. It occurred to her that Dan might decide to wear his, but then dismissed this. He would wear one of his beautiful suits as always.

Her heart was hammering, her hands clammy; it had been too long since they'd been together. She was nervous that for some reason he wouldn't feel the same about her. It was a short walk to the town hall, which was fortunate as she didn't think Oscar would have allowed Jane to come otherwise.

She wasn't carrying a bouquet – it wasn't her style. She was scanning the very smart group of people milling about at the bottom of the steps. Two men in police uniform, a girl in khaki, and one in air force blue.

Where was he? Then he stepped forward. He walked towards her, his eyes blazing, and with no walking stick or any sign of a limp.

Her feet moved of their own volition and she was in his arms. He picked her up and spun her around and then they kissed passionately.

'My darling, I can't tell you how much I've missed you.

You look absolutely beautiful. I'm glad you came in your uniform – it's who you are and it suits you perfectly.'

'It's been far too long, my love, and you look wonderful too. Are you going to introduce me to your friends or shall we wait until after the ceremony?'

'Afterwards – we've only got five minutes until it's our slot.' He grabbed her hand and almost ran up the steps. She scarcely had time to take in the difference in his appearance. Not just the fact that he could move freely but his face was no longer drawn; he looked rejuvenated and years younger.

She nodded and smiled at the group who'd accompanied him and then he whisked her into the room where she'd stood a few months ago witnessing David and Nancy's marriage. The vows they exchanged were the same as would be spoken in church – there were just no prayers, hymns or homilies.

Half an hour after entering as a single woman she exited as a wife. Dan remained glued to her side all afternoon. She was introduced to his godfather, the air commodore resplendent in his best blues, and his charming wife. Sergeant Wainwright and a senior policeman called Mike and his wife were guests as well as her friend Violet.

Betty and Billy were impeccably behaved and even baby Lottie remained cheerful and no trouble at all the entire afternoon. The buffet was everything she'd come to expect when Nancy was involved and there was more than enough champagne, beer and soft drinks to go round.

Uncle Frank, as Dan called his godfather, had somehow managed to arrange for a small charabanc to convey the guests to and from London. His sergeant had taken copious photographs and said he would get them developed and have them ready when they returned from their few days in Surrey.

'It's time to say goodbye to your friends, darling – the bus is here.'

'I've had such a spiffing time. I can't imagine a better day, a better husband or better friends and guests than we've had.'

They were standing on their own in the hall. He had his arms around her and she was leaning against him, struggling to believe that this amazing man was now her husband.

'I agree. We're spending tonight at the apartment and then going to Guildford first thing tomorrow. I've managed to get the house spruced up a bit and have taken on a family – they were bombed out earlier this year – to look after the place until we move in permanently.'

'Are there are a lot of Americans milling about in town?'

'Quite a few, but mostly the diplomatic types. The first influx of GIs won't be until the start of next year.'

Charlotte went in search of Jane who was sitting with her feet up on the sofa in the sitting room with Oscar perched on the arm beside her. He got up and moved away to allow them some privacy. 'We're going now. Let me know as soon as these babies arrive. If I get a twenty-four-hour pass I'll come and see you. It's only a short bus ride from Chelmsford to where you'll be living at the vicarage.'

'Please do, and bring your gorgeous husband if he can get time off. He's absolutely perfect for you. I know that both Oscar and David already like him. It's going to be wonderful when the war's over and we can all see each other whenever we like.'

'Our children will be best friends too – when I eventually have any.'

Nancy rushed across and flung her arms around Charlotte. 'I'm so happy for you, Charlotte. I knew there was someone out there for you as there was for Jane and I. Now Oscar's no longer flying ops, but running his flight from a desk, we don't have to worry about him being killed.'

'Dan's a senior officer and he won't have to attend every homicide or be as involved as he was before. I'm going to be stationed at Victory House again so I can live at home with him. Isn't that absolutely splendid?'

They hugged and kissed and Charlotte left knowing that these two would always be in her life. Violet was also a good friend and she fitted in the group perfectly.

They piled on the bus and everyone insisted that she and Dan took the back seat. There were several rows of seats left empty in front of them.

In the darkness she snuggled into his arms. 'Do they expect us to do something improper back here?'

He was nibbling her ear making coherent thought almost impossible. 'I'm game if you are.'

'Absolutely not. If you don't behave yourself, DCI Chalmers, I'll go and sit with Violet.'

He chuckled. 'Wainwright's already taken that seat. I think the two of them might make a go of it. I'm glad the poor chap feels able to move on after losing Davidson so tragically.'

'I've not been this happy since the night we had that dinner to celebrate our engagement.' He whispered into her ear, making her pulse race. 'I can assure you, my darling, that as soon as we're in bed, I'm going to make you even happier.'

Bibliography for the Girls
in Blue series

Ayto, John, *The Oxford Dictionary of Slang*, (2003).

Brown, Mike, *Christmas On the Home Front*, (2013).

Falconer, Jonathan, *RAF Airfields Of World War 2*, (2013).

Gane Pushman, Muriel, *We All Wore Blue: Experiences in the WAAF*, (2006).

Gardiner, Juliet, *Wartime: Britain 1939-1945*, (2005).

Geographers' A-Z Map Company, *A to Z: Atlas and Guide to London and Suburbs*, (1939).

Golley, John, *The Day of the Typhoon: Flying with the Royal Air Force Tankbusters in Normandy*, (1986).

Legrand, Jacques, *Chronicle of the Second World War*, (1994).

Longmate, Norman, *How We Lived Then: A History of Everyday Life During the Second World War*, (2002).

McKay, Sinclair, *Secret Listeners: How the Y Service Intercepted the German Codes for Bletchley Park*, (2013).

Opie, Robert, *The Wartime Scrapbook on the Home Front 1939-1945*, (2005).

Rice, Joan, *Sand in My Shoes:Coming of Age in the Second World War, a WAFF's Diary*, (2007).

Smith, Richard C., *Hornchurch Scramble: The Definitive Account of the Raf Fighter Airfield, Its Pilots, Groundcrew and Staff from 1915 to the End of the Battle of Britain*, Vol 1 (2002).

Thompson, Kate, *The Stepney Doorstep Society*, (2019).

Younghusband, Eileen, *One Woman's War*, (2013).

Acknowledgements

I want to thank Aria – Head of Zeus for their support over the last three years. My career has grown because of their excellent behind the scenes work. I'm proud of the seven books I've written for them and am sure these will continue to flourish.

About the Author

FENELLA J. MILLER was born in the Isle of Man. Her father was a Yorkshire man and her mother the daughter of a Rajah. She has worked as a nanny, cleaner, field worker, hotelier, chef, secondary and primary teacher and is now a full-time writer. She has over sixty Regency romantic adventures published plus four Jane Austen variations, four Victorian sagas and fourteen WW2 family sagas. She is a widow and lives in a small village in Essex with her British Shorthair cat. She has a son, daughter-in-law, and a grandson.

You can find Fenella J. Miller on her website fenellajmiller. co.uk and on Twitter as @fenellawriter.

Hello from Aria

We hope you enjoyed this book! If you did, let us know, we'd love to hear from you.

We are Aria, a dynamic fiction imprint from award-winning publishers Head of Zeus. At heart, we're committed to publishing fantastic commercial fiction – from romance to sagas to historical fiction.

Visit us online and discover a community of like-minded fiction fans.

You can find us at:

www.ariafiction.com
🐦 @Aria_fiction
📘 @Ariafiction